DEC 0 5 2022

D1802408

NANUET PUBLIC LIBRARY
149 CHURCH STREET
NANUET, NY 10954

The Guns of C.C. Ellis

The Guns of C.C. Ellis

Ralph Cotton

THORNDIKE PRESS
A part of Gale, a Cengage Company

NANUET PUBLIC LIBRARY
149 CHURCH STREET
NANUET, NY 10954

Copyright © 2022 by Ralph Cotton.
The Long Riders #1.
Thorndike Press, a part of Gale, a Cengage Company.

ALL RIGHTS RESERVED
This is a work of fiction. Names, characters, places, and incidents either are the product of the author's imagination or are used fictitiously, and any resemblance to actual persons, living or dead, business establishments, events, or locales is entirely coincidental.
Thorndike Press® Large Print Hardcover Western.
The text of this Large Print edition is unabridged.
Other aspects of the book may vary from the original edition.
Set in 16 pt. Plantin.

LIBRARY OF CONGRESS CIP DATA ON FILE.
CATALOGUING IN PUBLICATION FOR THIS BOOK
IS AVAILABLE FROM THE LIBRARY OF CONGRESS.

ISBN-13: 978-1-4328-9969-1 (hardcover alk. paper)

Published in 2022 by arrangement with Berkley, an imprint of Penguin Publishing Group, a division of Penguin Random House, LLC.

Printed in Mexico
Print Number : 1   Print Year : 2023

For Mary Lynn, of course

Part 1

PART 1

Prologue

C.C. Ellis and Jax Hoyt stood out front of the big ragged tent saloon in the soft rays of early-morning sunlight. They looked both ways along the bustling muddy street, amazed at how the little rail-siding town looked today compared to only a month earlier when they'd last ridden through. They'd been higher up in the foothills that trip, scouting out Henry Morrow and Sadie Long's Gold Bucket Gambling Hall farther up in the foothills. As it turned out, Sadie had recognized Hoyt from an encounter the two of them had when she was tossing her red skirts over her head atop a bar in Santa Fe.

That was . . . what? Two years? Three years? A few years back, he settled on.

Beside C.C. Ellis, Jackson Hoyt leaned on a newly built hitch rail. Jax shook his head, looking at piles and stacks of lumber, brick and roofing tin lying in town lots recently mowed and cleared, ready for whatever their new owners might want to build on them.

"I always hate seeing this happen to a place," Hoyt said as they watched even more delivery wagons roll in off the main trail.

"What's that?" Ellis asked, pretty sure he already knew what his friend was talking about.

"The way we rode through here last time and you could have shot marbles in the street, nobody to stop you," said Jax. "Now look at it."

"Didn't know you shot marbles."

"That's not the point," said Jax. "I'm just saying, if I wanted to, I could, is all."

Ellis waited for a second and caught a glimpse over his shoulder of two men who walked out of the ragged saloon tent and stopped behind them. From inside the tent, a piano played a peppy New Orleans version of "Oh! Susanna."

"What's your game, Jax, straight marbles or Knuckles Down Tight?" Ellis asked.

What the hell . . . ?

"Are you going to start on me — ?" Jax said.

But he realized something was afoot when Ellis nudged him farther along the hitch rail, getting away from where their horses stood right in the line of fire, should the two men from the saloon tent make a move, which his instincts had warned him in a split second that they would.

Catching a quick glance of the horses' position and having C.C. move him away from them told Hoyt everything.

"You there," one of the men called out, "you with the black hat!"

Ellis and Hoyt didn't answer. They moved away slowly, farther and farther from their horses. The two men followed at a distance of five yards until the tent was out from behind them and the horses were in a safer position.

"Don't act like you don't hear me!" the man called out.

Ellis and Hoyt stopped, keeping about ten feet between them.

"I hear you," said Ellis, the only one of the two wearing a black slouch hat. "What do you want?"

"I want *you,* Christian Clayton Ellis," the larger of the two men said. The other man had stepped away from him, the same way Hoyt stepped away from Ellis. "You've got something that rightly belongs to me, and today I'm taking it from you!"

People along the street turned toward the big man's raised voice.

"You know what it is?"

C.C. Ellis wasn't interested. "Don't know. Don't care," he said. "Whatever you're taking, try taking it."

"It's that big reputation of yours," the man explained anyway. "I'm hands down better than you with a gun, and I aim to prove it."

"Get to it," Ellis said quietly.

"One move out of you," Hoyt said to the other man, "and you'll die as quick as he does."

Inside his open riding duster, a long nickel-plated Remington stood diagonally across his belly. His right hand lay on the gun's butt, resting yet poised. Onlookers gathered on the busy street.

"Whoa now!" the voice of New Water Stop One's sheriff, Max Boyd, called out. "Any of you go for a gun, this double ten will lift you out of your boots."

None of the four men squared off could see the big ten gauge, but they all heard the metal sound as it opened and snapped shut.

"Go on about your damn business, Sheriff," the big man demanded, staring hard at C.C. Ellis. "This is strictly a private matter between me and this jake leg."

"All right, then," said the sheriff. "In that case, give me twenty-five dollars and go at it. I ain't wasting time arguing."

"Twenty-five dollars for what?" the man

shouted.

"That's what it will cost the town to pay somebody to gather chunks of your ass, box it and stick it in the ground once this ten gauge is finished with you." The sheriff called out to one of his two deputies on the scene, "Wade, show this fool your shotgun. See if it'll make a believer out of him."

The deputy raised the shotgun high enough to be seen.

But the man didn't even look at it. Instead, he made his move and let the fight start. He pulled his big Colt up from its holster and let out a yell. "Die, you sumbitch —"

But before he got out his words or his gun, two of Ellis's bullets pounded him in his chest, knocking him backward on the muddy building lot. A red haze of blood appeared in the air above the corpse, hung there for a second and vanished. A loud blast resounded from one of the shotgun's barrels, and Ellis and Hoyt spun in time to see the other man's gun fall to the ground. His hands went straight up.

"Quick thinking, Wade," said the sheriff. His deputy was still holding the smoking shotgun pointed at the sky. "You just saved the town twenty-five dollars."

He looked at C.C. Ellis, watching him replace the two spent bullets in his Colt as smoke curled from its barrel. "I don't think there's anybody watching here who'd call this anything but self-defense. What was his problem with you?" He nodded at the dead man lying in the dirt.

"I don't know, Sheriff," said Ellis. "Used to be I had a reputation for being quick with a gun. But that was a long time ago."

The sheriff's cordial smile disappeared. His deputies walked in closer and stood watching, listening, their faces serious.

"Don't count me as a rube," he said quietly. "You're Christian Clayton Ellis. I know *who* you are, *what* you are and what you've been from the war to now."

As he spoke, Hoyt eased in closer.

"I know you too, Jackson Hoyt. I mean, Jax," the sheriff added with a hint of sarcasm. Back to Ellis he said, "I was watching, is how come I saw what this fool had in mind, wanting to kill you."

Gesturing his deputies toward the other man, who still held his hands up, he said, "Wade, you and Bobby take this one over and stick him in a cell — one that's finished enough to keep him in it. And get this dead man off the street."

The sheriff stood with Ellis and Hoyt until his deputies and the prisoner were out of sight down the busy street.

"Fellas, I'm going to ask you both to do us all a big favor — for me, for Water Stop One and yourselves. I want you to get on your horses, or whoever's horses these are, and get on out of here and never come back. Can I count on you to do that for me?"

Hoyt's attitude started to curdle. "Sheriff, you just agreed there was nothing more we could have done but defend ourselves —"

"Okay," Ellis cut in. "We're leaving right now. We only came here looking for a friend we knew in Denver City. Seeing he's not here, we're gone. Obliged to you clearing up this mess."

He gave Hoyt a slight nudge toward their horses while the sheriff stood watching them closely. He continued watching until they reached the town limits and swung down the main trail, headed south out of the foothills.

"That didn't go real well, did it?" Hoyt said.

"Depends on how you look at it," Ellis replied. "Neither of us got shot. That's always a good outcome."

"Maybe so," said Hoyt, considering. "But we are going back, right?"

"Yes, we are," said Ellis.

He saw Hoyt slow his horse and start to turn it around. "But not today," he said quickly. "We looked the place over, met their *new* lawmen, and I found a good place to post a rifleman. What else do we need?"

Jax Hoyt straightened his horse and said, "Not a damn thing that I can think of. See you in a week, New Water Stop One," he said, tipping his hat to a small road sign alongside the trail.

They rode on.

Chapter 1

New Water Stop One
Seven days later

"Look at this dandy bob standing up ahead of us," said the railroad fireman. "He's wearing a string tie and all! Bet he can't tell his pizzle from a lampwick."

He stood at the open iron door to the firebox inside the large steam-driven engine, his knees feeling the heat through his coveralls as the dying coals inside the firebox cooled. He pointed a heavily gloved finger at the well-dressed traveler standing on the platform ahead of their slowing train, not recognizing Jackson Hoyt, who was shaved, trimmed and wearing a thirty-dollar business suit. The traveler looked back at them, waving, a wide flashy smile on his face.

"If he stands any closer, you can wipe his nose on an oil rag as we go by," the engineer said sidelong to the fireman without taking his eyes off of the platform as they drifted slowly past.

"I'm tempted to do it," the old fireman said. "Look, now he can't stop waving at us!" he said. "Must've thought we wouldn't stop for him. Bet he's drunker than a dog."

"Drunk or sober, I bet he thinks he's the berries," said the engineer. "He can't wait to get aboard the big choo choo!"

The engineer chuffed and repeated, "A jackrabbit, indeed."

Now the fool has forgotten his trunk and baggage! the fireman told himself, seeing the traveler step away from his large trunk and a leather valise, appearing to have forgotten the items in his rush.

Instead, the well-dressed traveler grasped the handrail of the barely moving train and swung into the engine's open door.

"Excuse me, sir!" said the fireman above the pulsing of the large steam engine. "You have forgotten your personals!"

The smell of rye whiskey wafted around the man. With it came the sour, bitter smell most frequently found lingering in a Denver City opium den.

"No, I have not forgotten anything, sir!" said the traveler, laughing under his breath.

Oh, yeah, this one is gone, drunk, doped.

God knows what else, the fireman told himself.

This new water stop hadn't been here a month, yet already the tents, the loose women, the cutthroats and various other ne'er-do-wells were all here. They had gathered on nearby streets and around the station as if they had come to witness some magnificent event.

The fireman knew that most of these people had migrated up from Denver City, following the new rails. Whatever else a man could do to himself here inside the saloon tent or at any one of the big tents outside of Boulder City, this well-dressed city fellow had already found and already done. But before the fireman could think much longer about it, a long Remington six-shooter came up from the traveler's waist and cocked inches from the fireman's face.

"Whoever wants to live, raise your hands!" he said loudly like some schoolmaster seeking class participation. He didn't sound as drunk or as doped up as his opium-lit eyes accused him of being. "I'm robbing this train." He jiggled the big gun in his hand — his hand now rock steady.

Both men's hands sprang up, the engineer actually turning loose of the engine's idle throttle.

"Sir, are you drunk? Are you funning with us?" said the fireman.

An iron coupling bar lay near his hand. He wondered if he could grab the bar in time to crack this man's head with it and take charge of the situation. A darkness in the man's eyes warned him against it.

The armed traveler steadied the big Remington in a one-handed grip, looking calmly and expertly down the sights atop its barrel.

"Yes, I am drunk!" he replied. "But, no, I am not funning with you!" he added, sounding miraculously sober.

The fireman and engineer saw gunmen scramble down from their saddles on the platform and hurry to push their way onto the train. A larger group of them headed into the open door of the express car — the money car, as some people called it. Others spread along the loading dock beside the train, rifles raised, taking charge of the station, the streets and the onlookers.

"Holy Moses! It is a robbery!" said the fireman. He took a step back, his eyes wide and frightened. "You're one of them, ain't you?" he said in a hushed tone.

"Yes, I am one of them," said Hoyt with a thin smile, his gun and his eyes steady, calm, in control.

The fireman leaned slightly and looked

back along the idling train where more gunmen had now gathered inside the reinforced express car. What he could not see were men gathered around the huge new safe standing bolted to both the floor and the thick walls of the car.

"You're fixin' to blow up the safe and open it, ain't you?" the fireman said.

"That is our plan this morning, yes," said Hoyt. "Now, stand there quiet-like so we won't have to kill either one of you."

"You'll get no guff out of us," the fireman said. He lowered a shaky finger enough to point at the big Remington in the gunman's hand. "Say now. Is that the new nickel-plated model everybody's talking about?"

The gunman turned the shiny six-shooter back and forth in his hand.

"I believe it is," he said, glancing down at the big pistol.

Along the loading platform more gunmen arrived, some holding the reins of the others' horses.

"My, my!" the fireman said, staring wide-eyed at the big Remington. "What I wouldn't give to hold a shiny beauty like that just once in my life!"

"Shut up, Lon!" shouted the engineer, whose name was Oscar. "You'll get us both killed sure enough!"

"I don't mean no harm, mister!" said Lon the fireman. "I'm just curious, is all!"

"I know," the gunman said quietly. "Here, Lon." He uncocked the Remington, turned it around in his hand and held it out, butt first, to Lon.

"Oh, my God!" said the fireman.

He looked at the big pistol, stunned at the suggestion of holding it. Yet without further invitation he took hold of the bone grips and hefted the gun up and down, getting a feel for it.

"Whoo-hee!" he said with delight.

As the engineer stared in disbelief, Lon held the gun pointed straight at the gunman's chest less than two feet away.

The gunman smiled. He placed a fingertip against the gun barrel and calmly nudged it away from his chest.

"Don't shoot me, Lon," he said affably. "You get all these long riders stirred up, no telling what they'd do."

"Oh, no, sir!" said the fireman. "I did not intend to —"

"It's all right," the gunman said.

He took the Remington as the fireman held it out to him. Cocking it, he held it loosely pointed at the two men. "What did you think of it, Lon?"

"It's a whole different feel from the Army

Colt," said the fireman. "Both fine shooting irons, I have to say. I never thought I'd get to hold one of them big Remmys!"

"I'm glad you got to do it," said the gunman.

Outside on the huge wooden platform, a masked rider came to a quick halt, leading a spare horse by its reins. Hooves clattered on the heavy plank surface.

"If you gentlemen will excuse me," said Hoyt, "I'll let you get back to running this railroad."

As he reached to open the small side door, Lon the fireman called out, "Wait, mister! I never heard the safe blow up."

"The rail clerk must have failed to lock the safe to begin with," said the gunman. "He must've just shut the big safe door behind himself."

"I'll be danged!" said the fireman. "Somebody will catch hell over that!"

The engineer and the fireman watched the gunman through the smoked and dusty window glass. The rider holding the spare horse in check moved in closer and pitched the gunman his horse's reins.

When the gunman fumbled as he caught the reins, the rider, Bailey McCool, called down to him, "Damn it, Jax, are you drunk?"

"No!" Jackson Hoyt said firmly, gathering his big silver-gray barb beneath him. "Why does everybody keep asking if I'm drunk?"

"I can only guess why!" she said. Her blue eyes shot him a harsh look between the edge of her bandanna mask and the lowered brim of her slouch hat.

Hoyt batted his knees to the horse, sending it forward, Bailey McCool right beside him. "Where's C.C.?" she asked, shouting above the sound of their horses' hooves on the platform.

Without answering, Hoyt nodded ahead at a fifty-foot wall of rock overlooking the rail siding.

"I told you he'd be nearby keeping an eye on us," Hoyt said with a smile.

The two raced on, their duster tails flapping on a breeze.

Watching behind the glass engine door as the two outlaws rode out of sight, the fireman looked at the engineer curiously.

"Do they really do that?" asked Lon.

"Do what?" asked Oscar.

"Just, you know, leave a safe standing open while they get tallied up and ready to leave the station?"

"Damned if I know, Lon," said Oscar, sounding a little agitated now at how his fireman had acted: holding the gunman's six-shooter, ogling it like a fool. "Maybe next time you can ask him!"

The two got quiet as a few horses ran across the platform and down onto the rocky trail, joining other riders.

"Nowadays they just ride in and rob us right at the station," the engineer said with a sad face. "Don't even give us time to pull away from the siding!"

"I'm sorry we're getting robbed," said Lon, "but that was as nice as anything that's happened to me in a long while, getting to check out that big ol' shiny Remmy —"

"You have no idea in hell who that was, do you?" the engineer cut in.

"Well, no," said Lon, "I can't say that I do. He was friendly enough."

"Friendly enough . . . !"

The engineer sat watching a large number of mounted gunmen ride off of the rail platform in a burst of dust. They rode strewn out along the trail in the direction of Denver City.

"That was none other than Jackson Hoyt himself!"

"Jax Hoyt? So he really is one of them," said Lon the fireman, sounding amazed. "One of the long riders?"

"He's not only one of them," said the

engineer. "He's one of the top men, right up there with C.C. Ellis, Holden Ryan and Poker Joe Elliot. We might be lucky to still be alive."

"Jackson Hoyt stood right here," said the fireman, pointing down at the iron floor in front of him. "I asked about his gun. Damned if he didn't hand it to me like we were ol' pals or something!"

"I had a hard time believing that myself!" said the engineer. "If I was you, I wouldn't be spreading that story around much. People will think you're touched."

"Hell, Oscar," the fireman said to the engineer, "you saw it with your own eyes!"

"Yeah, but I would keep quiet about it," said Oscar. "Ain't nobody going to believe it but you and me."

Outside on the trail, the new sheriff and his two town deputies galloped along behind the cloud of dust left by the many fleeing gunmen.

"Give them hell, lawmen!" the engineer said in a low half-joking voice.

The fireman chuckled to himself, then said aloud to the engineer, "Wouldn't it be something if this brand-new sheriff got shot by that big Remington I just now held in my hand?"

"Yeah," said the engineer, watching the

three riders tearing off in the direction of the gunmen. "But it ain't likely any railroad-owned jakes are gonna let themselves get close enough to stop a bullet, the cowardly sumbitches." He spit on the firebox and watched it sizzle. "Maybe our new sheriff and deputies will be better. We'll see."

Three miles from New Water Stop One, a huge boulder stood at a sharp northern turn in the trail. The fork merged onto a thinner trail running upward into a jumbled world of boulders and ancient pines. Farther up lay the heart of the Rocky Mountain range, gateway to countless hidden caverns and escape trails reaching in every direction.

Randolph Doss, former army colonel and recently appointed head of Colorado Western Express Railroad, was seated atop a tall chestnut stallion, and he turned his binoculars away from the rugged mountain peaks. He pointed them instead toward the long swell of dust rising along the trail from the new water stop outside of Boulder City.

"And now I'll soon have every last one of you bastards where I want you!" he said quietly to the long swirling dust.

He smiled indifferently around a stub of a black cigar clamped in his teeth. He lowered the binoculars, scowled toward the rising dust and turned to the man beside him.

"Scotty," he said, "bring Sonny Ryan over here. I want to educate him, show him how his pa dies today, choking on his own bleeding guts."

He smiled faintly at the thought and rolled the cigar stub around in his lips. The colonel lowered his binoculars and scowled and cursed under his breath toward the rising dust. Grumbling to no one in particular, he added aloud, "There's history fixin' to be made here today. Let every righteous man see it and know it to be true."

"Going right now, Colonel," Scotty Dowell replied, turning his horse toward a dilapidated miners' shack standing tilted in a small clearing among towering rock a hundred yards away. "I'm sure by now our guards have beaten him properly —"

"Wait, Scotty!" said Doss, stopping the aging trail scout and his horse in their tracks. "Refresh my memory."

The old scout turned his horse back to Doss and sidled in close.

"Well, Colonel," he said just between the two of them, "you told me to make sure they stick a feed sack over his head and beat him soundly with pocket clubs before you send his head to his pa."

Doss pondered for a moment.

"Yes, correct. I did say that," Doss replied. "By now I'm sure the guards have already beaten Sonny Ryan half to death. If we can drag in Holden and Sonny Ryan both together still alive, we'll decide then who gets to watch who die and who gets the other's head thrown on his lap. Are we clear on that?"

"Yes, Colonel, we're clear," said Scotty.

He started to turn his horse again. Doss stopped him with a raised hand.

"Oh, and Scotty," he said. He gestured toward a coiled lariat hanging from his own saddle horn. "Drag Sonny over here on the end of a rope. Don't dare trust that rotten sumbitch in a saddle."

"I can walk him over here on my rope, Colonel, if it's all the same to you?" said the old trail scout.

"No, Scotty," said Doss, "I think dragging him over here will be better for everybody overall. Good for morale. Folks like seeing justice at work in the flesh. It gives them hope!"

Seeing justice at work in the flesh? Scotty looked all around the empty endless land. *Gives them hope?*

With a proud look, Doss said, "We're doing a hell of a job out here, Scotty. Just make sure Sonny Ryan doesn't get his boots in a set of stirrups. Tell the guards to soften him up one more time. Then bring them with you. We won't need them over at the shack once Sonny is gone."

"Will do, Colonel."

In a moment Scotty was gone, his horse stirring up dust around its hooves.

Colonel Doss watched as the trail scout rode away at a quick gallop. He continued watching until Scotty slid his horse to a halt outside the shack a hundred yards away and bounded in through a side door.

Good man, Doss told himself.

He closed his eyes and enjoyed the feel of a cool wind on his face. He'd been here only a short while, but he was already seeing signs of the long riders, a gang of train and bank robbers, breaking up before his eyes.

He smiled. That was enough to keep him in this game, hot and heavy, he thought, drifting, catching flashes of the grueling trip he'd made here little more than a month ago. He reflected on the train ride from Gunn Point, almost nonstop down from the Medicine Bow range, along the mountain line toward New Water Stop One, through a dozen plank towns and mining camps in between, and now, at last, here he stood, the new vice president and security chief of the western rails region.

His eyes opened at the sound of the men leaving the shack and mounting their horses. He saw their prisoner wobble on his feet, his head covered by a blood-soaked feed sack as Scotty uncoiled one end of his lariat and tied it around his ankles. The colonel heard the bound prisoner try to shout something, but he was quickly knocked to the ground by guard Andrew Maggen's pocket club atop his head.

Oh, my! Poor, poor Sonny.

The colonel chuckled to himself, taking delight in the dazed man lying helpless in the rocky dirt. He watched the guard draw back a boot and kick the downed outlaw in his side.

Yes! That's the way. Give it to him, Andrew! Doss pounded a fist into his palm. *Give it to him hard and mean. Give it to him like the thief he is!*

The colonel stopped and took control of himself. Opening his tightened fist, he glanced around self-consciously, making sure no one had been watching. When he looked back at the guards, at Scotty and the man he dragged behind him, he kept his reaction to a guarded smile, yet he did let go an "Oops!" and a childlike giggle when he saw the bloody feed sack strike a large rock. As Scotty continued dragging the limp figure, the bloody feed sack and its contents time and again struck rocks large and small. Each time, the colonel winced, but then smiled and chuffed and kept himself from laughing out loud.

Inside the rail shack, Colonel Doss stood back, excited, fidgeting in place. "I hope to hell you haven't smothered him to death!" he shouted, watching the two guards and Scotty make their third attempt to get Sonny Ryan seated upright in a chair.

The first two times, Sonny had sat upright for only a few seconds. As soon as Doss stepped in front of him and repeated the same words — "Well, well, Sonny, what will your pa have to say about this?" — Sonny slid down from the chair to the floor. As if he were some boneless reptile, his motion was silent until he landed with his head thumping on the hard pine planks.

This time, Scotty stood behind the bound prisoner and held his head upright, as if his balance depended solely on the tilt of the head.

Doss straightened his white shirt, shot his cuffs and said, "Very well, where were we?" He kept his shiny boots spread wide and crouched forward, hovering like some predator from the wilds.

Gripping the bloodstained feed sack, Doss said for the third time, in the harshest tone yet, "Well, well, Sonny, what will your pa have to say about this?"

With his hand gripping the feed sack, he motioned for Scotty to turn loose. Colonel Doss grinned cruelly. "I suppose he'll realize that sometimes —"

Doss stopped his rehearsed lines as Sonny started sliding down again. The colonel gripped tighter, but the weight was greater than he had expected.

By hell, I'm losing him! Doss thought, feeling the weight pulling his hand down, and grabbed the chairback with his other hand for support.

I can't lose him! I can't lose him!

He held on a moment longer by sheer determination. But it wasn't enough. His prisoner was sliding down.

"Scotty! Grab him," Doss shouted.

The old trail scout gabbed Sonny's head on either side, but he grabbed too late. The feed sack string popped loose from around Sonny's neck and spread open, revealing a swollen, bloody chin and a blackly bruised throat and neck.

"Can you two help us out here?" Doss shouted at the guards, who stood watching in consternation as the feed sack climbed higher up the battered face.

They both jumped in, but also too late.

"Damn it, Sonny," one guard shouted. "I know you hear me! Lie still or I'll beat you worse!"

"Shut the hell up!" shouted Doss.

When Sonny slid from the chair for the third time, he landed between Doss's feet and left him holding the bloody feed sack. Without the weight on the chair, Doss couldn't keep it from flipping him up and backward. He got to his knees and slung the feed sack away from him. Scotty helped him stand.

"All right, damn it to hell!" shouted the colonel. "Enough of this foolishness!" He took a towel Scotty offered him and wiped his hands. "Throw water on this sumbitch and wake him up! I *am* going to talk to him right this minute!"

With a nod from Scotty, Andrew Maggen stepped over, picked up the house water bucket and dipper and dipped water over the swollen face.

"Sonny Ryan! Wake up in there, Sonny!" Maggen said. "I'll pour this whole bucket on you."

He dipped more water on the battered face. Dried blood met the water and was washed away, along with much of the dirt.

Maggen looked closer. The body hadn't moved an inch.

"Scotty, come take a look here," he said as quietly as he could.

Both Scotty and the other guard stepped over and looked down with Maggen.

"Holy Joe and Mary!" Scotty said in barely a whisper.

But Colonel Doss heard him anyway. "What is it, Scotty?"

"Colonel, Sir," said Scotty, "I don't know if this is good news or bad. It might be both."

"Then why don't you tell me, my good man!" Doss said sarcastically. "If it is such a puzzle for you, perhaps I can help figure it out."

"Yes, Colonel," said the aging trail scout. "The thing that's good is that Sonny Ryan is still alive. Far as we know anyway."

Doss gave him a dark stare.

"Okay, sir," said Scotty. "The bad news, depending on how you look at it, is" — he paused for just a second — "this poor sumbitch laying here ain't Sonny Ryan at all."

Chapter 2

At the edge of the standing rock wall where C.C. Ellis lay with a long rifle and scope in hand, he waited until Hoyt and Bailey McCool rode up at the same time as two others, Poker Joe Elliot and Filo Anderson. While the four milled below him on their restless horses, Ellis stood up, dusted himself off.

"Nobody's on your trail," he said.

A sigh went up and the four relaxed in their saddles. Bailey shoved her rifle down into its saddle boot.

"Which ones of us are carrying the you-know-what?" she asked.

She eyed a large leather bag tied down behind Poker Joe Elliot's saddle and an identical bag tied down behind Filo Anderson's. Both bags looked stuffed to the seams.

"Coming down," said C.C. Ellis. He stepped back out of sight.

The four sat their horses, waiting until he

walked around the bottom of the rock and stood among them, the scoped rifle in his gloved hand. With the other he patted the leather bag behind Poker Joe's saddle.

"It looks like all of you are alive and well."

The four riders nodded as one. Ellis looked them over thoroughly and saw no wounds on rider or horse.

Good! Damn good.

"As all of you know," he continued, "I have no idea where Harper Greer has taken the bags with the money in them. But these two locked bags are filled with old newspapers." He gave a slight grin. "That's why we call them decoys."

The riders chuckled softly.

Sitting close beside Bailey McCool, Jackson Hoyt spoke up. "If I was a betting man, I'd say that Greer and somebody else — maybe Kid Santa Cruz — have taken the real bags of cash and buried them out here somewhere for later." He looked around as he spoke. "Anybody want to join me the next few days? We'll turn over every rock out here, looking for it." He gestured across the broad rock-strewn terrain.

The group fell quiet, knowing the impossibility of what Hoyt was saying. Everybody here was certain that C.C. Ellis knew where Old Man Greer and whomever he'd partnered with these days had hidden the stolen money. This was the same outlaw ritual they went through after every job — a way of proving their trust in one another.

Bailey McCool sighed under her breath. "Okay," she said, trying not to sound bored, "wherever it is, we know we'll all get our share. We always do. Now that you've seen the four of us are alive and accounted for, can we cut out of here?"

"Sounds good to me," Ellis said.

"I'll second the lady's motion," Hoyt said.

The lady? "Watch your language," said Bailey, feigning offense.

Hoyt tipped his hat to her in apology. Then he stepped down from his saddle, walked around the edge of the big rock and came back leading Ellis's dapple gray gelding, Shadow.

After a second, Ellis said, "Okay, the four of you are clear and clean. You've done well." He looked from one to the other. "Now get out of here. You'll hear from me or another of us soon as the time is right."

The four riders separated, Poker Joe Elliot and Filo Anderson nudging their horses toward the trail at a walk. But before the two riders reached the trail, the sound of heavy gunfire resounded from the distant hillsides.

"Whoa now!" said Hoyt, pulling back on his horse's reins even though the animal was standing still. His big Mexican desert barb reared, but only a few inches, then settled.

"Who headed out that way?" Ellis asked quickly, gathering his restless barb beneath him.

Bailey sidled over closer, her horse feeling her tension in its reins.

"Harvey Brewer, Sammy Kendricks!" Bailey said. "And three new men: James Spivey and the Mexican brothers, Lejo and Juan Sanchez."

The rifle fire grew stronger as Ellis topped off his big-rifle ammunition and checked his Colt. Hoyt poked fresh rounds into a bandolier he slipped over his shoulder and across his chest.

Poker Joe and Filo Anderson turned and hurried back to the big rock, their rifles coming up from their saddle boots.

"What the hell is all this?" Poker Joe shouted.

"We've got five men who headed out that way," said Ellis. "We're going to make sure it's not them."

He checked his short double-barreled shotgun, clicked it shut and hung it from a clip on his saddle horn.

"Oh, are you now?" said Poker Joe in a

derisive tone. "And do what, jump in before you even see if it's our men being shot at?"

"You don't have to go, Poker Joe," said Hoyt.

But Joe didn't seem to hear. "And what if it's not our men under fire?" Joe said. "What, then? Listen to them damned rifles! It sounds like over a dozen. Filo and me ain't going!"

"You got that right," said Anderson. "I might could see it if we knew it's our men taking a starching. Hell, these could be deserters or slavers!"

"Or long riders like us?" Hoyt put in.

He reached over and grabbed a handful of rounds from the small wooden ammunition box resting on Ellis's knee and dropped them in his duster pocket. Shots exploded from the hillsides farther ahead.

"You and your mouth, Jax!" said Filo. "I'm sick of it!"

"I've got time to cure you of that sickness, Filo," said Hoyt quietly.

"That's enough!" said Ellis.

He glared at Filo Anderson and Poker Joe Elliot. Filo's hand rested around the chamber of his rifle, his thumb on the hammer. Hoyt only sat comfortably slumped in his saddle, his right hand gloveless, only inches from his big shiny Remington.

Ellis knew what would come next. "I told you. Neither of you has to go," he said.

The rifle fire ahead of them was growing worse. Ellis could see it being his men pinned down now, needing help bad.

"Let me in!" said Bailey, bumping her horse against Poker Joe's.

"What are you doing, Bailey?" Ellis asked her roughly.

"What do you think?" she said. "I'm getting some ammunition from you."

Reaching in, she grabbed a handful of rifle rounds.

Ellis gazed calmly at Poker Joe as Bailey raised her rifle, laid it across her lap and started topping it out with ammunition.

"Damn it! Damn it! Damn it to bloody blue hell!" shouted Poker Joe.

He yanked his big Colt from a flowery-rosette-engraved belly holster, checked it and stoved it back down into place. He turned a heated stare to Jax Hoyt.

"It amazes me that somebody hasn't already shot you a dozen times in the head! I would gladly hold their horses while they did it."

Without saying a word in reply, Hoyt reached over, picked up the ammunition box from Ellis's knee and held it out to Poker Joe — as a peace offering? Mockery?

"This son of a bitch!" Poker Joe grumbled under his breath, yanking on his horse's reins. "All right. Let's go shoot the living hell out of these slack-jawed jakes! Get it done and over with!"

Hoyt gave Bailey McCool a faint smile. "They'll be all right once they start fighting."

Harvey Brewer, a former rider with the James-Younger Gang, had been given charge of a four-man unit before riding to the rail station at New Water Stop One. The robbery itself had been a piece of cake. The big walk-in safe had been left unlocked. Brewer didn't know if the conveniently open safe had been a setup or a foul-up. He might never know, he told himself. But that was all right with him. He saw huge banded stacks of cash go into leather bags with locks on them — payroll money intended for the commercial mining operation. He would be there for his share when those locks were removed. He smiled to himself, feeling good thinking about it.

But that had been an hour ago, he reminded himself as he huddled down behind a rock while bullets streaked past overhead and careened off the stone-covered hillside. Now only he, Sammy Kendricks and Juan

Sanchez were still alive, and Juan lay bleeding from a bullet hole in his chest. The other two, Lejo Sanchez and James Spivey, had fallen dead on the rocky trail twenty yards away, where the railroad security ambush had started.

"Is Juan going to make it?" Brewer asked Kendricks during a short lull in the rifle fire.

"I don't know." Kendricks looked down at his bloody hands. "I packed his wound with a shirt from his saddlebags. That's all I can do for now. He needs a doctor really bad."

"I know," said Brewer. "Damn it, I should have seen this coming."

"You had no way to see it coming," said Kendricks. "I think that's why it's called an ambush."

"Still," said Brewer. He was about to say something else but stopped as he heard the rifles start firing again.

"Wait a minute!" he said, hearing no bullets hit the nearby rocks, only higher up the hillside. "What's going on here? They're not shooting at us!"

"They damned sure ain't!" shouted Kendricks, quickly levering a round up into his rifle chamber.

Atop the hillside more rifle shots joined in. The riflemen above them jockeyed all around for better position. One rifleman let out a sharp yelp and fell among rock and brush. Brewer gave a strange, wild grin.

"Hear that, Juan? We've got pals up there!" he yelled to Juan Sanchez, who held a blood-smeared Colt cocked across his lap, in case he decided to use it on himself, should their situation get any worse.

"Give them . . . hell, *mis amigos,*" Juan replied in a failing voice. He smiled a bloody smile and tipped his gun barrel toward them. "If you help me sit up, I'll kill more of these *bastardos!*"

"Obliged, Juan," said Brewer, "but you lie still there and stop bleeding. There's going to be plenty of *bastardos* to go around."

Listening to the fierce rifle fire still raging atop the hills, Kendricks said, "I don't know who's up there saving our asses, but I'd sure like to walk up there and shake their hands."

"Go ahead, Sammy," said Brewer, "I'll wait here and keep you covered. Thank them kindly for their help. Have them send me down a bottle of rye if they've got one to share."

A hard barrage of gunfire resounded from their right.

"What the hell?" said Sammy Kendricks, looking in the direction of this new gunfire. "Sounds like more folks coming to attend our little shindig!"

Brewer continued firing as he said, "Better hope to hell they're not more railroad security!"

Chapter 3

Bailey McCool rode the wind down.

She neither heard nor felt the bullet that knocked her from her saddle and sent blood gushing up into her face. A hard shuddering feeling had overcome her like a sharp bolt of lightning. Something warned her she had just been shot, and the warning was correct.

She was not conscious or completely unconscious. Her first instinct was to hold on, stay in the saddle.

Like any hard-assed outlaw, she thought. But the horse, the saddle and all of the other elements involved, including the pain that had half circled her body, were having none of it. She tried, though.

Damn right I did! But at the last second, when she'd done all she could to stay in the saddle, an edge of darkness fell across her and told her that it was no longer within her power to stay. She accepted the realization.

All right, I can let go now, I suppose.

She lifted her boot from the stirrups and leaned back rather than snag her spurs and cause herself to be dragged to death. She let the reins slip from her hand and felt the saddle melt away beneath her, remembering somewhere in her childhood old vaqueros and wranglers murmuring, *Ride the wind down, child.* So she did or at least her interpretation of it.

Now she felt a cool breeze move easily across her face and the open wound on her bare chest. The canvas sides of the small medical wagon were rolled up and tied in place, offering light for the young doctor fella seated beside her to do his job. The canvas had protected them from a hard rain they had passed through earlier. She recalled the sound of heavy thunder.

As she awakened more, she saw the young doctor push the man standing beside him away from her cot.

"Stand back, Cal Lindsey!" he said to the hovering rifleman. "Give her room to breathe!"

Lindsey moved only an inch farther, then stopped and stood his ground.

"The chief said to keep my eyes on her,

Doc. By God that's what I'm doing!"

"I see you are, indeed!" said the doctor, Douglas Gray.

"What are you saying, Doc?" said Lindsey, catching the accusing tone of the young doctor. He took a threatening step closer to the doctor.

Dr. Gray, hired as a railroad security gunman owing to his medical training, raised a .36 Navy Colt quickly from the cot beside Bailey and swung it around, then cocked, leveled and aimed it at Cal Lindsey's face. Lindsey stopped cold. His hands went up defensively and he stepped back.

"Smart move," said the doctor. "Now turn and look away while I finish bandaging this young lady's side."

"Young lady?" said Lindsey. "Ha!"

But in spite of his attitude, he turned and looked out the open side into the rocky hills beyond the tracks running from Denver City.

Leaning down close to Bailey, who'd been watching and listening, the doctor laid down the Navy Colt and whispered, "Don't worry. It's never loaded."

Then he slipped a hand under her shoulder and said, "If I help, do you think you can sit up long enough for me to get your side bandaged?"

Lindsey looked back over his shoulder. "I'll hold her up, Doctor. That's why I'm here, to help you with her."

The doctor saw the look on the woman's face and murmured, "I understand."

He turned to Cal Lindsey and said, "Oh, all right, if you can behave yourself."

"Oh, I can, Doc!" said Lindsey, "I swear I can!"

He turned around and saw the woman lying bare chested, the doctor holding a cloth pressed against a thin seepage of blood on her side.

"My, oh, my!" said Lindsey, struck dumb by the sight of the beautiful woman's breasts. He stepped closer. "We have got to do whatever it takes to save this woman's life!"

"That's the spirit I'm looking for, Lindsey."

The doctor pressed Bailey's hand over the cloth covering the wound and causally flipped a sheet up over her, wound, breasts and all.

"Now, then," he added, "take this medical flask and go to my horse. There's a bottle of medicinal whiskey there in my saddlebags. Fill the flask halfway full of whiskey. Then take it to the little brook right over the hill and fill it the rest of the way with fresh brook water."

He gave Cal Lindsey a serious look. "Will you do that for me, Cal? For us?"

He gestured a hand toward Bailey. She gave Lindsey a faint coy smile, making herself a part of whatever the doctor was up to.

"Oh, yes!" Lindsey said. "I can do all that!" He fumbled with the flask, almost dropped it.

"Well, Cal," the young doctor said, "what are we waiting for? The rain has moved out. When you get back, you'll have to help me get the rest of her clothes off and hand-bathe her all over."

"I can do that too! I swear to God I can!" said Lindsey. "Whatever it takes to save this woman's life!"

The two watched as Lindsey hurried out of the wagon toward the rope line of security men's horses.

"Okay, let's get busy," said Dr. Gray. "We're less than half a mile from the brook. I estimate his trip at around fifteen minutes there and back."

As he spoke, he pulled back the sheet covering her. "Time to get you undressed and into one of our cloth surgery gowns, dress the wound and get you cleaned up before he gets back. Are you with me?"

"I'm with you," Bailey said, already pushing down her trousers.

As he helped her undress quickly, he asked, "Were you riding with the good guys or the bad guys?"

"How do you tell them apart?" she asked.

"I have no idea," Gray said. "Anyway, I'm nobody's judge."

He helped her ease back down on the cot, her trousers, socks and undergarments in a pile on a folding chair. "If they're not shooting at me, I figure they are the good guys."

"That's how it was with me," Bailey said. "I was on my way to visit a family I know. All of a sudden, I was between two groups of men trying to kill one another. All I wanted to do was get out of there! Instead, I got shot!"

"Listen," he said, picking up the bandage wrapping and scissors, "I don't know if that story is true or not. I don't care. But whatever you do, stick to it."

"It happens to be true," Bailey said.

"Good!" said the doctor. "If you're clean — no charges, no bounty on you — they'll have to let you go."

"That's a relief," Bailey replied. "Out of curiosity, what would have happened if I was one of the riders they're after?"

"This is the railroad," said the doctor.

"They hang people if it suits them or they shoot them down like dogs and leave them lying where they fall."

"Why are you with them, Doctor?" Bailey asked.

"They were looking for a security agent with medical experience. If I stay for a full year, I get a nice bonus. I've got only a few weeks to go." He raised his crossed fingers. "Wish me luck."

"Good luck, Doctor," she said, raising her crossed fingers in reply. "I hope you'll wish me the same."

"I do," he said.

He saw her wince a little in pain from the wound. The bullet had struck her in the ribs. Instead of entering her chest cavity, it had followed her rib cage, leaving a purple-red welt of swollen fresh that might have otherwise been made by some hungry carnivorous creature. The bullet had circled around to her back and exited a few inches from the center.

"I can give you some tincture of opium for the pain," he said. "But it's going to hurt for a while, I'm afraid, and we don't want to turn you into a hop."

"We don't?" she said, partly joking. "Not even just a little?"

"Okay, if you think you need it."

"Oh, I need it."

He turned to his medical bag and took out a small blue bottle and a spoon. As he opened the bottle, he gave her a cautioning look.

"Don't worry," she said. "I know better than to start using it too much."

"That's good." He poured a small amount into the spoon and held it out to her. "Its name is laudanum. Folks here call it Blue River. You should need it for only a day or two."

"Blue River," she repeated. "I've heard of it somewhere. Laudanum. It does wonders for pain too."

Bailey took the bitter dose and lay back on the cot. A few moments later, she felt the warm glow of morphine moving all through her, all around her.

Oh, Doctor, she thought, *you've touched me in a warm, soft spot. . . .*

She smiled to herself, floating, drifting, free of bullet holes, free of the biting stiches holding the tear in her back together.

"Here comes Cal Lindsey with our brook water now," she heard the doctor say as from the other end of some long corridor.

She wouldn't let him know this was not her first time using tincture of opium, though it was her first time using it for medicinal purpose.

Blue River. That's funny. She smiled and continued to drift as she heard boots climb the steps into the wagon.

"Here's the flask," Lindsey said, a little out of breath. "Let me give it to her, okay?"

Bailey lay only half asleep, listening, her eyes closed.

"No, stay right there, Cal," said the doctor. "She's asleep. What the hell kept you anyway?"

"Nothing!" said Lindsey. "I hurried to the brook and right back here!"

"Well, as you can see, she's asleep. I gave her some Blue River laud. She fell under right away. I had to undress her, wash her, put her in a sleeping gown and do everything myself."

"Damn it!" said Lindsey. "Are you sure I shouldn't go ahead and just look her over good, make sure —"

"Put it out of your mind, Cal," the doctor said, cutting him off.

"I'll be damned if I will!" Lindsey said.

He trembled in rage — rage fueled by his growing need for laudanum, which he'd acquired over the past month.

"Hey, take it easy, Cal," said Dr. Gray. "Tomorrow's another day." He picked up the little blue bottle, uncorked it and held it out to the irritated gunman. "Here, have a shot. It'll settle you down. Next time, when I send you to do something, don't dawdle."

He watched Lindsey take a good-sized swallow straight from the bottle.

"Ah, yeah. This will do for now," the man said, looking down at the dozing woman. "But I swear, I want this woman bad," he murmured.

"I can see you do." The doctor nodded at the blue bottle in Cal Lindsey's hand. "But you'll have to wait. Why don't you stick the bottle down in your pocket, Cal? I ordered plenty this month."

"Yeah?" Lindsey said, already feeling the drug moving in his chest. "It feels like you've beefed it up some too."

"I always do," the young doctor said. "It happens to be my specialty."

"It's mighty good," Lindsey said.

He chuckled, feeling the Blue River run up and down him like a pair of warm friendly hands.

"All right, then. Let it take the edge off of your lustful urgings, Cal," the doctor said. "You can pay me for it come payday."

Two days earlier
Since the gun battle ended, Kid Santa Cruz had been busily separating the living from

the dead. He stopped when he saw Brewer, Kendricks and Juan Sanchez, wounded, riding into the camp. The Kid took note of a fourth man sitting slumped on his horse between them, his hat brim lowered and a bandanna masking his face.

A stranger! The hell is this, the Kid asked himself, his Colt smoking in his hand from shooting badly wounded security agents where they lay bleeding in the dirt. He'd always had a problem with strangers, had all his life.

The Kid had grown up with a bad stutter. None of the outlaws he rode with dared mock, laugh or in any way make fun of him. He could tell there were times when one might mistake the stammer in his voice for some flaw in his mental capacity. But that was a belief he quickly cured them of if he allowed himself to take offense. Mostly he let it go. But strangers almost always required a reckoning of some sort.

Not so with C.C. Ellis. The Kid and Ellis always seemed to understand what each other meant.

"Don't nobody shoot," Brewer called out then, gesturing at the masked stranger riding beside him. "He's with us."

Kid Santa Cruz saw a swollen black eye above the stranger's mask.

The hell is this? he asked himself again.

"Hey, Kid," Kendricks said, "you want to give me a hand getting Juan down? He's shot bad."

He swung down from his saddle and the Kid walked over to him, holstering his Colt.

Brewer cut in. "Hey, give us a minute here, Sammy! I want Ellis to see our surprise."

Ellis appeared from behind a twisted ancient juniper, a rifle hanging in his hand. He motioned for the Kid and Kendricks to go on and get Juan Sanchez down from his saddle. Blood dripped from both stirrups.

"Look what I've got here, C.C.!" Brewer gestured at the masked stranger. "Guess who this is!"

Ellis gave the stranger a quick once-over — the black suit a little tight across the shoulders, the trouser legs too short, leaving a full view of battered boots that Ellis would have recognized anywhere. Yet he went along with Brewer's gag.

"I'm guessing a railroad agent," Ellis said. Looking at the black eye, he added, "One who let himself take a recent beating from some drunken cowhand and lay there, begging him to stop."

"Not on your worthless life," said the stranger. He jerked down his mask as he dismounted.

"I'll be damned! Sonny Ryan!" said Ellis, looking as surprised as he might have been expected to be after a long hard gun battle, the smell of it still looming on the still air. "We all figured you'd stumbled around and got yourself killed!"

Sonny and Ellis both laughed.

"What happened to you, Sonny?"

"I got away, as you can see," Sonny replied. "I heard somebody needed to get over here and save your skin, so here I came running!"

Now that they had spent enough time razzing each other, Sonny cleared his throat and said, "Truth is, Freddie Bell and Hawk Creek Evans tracked me to a shack the new security chief was holding me in. There were two guards in there working me over, as you can see. Freddie and Hawk Creek weren't there two full hours, and they grabbed a lone rider sneaking in unannounced. They waited until the two guards went out front to have a chew and a smoke. They eased in, knocked the man colder than a day-old dog turd and traded him and me places, clothes and all. Turns out, the rider was the railroad owner's new son-in-law! Owner sent him all around to learn the business!"

The men in camp who had gathered

around at the news of Sonny Ryan's arrival roared with laughter.

"They had the son-in-law gagged with a bandanna, and they stuck a flour sack over his head! That's the same way they did me!" Sonny said through the laughter. "I expect the guard might have beat him to death before they found out who he was." He settled himself and said, "I wouldn't be laughing, except I learned he's been going around killing prisoners himself, after seeing he couldn't get any information from them. I hope they beat that sumbitch to death!"

"Well, you're back in the fold now, Sonny," said C.C. "Have some coffee while we fix you a steak."

"Obliged," said Sonny, looking all around. "Where's Bailey?"

"Bailey took a bullet," said C.C., "and it knocked her from her saddle. She was alive the last our men saw her. They said security men were carrying her off the trail."

Sonny's expression turned angry. "What are you doing to find her, C.C.?"

"I've got men covering every trail and game path in these hills, searching for her," Ellis replied. "I was on my way when you and Brewer rode in. You want to come along?"

Sonny calmed down and let out a breath.

"I was getting a little edgy," he said. "I know you're doing everything you can. Sure, I'll ride with you."

Ellis looked at the man standing beside the campfire, a long meat fork in his hand. "No steak for Sonny or me right now, Charlie," he said. "Fill us a couple of canteens with coffee. We'll take them with us."

"Aw, you both got to eat," Charlie Hodges said.

"We'll eat when we get back," said Sonny, checking his Colt and slipping it back into his holster.

"When's that going to be?" Hodges asked.

"When we find Bailey McCool," said C.C. Ellis.

Kid Santa Cruz and Sammy Kendricks had returned from carrying Juan Sanchez to a canvas overhang set up for treating the wounded, and they immediately started readying their horses for the trail.

"Hey!" Sonny said. "Where do you two think you're going?"

"To fi-fi-fi-fi —"

"To find Bailey McCool," Kendricks cut in, helping the Kid out.

Kid Santa Cruz nodded and said clearly, "That's right!"

Sonny saw the determination in their eyes.

"All right," he said. He looked around at the rest of the men. "After you eat, catch up with us on the trail." He paused, then added, "Bring your own coffee!"

CHAPTER 4

Before leaving the shack where the railroad owner's son-in-law had been killed, Security Chief Randolph Doss made sure his trail scout, Scotty Dowell, and the two guards got rid of any evidence that might link the colonel to the young man's death.

The colonel even saw to it that the battered body was cleaned up and buried in a pine coffin in a shallow grave. The grave was then covered with stones against an invasion of coyotes or other frontier predators.

What killer would have gone to such trouble as that? He smiled to himself.

Should the story ever come to light, it was Sonny Ryan — that craven, bloodthirsty, fiendish bastard — who had beaten the poor man to death before he made his getaway. *Something along the line,* Doss had decided, but he wasn't going to worry about it right now. He had this all going according to his new plan.

He watched flames seep up as from the bowels of the earth and spread. When the shack was no longer distinguishable from a roiling fireball, he saw Scotty and one of the guards throw what was left of their shortening torches into the flames and come trotting back to the horses, like obedient hounds from a hunt. At that point he was certain none of these three witnesses would ever turn on him.

In this vast, wild, dangerous land, men died every day. Some were thrown from their horse and trampled under hoof. Some slipped from the edge of a high cliff — oops! — and were never seen again. Some had their brains bashed out in raging rivers, others grabbed bull rattlers from their saddlebags, and Doss knew of men blowing their own heads off in the middle of the night, owing to anything from faithless love to dark, violent war memories.

"Ready to go, Colonel?" Scotty asked, seated in his saddle beside him.

The colonel looked at each of the three with a faint smile. It was as if parts of this violent land had been created in hell specifically as a place for man to kill man with almost total impunity.

"Tell me, Scotty," he said, quietly, still

smiling. "Do you ever think about the war? Do they ever bother you, the things you did, the things you saw?"

"What war is that, Colonel?" the aging trail scout replied, turning his horse to the trail. "I've been in a war of some kind or other since I was seven."

"None of it ever bothers you?" the colonel pressed.

Scotty shook his head. "Hell no. What's to bother about? I kilt everybody that couldn't kill me first! Had they kilt me first, I wouldn't've known it. So it wouldn't have mattered much, would it?"

"Exactly," the colonel said, and he was done with the matter. Backing his horse a step, he turned it to the trail and put it forward. *Nothing to worry about . . .*

Scotty and the two guards looked at one another, shrugged and rode off behind him.

Atop a stony rise, Sonny Ryan and C.C. Ellis sat their horses on a ledge partly hidden by a heavy growth of juniper, aspen and pine. They looked all around at the hillside saturated from two days of storms. Rivulets still trickled between rocks and ran down. In the northwest sky above a line of spiky foothills, new storm clouds gathered and thunder rumbled.

"Damn it," said Sonny, looking off at the Rocky Mountain line. "Looks like we're in for a full run of storms. These fronts can last a week or two, one blasted storm right after another."

"Or longer," Ellis put in. He hitched a thumb at an overhanging ledge behind them. "Looks like we can get the horses out of the rain at least, if it gets blowing hard."

"Yeah, lucky us," Sonny said, dryly. "We get to sleep with two wet horses under a rock."

Ellis chuffed and shook his head. "Sonny, you'd complain if you lost an ear," he said.

"One ear? No," said Sonny. "But two, yeah, I'd grouse like hell."

"That's what I thought," said Ellis, swinging down from his saddle. "Of all times to get stormed out," he said. He raised a palm to the fine gray mist of rain starting to fall more thickly around them. "We'll never pick up any trail sign after this."

"I'm afraid she might have left something but maybe we've missed it," said Sonny as he dismounted.

"Watch your language," said Ellis. "Something as important as us finding Bailey McCool, I wouldn't miss a trail sign, even if I had to make one up to keep us going."

Sonny let out a breath. "I know that," he

said. "If you did make one up, I'd follow it with you anyway."

The two fell quiet for a long moment.

"Well, I've got the horses," Sonny said.

They both stood up. Sonny dropped their saddles near the fire and tended to the tired animals while Ellis walked farther back into the gradually narrowing overhang and came back with an armload of dry kindling and downfallen limbs. When a small fire stood banked in its rock-lined bed, and the horses were grained and stood resting where their ears touched the stone overhang, Ellis and Sonny sat at the fire drinking tepid coffee from their canteens.

"How far you figure the other six men made it today?" Sonny asked.

"Not far," said Ellis. "I told them to turn back when they got to the big rim. That's about seven miles ahead. I asked them to send us some food and more grain for the horses. They should catch up to us by midmorning." He paused, then added, "I wish I knew something else we could do right now to get her back. We don't know where to search. The fact is, we don't even know if she's dead or alive."

"With this blasted rain washing us out, they could have taken her anywhere. We wouldn't know it," Sonny agreed. "But I don't like thinking she might be laying dead somewhere. Bailey's as tough as they come."

"Yep, but we've got to look at every possibility if it'll help us find her."

"The only people there were ours and the railroad security men," said Sonny. "If we get as far as New Water Stop One with no sign of her, we'll have to find where the railroad men are camped. We'll grab one and see what he can tell us. I've got enough money to open somebody's mouth."

Ellis didn't like the idea of taking one of the railroad agents captive and asking about Bailey McCool. For now the fewer people who knew she was missing, the better. But he wouldn't mention that to Sonny just yet.

"Wherever she is," he said, "you can bet she's doing everything she can to get away."

"Thing is," said Sonny, "if she gives them too much trouble, they'll turn her right over to Willis Dan's Comancheros."

"I still know Willis Dan well enough to talk to him," said Ellis. "Tomorrow after New Water Stop, we'll see about drawing his warriors out of the rocks and have them take us to him. Willis Dan knows something about everything that happens out here."

"He might tell us something about Bailey," said Sonny. "But we'll have to keep him from trying to get his hands on her, if he hasn't already. He knows of places farther south than Mexico where he can get top money for a fiery young woman like her."

"Enough of this," said Ellis. "Let's quit thinking something bad has happened to her. Like as not, the railroad security grabbed her. She's going to deny anything to do with us, and unless they can prove otherwise, they'll turn her loose."

"Yeah, like they did me?" said Sonny. "I'd be beaten to death by now if it hadn't been for Freddie Bell and Hawk Creek Evans looking for me around the old tool shack."

"The rail security men knew you by sight," said Ellis. "I don't think anybody recognized Bailey. When they saw it was you, they got a high killing fever. If I know Bailey, she'll hand them a story they can't argue with." He grinned a little. "That's just one simple advantage women outlaws have over us men."

"Didn't you say she was already on the ground the last you saw of her?" Sonny asked.

"No, Sonny," Ellis replied with irritation. He'd been asked the same question several times in different forms. "Listen real close 'cause I'm not telling this again."

Sonny leaned in, listening. He poked a small branch around in the firebed with his left hand. His right hand lay loose yet poised an inch above his holster.

"We rode in shooting. The railroad men met us head-on as well as on our right flank. I fired straight ahead, then looked to my right. I saw Bailey's horse running forward, wild as hell, but the saddle was empty."

"And you never saw her on the ground, heard her scream or nothing?" said Sonny.

Ellis just stared at him. "I never once in my life heard Bailey McCool scream in the middle of a gunfight, Sonny. Have you?"

"I've never heard her scream at all," said Sonny. "Bailey's not the screaming type. Wherever she is, I figure she's trying as hard to get away as we're trying to find her. The only screaming going on will be from anybody who tries to stop her."

Ellis nodded in agreement.

"She knows that seven days from now we're going to hit the Duncan Mine payroll coming in. I've never known of her missing a job, especially one this big. Maybe she's laying low somewhere until then. Maybe she'll surprise all of us."

Seven days from now? Ellis thought about it.

"How do you know the date?" he asked.

"I found a little twelve-month almanac in the clothes of the man that the guards beat up," said Sonny. "Thought I'd hold on to it, in case I ever want to know where I am any particular month or day. Thought it might be interesting."

Instead of replying, Ellis just stared into the fire. He knew if they hadn't heard anything from Bailey before then, she was probably dead. He thought it, but he kept it to himself. He turned and pulled his saddle closer and rested back against it. Outside the overhang, a new storm had rolled in. Looking out, Ellis watched lightning twist and curl in the black sky.

In the middle of the third stormy night in a row, Bailey awakened on the cot that had become her bed. She didn't move or open her eyes right away, a habit she had taught herself long ago as a child.

As she awakened, she imagined she had felt a soft touch on her forehead, then her face, then her throat.

As the thin veil of sleep stirred from her consciousness, she realized this had nothing to do with her imagination! The hand still rested at her throat; then she felt it move ever so slowly, so gently, loosening the top of her sleeping gown and burrowing softly down under it.

Dr. Gray? she almost asked herself aloud,

yet the same self-preservation she'd taught herself as a child was still strong and well inside her.

She managed to remain silent, knowing that the small dinner knife she'd stuck between the two folded blankets padding the cot was still there, easy for her to grab when and if that time arrived.

Was it Dr. Douglas Gray? Yes, she was certain of it. The hands that traveled over her were smooth, soft, almost feminine. The hands of the young doctor, not those of Cal Lindsey.

She remained lying perfectly still in the wake of the passing storms, even for a good while after the hands had taken satisfaction in their full account of her. Even when she felt certain whatever she'd been involved in was over, she still refused to allow herself to so much as raise her fingertips and wipe the welling of tears from her eyes. Instead, she closed her eyes tighter and let tears run down her temples onto the flat, misshapen pillow.

In the grainy morning hour, she reminded herself that these were not real tears in the present moment. These were tears from a long ways off, tears of a frightened child in some distant place and time.

Stop it! she told herself.

She had heard nothing from that frightened child for a long time, and she didn't want to hear from her now, knowing full well she had taught that child when to cry and when to stop. She sat up on the side of the cot.

As a silver-gray mist crept in and surrounded the wagon and water dripped from its canvas cover, she stood up and stepped out of the gown, naked in the shadowy morning light, knowing that if he wanted to see in full what he had fondled and taken pleasure in, he would never have a better chance than now.

"Are you asleep?" she whispered. She took her time, dressing in the clothes she'd been wearing during the gun battle. Without buttoning her shirt, she stepped over to his small bed, her feet bare. "Are you asleep, Dr. Douglas?" she whispered again. "Dr. Douglas Gray?"

She paused for a second. When the doctor still didn't answer, she picked up an open bottle of Blue River and took a longer-than-usual drink. Seeing the doctor had left an open crate padded with wood shavings and unopened bottles of Blue River, she immediately wrapped the crate in the sheet from her cot, and in spite of the pain from her injured side, she hiked it up over her shoulder.

When the doctor still didn't make a sound, she corked the open bottle, stuck it down behind her waist and leaned down over him, her breasts dangling out of the shirt and close to his face. She swooned from a soft, warm rush of the laudanum.

"Too bad," she whispered. "You got me all warmed up."

She stepped into her boots and picked up the unloaded Navy Colt he'd carelessly left on a small table beside his bed. She buttoned the fly of her trousers and shoved the Navy Colt down into their waist. Beside the Navy Colt, she shoved another unopened bottle of Blue River and walked down the steps from the wagon.

Taking her time, she walked from the wagon to a rope line of seven horses, where a guard sat atop a pine stump dozing, his chin on his chest. In the dark distance, she knew the two wagon mules had been hobbled some fifty yards from camp, grazing on sweet wild grass. Rather than taking a chance on their temperament, she left them there.

Still in no hurry, she looked all around, growing giggly on the dose of laudanum. With little effort, she slipped the guard's rifle from the crook of his arm and held it while she walked to the line of horses. Setting the sheet-wrapped crate on the ground, she loosened the rope line and fashioned it quickly and expertly into a lead rope, which she then ran from horse to horse. When she'd finished, she reshouldered the sheet-wrapped crate and climbed atop the horse she'd chosen for herself. With the guard's rifle across her lap and the lead rope in hand, she leaned forward close to her horse's ear and chuckled almost uncontrollably through an aching, fun-filled laudanum glow.

"I don't know about you," she said merrily with only a minimum effort at restraint, "but I'm ready to leave if the rest of you are."

Chapter 5

Near dawn the two hobbled mules, Elton and Champ, had short-stepped their way, ten inches at a time, until they'd reached the empty blanket bedroll of Cal Lindsey near the waning campfire. Elton, the elder of the two mules, raised his snooping nose from Lindsey's empty bedroll and looked back to where Champ stood watching in the grainy light twelve feet behind him.

In the silence of morning, for reasons no one was likely to ever understand, Elton raised his head to the sky and without warning began braying loudly, as if rough hands had sprung up and were suddenly attempting to skin him alive where he stood.

"My God, man!" a voice shouted. "Lindsey! Shut that sumbitch up or I'll cut his throat!"

"Shoot him!" another sleepy voice shouted.

The sounds of the men's voices caused

Champ to join in, braying straight up. His head, between brays, pointed somewhat in the direction of the brook where Cal Lindsey had tied his horse to a pine the night before. Later it would be discovered that Lindsey's horse was also gone.

A pistol shot streaked upward in warning, yet neither mule gave an inch. If anything, their braying grew louder.

The security squad leader, Detective Lawrence Sterns, jumped into the firelight, a shotgun in his hands.

"Cal Lindsey!" he shouted. "Shut them up before they get the horses riled!"

When Lindsey didn't reply, nor did the horses get riled, Sterns yelled, "Somebody's ass is going to swing from a tree over this!"

"Where are the horses?" a voice called out.

When the shot had been fired, the man guarding the horses had jumped up from the stump where he'd sat sleeping and looked all around.

Nothing!

The horses were gone! His rifle was gone! He gripped a half cup of cold coffee in his hand.

"Where in the living hell are the horses, Baggs?" Sterns bellowed in his face.

"The horses are gone!" Menard Baggs replied. "Everything's gone! We've been robbed!"

"And you saw nothing? Heard nothing?" Sterns shouted.

"They were like ghosts, Mr. Sterns! I never heard them or saw them!" The cup of coffee trembled in Baggs's hand.

"He was asleep," said a man named Ave Pettigo. He stuck a finger in the tin cup of coffee, then raised it and flicked it in Baggs's face.

"Look at this!" Pettigo said, yanking the cup away from Baggs and thrusting it toward Sterns. "This coffee's colder than a witch's teat!"

Sterns dipped his fingertip into the coffee.

"Yes, so it is," he said, staring hard at Baggs in the first rays of sunlight. "You're lucky I don't want to waste a bullet on you," he added. "I would blow your brains into the next territory!"

Pettigo raised a big Starr .44 from his waist and nudged it to Sterns, butt first.

"Here you are, Mr. Sterns," he said. "I'd be honored if you use my gun."

Baggs came slightly out of his frightened stupor and glared at Pettigo with pure shock and hatred. Pettigo gave him only a smug look.

Sterns took Pettigo's big Starr and turned it back and forth in his hand as if considering Pettigo's suggestion. He raised the gun and reached his thumb up to cock the hammer. But the hammer was taller than he was used to with his Colt. Instead of readjusting his grip in front of the men, he handed the Starr back to Pettigo, butt first, looking a little embarrassed.

"Obliged for your offer, Ave, but I won't use it today," said Sterns. "Maybe Baggs has learned his lesson."

Looking at him curiously, Pettigo took the Starr back but said almost insistently, "Are you sure, Mr. Sterns? I don't mind at all."

"You son of a bitch!" Baggs shouted, awake now and fired up.

He knocked Pettigo's pistol from his hand and fell upon him, taking him to the ground, beating him in the face with the coffee cup. Cold coffee flew. The edge of the metal cup left a bloody half-moon cut every time it struck Pettigo's cheek, his chin, his forehead.

"Hold it, damn it!" shouted Sterns.

He and three other men jumped in and pulled apart the two on the ground. The cup was so battered, Baggs couldn't turn it loose. He yelped loudly when someone tried taking it from him, which caused the mules to start braying again, this time more angrily.

Another man jumped in and shouted to Sterns, "Cal Lindsey and his horse are gone too!"

"The hell?" said Sterns.

Except for the braying mules, the camp fell silent for a moment in contemplation.

"So is the woman," said Dr. Gray. He had flipped the canvas up from the rear of the wagon and stood there shoving his shirttails into his trousers. "She's gone, and so is my new shipment of medical supplies."

"This settles any question I had about whether or not she's one of the long riders!" Sterns shouted. "She's in with them up to her pretty little neck!" He pointed at Dr. Douglas Gray. "And you thought she was just some traveler who got tangled up in our ambush!"

"I was giving the young lady the benefit of the doubt," the young doctor said in his own defense. "After this, I might very well have to change my mind about her!"

"Change your mind while you're walking your sorry ass down the trail!" Sterns barked. "You are fired, Doctor! Never show your face in my camp again, or I will have you —"

Sterns stopped abruptly as if stricken to silence at the mere sight of Security Chief Randolph Doss, his trail scout, Scotty Dowell, and the railroad guards Andrew Maggen and Billy Tobin. The four sat their horses abreast, staring down at him.

"What brings you here, Chief Doss?" Sterns managed to say in his best subservient tone of voice. He raised a hand toward his gathered men, quieting them.

The colonel kept completely silent until every eye was upon him and not a single sound could be heard among the men. Finally, he said, "I heard gunfire." He inclined his head toward Elton and Champ and added, "And these two mallet heads, of course."

"We were robbed in the night, Chief Doss," said Sterns. "I hate to admit, we had a prisoner — a member of the long riders, I'm certain. But the gang swept through in the night and sacked us. Took our prisoner, took all of our horses. Even took our former doctor's medical supplies!"

"Your former doctor?" said Doss, looking over at Gray.

"Yes, that's correct, Chief," said Sterns. "I have fired him. He's lucky I haven't flogged and hanged him —"

Doss cut him off, saying to the doctor, "You lost all of your medical supplies to these long riders?"

"Yes, that's correct," said Dr. Gray.

"And a single prisoner is responsible for all of this?" Doss gestured around the campsite.

"Yes, one prisoner," said the doctor. "That is, if she was even in on it. We have nothing to prove she was."

"Oh! She was in on this!" shouted Sterns. "Believe you me!"

"Scotty," Doss said to his scout, who had inched up on his left side, "if Sterns opens his mouth again, mash it good and hard with your rifle butt."

Sterns shut up, trembling with rage.

"One of our men — my personal trail scout, Calvin Lindsey — might very well be on the woman's trail right now," the doctor continued. "Both he and his horse are gone."

Doss shook his head.

"In union with the woman, perhaps? This is all very bad," he said to Sterns. "You've blindly allowed a woman to come in, set you up for a gang of outlaws, take off with your trail scout, your medical supplies and every damn horse you had in camp?"

Sterns raised his hand like a child in school.

"May I say something?" he asked.

"Yes, by all means, please do," said Doss.

He gestured to Scotty to stand down on

cracking Sterns in the mouth with his rifle butt.

He listened to Sterns's version of what had happened overnight, shaking his head now and then in critical disapproval. Yet nothing being said came close to what he and his men had done, beating the railroad owner's son-in-law to death. Or if they had not beaten the ill-fated young man to death, they had, perhaps even worse, washed his tortured face, combed his hair, dusted him off and buried him alive.

As an experienced leader of men, first in the military and now in civilian life, Doss knew that just as important as assigning the mantle of duty was tactfully attaching the yoke of blame.

"Sterns," he said gravely, "owing to the terrible mess the young woman has left you in, I'm assuming your command until we can get everything straightened out."

My command? Sterns felt a cold slap of defeat across his reddened face.

"Chief Doss," he said quickly, "if I may impose on one of your men for the use of his horse, I'm certain we can continue discussing matters while we ride —"

Doss cut him off, motioning toward the supply wagon, where the two mules were now being hitched.

"Men, listen up!" Doss called out a little louder than necessary to Scotty and the two guards, who had sat their horses a few feet behind him. "Would any of you like to ride aboard the mule wagon and volunteer your horse for Mr. Doss to ride?"

"In the mule wagon?" Scotty chuckled. "I don't think so."

Waiting no more than a second for any further reply, Doss said, "There you have it, Mr. Sterns. No volunteers. My men know the value of a good horse. They keep their mount close at hand and allow no one to slip away on it in the dark of night."

He looked around at the faces of Sterns's men, seeing how well they had taken his words.

Sterns stood crestfallen at how mercilessly he had been maligned by his superior in front of every man in camp.

"From now on," Doss continued, "anything that you felt you needed to say to Sterns, you will bring instead to one of these three men gathered around me." Doss indicated the two guards and Scotty Dowell. "I am taking charge of this outfit until it is once again being run properly!"

His words brought some whistles and applause. Dr. Gray gave a quick cheer, but hurried back inside the wagon to let up the canvas side flaps and clear space for himself and whoever else would be reduced from horseback to riding in the mule-driven rig.

New Water Stop One

At daylight, C.C. Ellis, Sonny Ryan and Jax Hoyt stood drinking coffee out front of the large ragged tent saloon. They watched for arriving members of their group and gave them directions to an abandoned mining camp a few miles out of town, up off of the main trail. The new arrivals followed their directions, turning their horses and leaving, but they did so with dark grumblings and hard stares at the ordinary-looking railcar sitting at the siding platform. The railcar had not been there a few days earlier when they'd robbed the safe on the train that had stopped to take on water. This railcar, which had appeared there mysteriously, would draw any train robber's attention at first glance, the way it had C.C.'s and the other two's.

"How long are we going to stand here telling our own people to leave town? Even the saloon owner is getting the jaws over it. He keeps looking out here."

"He's losing some money," said Sonny. "But not much. Our riders always spend like money's gone out of style."

"But he hasn't lost a dime on us yet," said C.C. "We bought two cases of his rotgut and sent it on up to the mine camp first thing. He knows our riders will be back for more."

"Yeah, we draw more business here than we run off," said Jackson. He started to say more but Sonny interrupted him.

"Want to see some no-account sum-bitches, look who's coming right at us," Sonny said.

They all stared at the far end of town, where the sheriff and his two deputies, Wade Parnell and Robert Flitz, came riding in slowly. The deputies and two other men rode on either side of Sammy Kendricks and Kid Santa Cruz, with Sheriff Max Boyd bringing up the rear. Bystanders slowed and watched from either side of the street.

"Looks like we're fixing to have a parade," said Jackson, smiling.

"We're about to bury every lawman this dung heap has," said Sonny Ryan. He lifted his rifle from his side and laid it in the crook of his arm for easy reach.

"At least the sheriff was smart enough not to try taking their guns," said C.C.

"He's making a show for the townsfolk," said Jackson, "bringing in some wildlife for them to look at." He chuckled and muttered, "Sheriff, you have no idea how close you are to meeting Jesus right now."

"I've met the sheriff. I might be able to talk to him," C.C. said over his shoulder to Sonny.

"Be my guest," replied Sonny. "I know you've got us covered."

"You're right." C.C. nodded. "One of you take the street. One drop back behind me."

Without a word, Sonny casually veered away from the other two and stepped off the boardwalk into the dusty street. Jackson slowed his pace and let the distance between himself and C.C. lengthen.

C.C. Ellis stopped at the edge of the boardwalk and waited until the sheriff and his two deputies took note of him and rode over closer. Kendricks and Kid Santa Cruz stopped their horses dead in their tracks until a short nod from C.C. got them moving along with the deputies.

Sheriff Max Boyd swung his horse forward and rode around from behind the deputies in time to make an impressive stop where Ellis stood waiting at the boardwalk, a cup of coffee in his left hand.

"Morning, Sheriff," said Ellis.

"Morning," Sheriff Boyd replied in a restrained, tight-lipped manner. He looked at the cup in C.C.'s left hand, then at his right hand resting close to the butt of his big Colt. "As you see, I met a couple of your men on the trail and brought them here under guard."

"Under guard?" said Jackson Hoyt, a few feet behind Ellis. "I'd give a gold pocket watch to see you and your two monkeys take their guns —"

Ellis gave Jackson a look that shut him up. Sonny Ryan stood in the street, watching for railroad security men in either direction. The security men were around, but they stayed back and gathered on the platform near the railcar. By now Ellis was sure that they'd heard the news of Sonny escaping custody. *If the news has been released, that is.*

"I see," said Ellis. "I don't know what serious laws they've broken. But I see they're still wearing their guns."

"They've broken no major laws yet," said Boyd. "I asked them a few questions. They refused to answer. I brought them here to question them again. I could have arrested them for threatening violence and blackguarding an officer of the law."

"But you didn't arrest them," said Ellis. "Are they under arrest now?"

"Well, no," said the sheriff. "I wanted to question them, see if they're a part of your bunch. Now I see that they are, so I don't have to ask. I doubt if either of them knows anything about the safe robbery here the other day." He gave Kendricks and Kid Santa Cruz a dubious look, then added, "If they did, I'd have to tell them to take it to railroad security."

"So they're both free to leave, I take it." Ellis realized he'd been right moments ago when he said Boyd was bringing these two in strictly for show.

"Yeah, they're free to go," said Boyd. "All of you get out of my sight," he added, raising his voice, letting both the townsfolk and the railroad men know firsthand that behind the badge on his chest stood the new top dog on the block.

Good enough, thought Ellis.

He stepped back and touched his hat brim respectfully. But before he felt the tension that had set in begin to lift from the street and the siding platform, he heard the rumble of hooves and looked toward the sound.

"I'll be damned!" said Jackson Hoyt beside him. "Look who's coming here!"

"Is that who I think it is?" Sonny asked, joining them from where he'd stood in the street.

"If you think it's Bailey McCool, you're

right!" Ellis said.

There she was at the head of the oncoming herd, lying low on the front horse, riding bareback, her boots flapping against the dapple gray horse's sides. Beside her, a large buckskin raced along battling, side-slamming and snapping its teeth at Bailey's mount, trying to take control of the herd.

The sheriff seemed dumbfounded. People leaped off the street into any open door they could find. The horses kept rumbling forward, dust churning thick behind them.

"Open the corral! Round them in!" Ellis shouted amid the commotion.

A large new corral stood between the town livery and the new rail platform.

"It won't stop them!" the sheriff shouted. Yet he drew his gun to direct the out-of-control horses.

"It's a start," Ellis shouted back, his Colt up, ready. He waved down three riflemen he'd posted just in case on the roofs above the street. Railroad men hopped down from the platform and took up positions along the street, waving rifles, shouting at the animals.

The street suddenly turned into a gauntlet of gunfire, slapping of coiled lariats, whistling and catcalls as men cursed, threatened, bullied and cajoled the animals into the open corral gates.

Inside the corral the mass of animals ran in a tight, fast circle, tails and manes flying. But after only a few minutes, they slowed down, finally stopped and milled around as if nothing had happened.

Ellis hurried over to the corral railing and grabbed up Bailey when her horse circled and slowed. She held the sheet-wrapped crate of laudanum firmly against her as Ellis helped her down and out of the corral.

"Oh, no!" she whispered, seeing the sheriff hurrying toward her. "What am I going to tell him?"

"Tell him the truth, Bailey," said Ellis. "You were on your way here to meet me, and you found all these horses wandering around loose."

"Good idea," she said quietly. "The truth is always best." She muffled a little giggle.

Ellis saw the relaxed glassy look in her eyes as she took off her hat and slapped off the dust. "Most of the time anyway."

Chapter 6

Sheriff Max Boyd and one of his deputies hurried from the corral gates to where Bailey McCool and C.C. Ellis stood talking.

"I'll have a word with you, C.C. Ellis!" he called out angrily, pointing a firm finger at C.C.

Ellis watched him stride rigidly toward him along the boardwalk. Jackson Hoyt and Sonny Ryan came over and looked through the corral rails at the horses, or so it appeared.

The main street had settled down quickly without the thunder of hooves pounding on it. The sheriff and his deputy looked in surprise at the hidden riflemen C.C. had positioned along the rooftops who were now standing at various intervals, watching the railroad men gathered by the "ordinary" railcar. They too looked surprised at the riflemen's sudden appearance.

"Dang, Sheriff," Deputy Parnell whispered, "these fellas mean business."

Dang is right! The sheriff had seen no sign of Ellis setting the town up this way. He wondered how many more unseen guns might be pointed at him. He tempered his attitude down a notch as he turned to Bailey McCool.

"Young lady," he said, managing a smile that had been heretofore unplanned, "I hope you'll give me a good reason for charging in here with a dozen half cayuses chasing you down the middle of our street! My goodness, you could have been injured!"

"Sheriff, I truly am sorry!" Bailey said. "There were only eight horses before the other four joined me along the way. Once I saw them with us, I hadn't the heart to turn them away."

"I can understand that, ma'am, being a horse lover myself," said Boyd. "Horses will join a herd mighty quick if they're running alone or in small numbers in wolf or big-cat country."

"Wolves? Big cats?" Bailey looked all around, wide-eyed, as if frightened at the thought of roving predators.

She had set the small sheet-wrapped crate of laudanum at her feet. The sheriff looked at it, but didn't inquire as to the contents.

Instead, he said, "Yes, ma'am. Some of the biggest, meanest hill cats and lobos you'll ever see. Keep that in mind before you go riding out of here alone without a man watching out for you."

"Oh, my, yes! I will," said Bailey, scooting closer to C.C. Ellis's side. "Will you watch over me, sir?"

She batted fetching blue eyes. Only Ellis noticed the glassiness.

"I would be honored, ma'am," he replied.

"All right, both of you, cut it out," said the sheriff, wearing his smile. He was genuinely more sociable now with a lovely woman standing before him — and an undetermined number of firearms surrounding him. "Don't try to kid a kidder. I could tell the two of you knew each other when the lady got down from her horse."

"You're right, Sheriff Boyd," Ellis said. "We do know each other —"

"I'm Miss Violet Thune," Bailey cut in, offering her hand. "Call me Miss Violet, Sheriff, if you please."

As the sheriff lowered his face to kiss her hand, Deputy Parnell stepped in closer.

"Deputy Wade Parnell. Most pleased to meet you, Miss Violet."

"Did I hear you say you were coming here with eight horses, and you now have twelve,

Miss Violet?"

"Yes, it is the strangest thing," Bailey said. "The other horses came to my aunt's house before daylight. I awakened and fed them and gave them water, and they simply stayed! When I left this morning, they followed right along with me. Poor things must've been hungry, do you suppose, Sheriff?"

"I can't see how, Miss Violet, if you'll pardon me for saying so," said Boyd. "They had the meadows and foothills, the whole Rocky Mountain range standing over them."

"Yes, Sheriff, you're right," Bailey said. "I feel so foolish now."

"Don't feel foolish, Miss Violet," the sheriff said. "How were you to know?" He returned her hand to her. "And please forgive me if I have rambled on too long about horses. I seldom get the opportunity to meet someone so —"

"Sheriff Boyd," Ellis interrupted, "you said you'd like a word with me?"

"Oh, yes, I did!" said Boyd, catching himself.

He beckoned Ellis aside, with eyes following them from every direction. Sonny remained standing at the corral rails. Meanwhile, Jackson followed Ellis and the sheriff a few steps and repositioned himself, his

Remington in full view across his flat belly.

Out of earshot, the sheriff continued to Ellis. "Don't go thinking I'm only being polite for the woman's sake," he said.

"I'm not," Ellis said in the same affable tone. "I think it's because you saw more of my men and it dawned on you I've got this town by its little red cherries if need be." He smiled slightly.

"Hell no," said Sheriff Boyd, "that's not it either! These detectives would back my play in a second if I decided to take you men to jail —"

"You're dreaming, Sheriff Boyd," Ellis cut in. "These railroad jakes won't lift a finger without an order from the home office. If they had any evidence against us, they would have wired every law enforcement office in the country and gotten them on their side. You're a sheriff; have you ever seen a railroad make a move unless all the numbers were tilted high in their favor?"

Max Boyd hesitated for a second, then said, "No, I haven't. That's because they have to look out for the good of the public."

"Ha!" said Ellis. "Big numbers and bigger rewards, Sheriff. That's all that ever stopped anybody. You and I both know it. I bet when you came here just now, you were all set to tell me and my men to leave town. Then you saw the extra gunmen. Then you saw the woman. Now look at us talking like two gentlemen."

"Make no mistake, Ellis," said the sheriff. "I did come here to tell you it's time you and your men get out of town. I'm still telling you the same thing. If those jakes get orders or the home office issues a bounty, they will kill you. I'll have no choice but to join with them, but if I can keep from it, I don't want to be a part of it."

"Well spoken, Sheriff Boyd," said Ellis. "I knew we could talk on the square when we put our minds to it."

The sheriff almost smiled, but remembering that the railroad men were watching, he stopped himself. He raised his voice and hardened his tone.

"You've got an hour, C.C. Ellis. I want the lot of you off my streets."

"An hour it is, Sheriff. You have my word," C.C. replied in the same tone of voice without touching his hat brim.

As the sheriff and Deputy Wade Parnell walked away, the townsfolk along the street nodded with great respect.

Jackson Hoyt came strolling up the hard pine planks of the sidewalk.

"If you're all through winning over the local law," he said, "how 'bout I see to Bailey and sample a modest amount of her Blue River?"

"How do you know that's what it is?" Ellis asked.

"Only thing that makes Bailey McCool's eyes shine that bright is the jingle of stolen gold or a dose of good strong hop."

"Don't get too lit up, Jax. We're heading back to the mine camp within an hour, as soon as everybody's ready to ride."

"I'll be ready, C.C.," Hoyt replied. He inclined his head toward the railroad men, who stood across the street watching them. "These jakes are acting a little bolder each day. What's it going to take to get them to make a move?"

"They're still a few men short," C.C. replied, recalling his exchange a moment earlier with Sheriff Max Boyd. "As soon as the railroad posts a bounty or sends in a few more men, they will be coming at us with their claws out."

"I can't wait," said Jackson. "Meanwhile, I'm going to paddle my way up Blue River."

CHAPTER 7

As Ellis and his men rode out of New Water Stop One, ten of their outlaw gang joined them, staring hard at the rail platform and the railroad's paid gunmen surrounding the "ordinary" railcar sitting against it. Before they had ridden five miles, a half dozen more men had come down from their hiding place in the low hills and joined them.

C.C. Ellis, Sonny Ryan and Jackson Hoyt all knew the men were drawing together for the big payroll robbery coming up at the Duncan Mine and Silver Works. Ellis figured on twenty to thirty men by the time they pulled the job. That was all right. There would be plenty of cash to go around.

The day after leaving New Water Stop One, Ellis and Ryan rode off and retrieved the leather satchel of cash from under a short pile of hillside rock where Ellis had buried it days before. Returning with the money, Ellis stood distributing the money to the ones who'd been involved in the robbery.

"Whoo-hee!" Jackson Hoyt hooted. He held up his share of the loot in both hands. "This doesn't even feel natural!" He laughed. "I've never collected this much big cash while I still had money from the last job burning my britches! Somebody stop me! I might break and go running off to some smoky opium parlor or a big ol' faro table."

"Suit yourself," said Ellis. He pointed south at a line of low hills. "Head southwest, around five hundred miles, down through *Nuevo México* Territory. If you get to El Paso, you've gone too far."

The men chuckled.

"Don't worry, Jax," said Bailey. "If you get lost, we'll come looking for you!"

"Forget it," Jackson said. "I'm staying right here with my money! I don't trust none of you as far as I can spit." He lowered his voice. "I've heard rumors that some of you have rid with the James and Younger brothers out'n Missouri!"

"Watch your language!" a voice called out. The group laughed.

When the stolen money had been divided among them, the riders dispersed, some of them to bury the bulk of their share among the rocks or hidden away within their personal belongs. Reassembling at a nearby water hole, they stood beside their horses as the animals drank their fill. With the tepid contents of their canteens emptied and refilled afresh, and in the long shadows of evening that stretched across the land, they rode on.

To avoid being seen arriving in New Water Stop One in broad daylight by way of mule wagon, security squad leader Detective Lawrence Sterns stepped down from the crowded, demeaning wagon and walked the last mile into town. Behind him walked Ave Pettigo, Menard Baggs and Dr. Douglas Gray, who stayed back and tried to go unnoticed. As soon as he got a horse under him, he would be gone.

The three quickly realized they would have to slow their normal pace to avoid passing the mules and their cargo of gunmen! The canvas sides and top of the wagon had been raised and a lantern lit inside, giving off a swaying, bouncing announcement of some carnival of scoundrels arriving in the dark of night.

It won't do, Sterns told himself.

"All right," he said firmly, after seeing in ten passing minutes that the wagon was making little headway, "Menard Baggs, guide us over these rocks and into town on some lesser known back trail."

"But, Mr. Sterns!" Baggs said, eyeing the black silhouette of rocky hillside standing high alongside the darkening trail.

"Do not *but* me, Baggs!" Sterns barked. "Take us over these rocks and into town without us being seen! Can you — will you — do that for us?"

"Yes, Mr. Sterns." Baggs looked all around and fell silent, glad that he and Ave Pettigo could not clearly see each other's face in the dark.

"Proceed then, Baggs," Sterns said, stepping back to allow Baggs to get ahead of them up the sharp, dangerous hillside.

Dropping a few steps farther back, Ave Pettigo sidled up to Dr. Gray and whispered, "I saw you jump down and join us. Don't worry. I'm not telling Sterns."

"Obliged," Gray whispered.

"Are you thinking what I'm thinking, Doc?" Pettigo asked.

"I don't know. What are you thinking?"

"I'm thinking that we should have killed Sterns when we had the chance."

"We still have that chance," said the doctor. "But we'd have to kill Baggs too. He's starting to follow Sterns like some skull-cracked cousin."

"I know, but I hate killing an innocent man," said Pettigo.

"Innocent of what?" said the doctor. "We wouldn't be walking right now if he hadn't let our horses get stolen!"

Pettigo didn't reply.

"That's what I thought," said the doctor after an extended silence.

"Oops!" Sterns suddenly called out over his shoulder. "It appears that our man Baggs is floundering again."

"Jesus!" said Pettigo.

He hurried forward. The rocky dark terrain was such that every few yards, Pettigo had to step ahead of Sterns and help Baggs to his feet.

Sterns would wait until Baggs was collected and upright, and Pettigo was back in place. Then he would announce, "Forward, men, for glory or death!"

"He's lost his mind," Pettigo whispered. "We might be surprised if we asked Baggs. He might want to kill him too, skull-cracked cousin or no. Did you see his shins? Even in the dark, they look like chopped meat on sticks!"

"I saw them," said Gray. Then he jutted his chin toward a light that came into view. "Look at that. Let's talk again later."

The barn door swung open, revealing more light from inside. Sterns started to call out, but he stopped short and ducked down as a rifle shot exploded and streaked skyward.

"My holy mother! Don't shoot!" he shouted, crouching behind a rock, Baggs right beside him.

A few feet back, Pettigo did the same.

"Who goes up there?" a loud voice called out from the livery barn. An echo rolled from one distant end of the hill line to the next, the sound clear and sustained.

"Why doesn't this damned fool just get himself a megaphone?" Sterns said to Baggs.

"He doesn't seem to need one of those, Mr. Sterns!" Baggs replied. "Stay down!"

"I'm being sarcastic, Baggs!" Sterns said, hunkering closer to the ground behind the rock.

"Identify yourselves up there or I start shooting!" came the voice from the livery barn.

"We're railroad security men!" shouted Lawrence Sterns. "We need horses!"

"Then get down here to where I can see your faces!" the voice shouted. "I don't sell horses by mail, do I?"

"He's got a point, Mr. Sterns," said Baggs, trying at every opportunity to calm Sterns and make up for losing the horses.

"Of course not! Here we come!" Sterns called out to the livery barn.

As he, Baggs and Pettigo started walking slowly down the hill, picking their way over thick gravel beds and large stones, Pettigo looked around in the darkness for Dr. Gray, but saw not a trace of him.

"Stop trying to be my warm-nosed friend, Menard Baggs," said Sterns. "Just keep your mouth shut and do every damn thing I tell you to!"

"You got it, Mr. Sterns!"

Slithering down the rocky hillside, up, around and over rock like some half man half reptile, Dr. Gray swung wide around the livery barn to the dark front door. He paused for only a few seconds, listening to the sounds of the other three making their way down to the glow of the barn's open rear door.

A long row of occupied stalls lay before him. Horses stood with their necks craned and cocked, looking down at him. At the first stall, he saw a saddle hanging over the rail, as if horse and saddle had been standing there just waiting for him. The butt of a rifle stood in the saddle boot. A canteen hung from the saddle horn.

All right!

In what seemed like a few passing seconds, he'd saddled the horse and led it out the darkened front door. He climbed atop the tall chestnut barb and moved away from the barn quietly, the rifle out of its boot and in his hand. He didn't check it until he reached a patch of woods stuck among a cluster of large boulders. When he did lever the rifle, easy-like, he let a bullet fall over in his palm and felt another round slip in the chamber to take its place.

A rifle loaded and ready. How about that! Slipping the first levered round into his shirt pocket, he tapped his bootheels to the chestnut's sides, and rode off contentedly toward New Water Stop One.

Well after dark, C.C. Ellis, Jackson Hoyt and Bailey McCool topped a purple moonlit ridge and looked down at a single low burning lantern on the far side of the deep valley below them. They knew from experience that the light could be seen from no ridge other than the one upon which they were stopped.

"Here it is now," Bailey McCool said under her breath. "Nature's gift to the outlaw kingdom."

She sounded lit up, but Ellis had seen her in worse condition.

"Home at last!" said Hoyt, sounding half asleep in his saddle.

He and Bailey had sipped on a bottle of laudanum they had poured into a canteen of fiery rye whiskey for the trail. At the ragged tepee of an old Mexican bruja outside a small siding town, Bailey had acquired the herbs, mushrooms caps and grain alcohol necessary to give the concoction the powerful punch her brew was known for.

She'd mixed it all together from her saddle as they rode away from New Water Stop One, and let it sit and ferment all day in the sun.

"See why I love you, my sweet mystic Gypsy princess?" Hoyt said to her, slurring his words.

"Both of you listen up," Ellis said. "I'm counting on you to remember this."

They turned their dozy, watery eyes to him.

"Tonight, everybody gets to sleep until dawn. Then we're all heading out, the same way we came here, in twos and threes."

Bailey and Jackson straightened up a little more.

"Wait a minute," said Jackson. "We can't sleep until dawn, then get up and ride to the Duncan Mine in time to rob them. We'd have to fly there like birds!"

"That's our plan, Jax."

"Hell, that's not any kind of plan, C.C. That's plain craziness!"

"Oh, you think so?"

"Yeah, I think so!" said Jackson. "I could ride from here to there without stopping and wouldn't get there before they close tomorrow evening! Get serious!"

"Okay, now I'm serious," said Ellis. "We've let the word get out among our riders for a month now. Only tomorrow, instead of robbing the Duncan Mine, we're going to rob Gadsen Mining and Excavation. Maybe that helps your calculation some?"

Jackson stared, trying to think, letting his gaze get settled.

"You heard right, Jax," said Ellis. "The Duncan Mine is our decoy, in case word got out. While railroad security is sniffing the trail toward Duncan, we'll be trimming the Gadsen Mine to the bone." He looked toward Bailey for understanding. "We have to do it this way. We've got too many eyes on us right now."

"Don't apologize for looking out for us, C.C.," said Bailey.

"Yeah, we're good with it," said Jackson. "Everybody else will be too unless they're the railroad spies among us that we're trying to flush out."

"Let's not start accusing anybody, but that's how I look at it too," said Ellis. "I'm letting the two of you know. Sonny's letting some others know before they get here. The only ones who won't know that the Duncan Mine is a decoy are the ones who've caused suspicion lately. As soon as we all leave here, nobody will be allowed out of our sight until we hit Gadsen Mining."

While they waited for the others to ride in, Ellis lit a small lantern he'd taken from his saddlebags. He waved the lantern back and forth three times, then turned it off. In a moment the light down on the valley hillside also turned black. The wide valley before them turned into a bottomless black abyss.

Part 2

Part 2

Chapter 8

Before dawn, in a long-abandoned mining project on Rattlesnake Ridge, C.C. Ellis and Sonny Ryan stood beneath glowing lanterns they held overhead. On the long cavern floor, they watched their riders awaken amid whispered cursing, muttered threats of violence and the sound of outlaws letting down cocked hammers on firearms that had shared their bedrolls.

The ten riders, nine men and one woman, were the ones Ellis had picked to go inside the Gadsen Mine security office and bring out the highly protected payroll waiting there. Eight of the outlaws stirring from their short night's sleep had bedded down on the stone floor.

Bailey McCool and Jackson Hoyt had dozed instead, sitting up against the stone wall, each wrapped in their own blanket, their saddles and gear lying between them.

"Look at this," Ellis said to Sonny Ryan.

"Ten riders here and six more joining us on the way to Gadsen. A few years back, four of us would ride in, whooping and shooting, on a job this size."

"Yeah. This is what it's come to," Sonny replied in a low voice. "The railroads keep coming up with ways to keep us from them, and we just keep coming up with ways to rob them anyway." He laughed. "The main thing these days is that nobody gets a chance to sell us out." He studied the outlaws as they rose.

"Nobody has left this snake den all night," murmured Ellis, "and the six waiting outside are trail guards and scouts who know only the false information I've helped spread."

Sonny Ryan shook his head. "It's sure different from when my pa ran this bunch," he said.

"Got a complaint?" Ellis asked flatly.

"No. Hell no!" Sonny was quick to respond. "Just an observation, is all."

"How is your pa these days?" said Ellis, lightening his tone. "Or do you call him Old Man Ryan?"

"Holden Ryan is doing all right," said Sonny. "I slip up and call him Pa only now and then. He always asks about you. Wants to know how you like running things."

"What do you tell him?"

"I tell him you take things as they come and deal with them best you can." He scratched his chin and said, "He always says that's what it takes, and that's what put you here."

Ellis nodded, not taking his eyes off the outlaws sorting their gear and rolling their bedding in the lantern light.

"Does he still ask you to take over?" he asked.

"No," said Sonny. "We settled all that long ago. He knows I don't want to lead. He's my pa, and you and I are near the same age. But you rode with him and the old-timers longer than I did. You got the chance to pick up more of the old ways."

"I think of getting out the business sometimes, doing something else," Ellis said.

"If you ever do," said Sonny, "I'll run things just as long as it takes for me to change my name, burn all my belongings and move to South America. Give up my guns and teach parrots how to talk."

"Good luck," said Ellis. "In that case, I'll stick right here and run this show."

"Good to hear," said Sonny.

Jackson and Bailey approached, looking disheveled, their blankets hanging over their shoulders.

"Did anybody think to make some coffee?" Hoyt asked in a gravelly voice.

"They sure did," said Ellis. "Right out front. Get your coffee. Go to your horses. They're fed, watered and waiting to ride. Saddle them to suit yourselves. But nobody leave until I say so."

He walked down to where the riders were lining up in a loose fashion, their saddles hiked up on their shoulders or under their arms.

"Any chance of us getting a little eye-opener?" Poker Joe Elliot asked.

"No," said Ellis. "No drinking until we get this job finished."

"Uh-oh. I might have already jumped the gun," said Poker Joe.

"Don't jump it again, Poker Joe," Ellis said in a firmer tone. He looked all around, letting his gaze come to rest on Hoyt and Bailey. "No drink, no hop, no nothing."

"Don't worry about Poker Joe," said Harvey Brewer. "I'm watching him."

"S-s-s-so!" Kid Santa Cruz stuttered.

"So is Kid Santa Cruz," Brewer said, interpreting for him. "We'll both be watching him. He owes us money!"

The Kid gave a crooked little smile.

■ ■ ■ ■

Gadsen Mining Company

"Well, there it is, Jax," said Bailey McCool.

After a long, hot, all-day ride, the two had left their horses out of sight among long shadows and scrub juniper a few yards away from the fence surrounding the mining site. They had crouched and belly-crawled their way closer and now lay side by side behind a rock.

"Whoa, this looks worse than I thought it would," Jax whispered.

The fence, wire mesh woven into four-inch squares, with barbed wire running through every third row, surrounded the entire property, running in and out of sight around a hundred forty zigzagging acres of broken boulder, rock and gravel. Behind them, the other riders had spread out among the rocks and sparse patches of timber. They had taken turns creeping out for a look at the fencing, the lay of the land and the distant thirty-foot-tall guard tower.

"How's your headache?" Jackson asked.

"Better, thanks," Bailey said. "I have to admit these eye shades do a good job keeping out the sun."

She adjusted the dark-green-shaded spectacles he'd given her earlier on the trail. He'd also put on a pair of shaded spectacles himself. He grinned and waved at her from three feet away.

"I see you didn't listen when C.C. said no alcohol or hop until we're finished here," she said.

"He didn't mean you and me," said Jackson. "He meant all these others." He looked her up and down. "Anyway, I see you wasn't listening either."

"I won't tell anybody if you won't," Bailey giggled. "I took only a little sip, just enough to steady my hand."

"Yeah, me too," said Jackson. "I can do anything as well drunk or hopped up as I can sober. I just need applause a lot more when I'm finished."

In the grainy evening light, C.C. Ellis crawled in quick and quiet on Bailey's other side.

"What's going on here?" he asked purposefully.

"What do you mean?"

Bailey kept her gaze on the other riders, who lay spread out along the scrub line twenty feet away. They looked back at her.

"I didn't hear her," Jackson said.

"Don't fool with me, Jax," Ellis warned. "We've all got a lot riding on this."

Before Jackson could reply, Bailey cut in.

"I'm sorry, C.C.," she said, lowering her voice. "I'm just restless, wanting it to hurry up and get dark so we can go in there and ply our trade."

"All right," said Ellis. "Both of you get ahold of yourselves and keep quiet over here. We won't be waiting much longer."

Before crawling away, he looked back at Bailey and said, "I like your new spectacles."

"Why, thank you, Mr. Christian Clayton Ellis," she said playfully.

As C.C. departed, Bailey pulled her dark spectacles down onto the bridge of her nose.

"Hear that, Jackson Hoyt?" she said with a smile. "C.C. Ellis likes my new dark spectacles. What do you think of that?"

Hoyt didn't answer. Instead, he looked down at the dirt so close beneath his face. He knew it was teeming with life down there, tiny, unseen. He chuckled to himself.

"Can you believe this?" he asked no one in particular.

Almost as soon as he'd left the livery barn in New Water Stop One, Douglas Gray, formerly Dr. Gray, discovered his former trail scout, Cal Lindsey, following close behind him. Rather than start trouble there in the dark within walking distance of the town's new sheriff and his two deputies, the doctor decided to allow Lindsey to continue following him until they reached an isolated stretch of rocky trail.

"Easy, boy!" Cal Lindsey said an hour later, settling his nervous horse in the purple moonlight. "Whatever's got you spooked, we're going to find it right now!"

He swung down from his saddle and led the horse along beside him. He crouched, staring down at the shadowy dirt and gravel trail. Then he stopped, stooped and placed his fingertips on fresh hoofprints.

He listened closely to the sounds around him. He looked all around the rugged terrain, then sank down, his rifle resting across his knee. Relaxed, he breathed in the chill of night air, realizing dozily how bad he missed the laudanum. He suddenly realized that the strong grip the laudanum had on him had caused him to start losing track of time.

He wasn't missing great amounts of time, not yet anyway.

He had caught himself losing a minute or two here and there, dropping his train of thought, never to get it back. Only just now he'd felt himself slipping away as if being drawn down some long silent tunnel.

Damn.

The only thing that stopped him from disappearing was the cold feel of a gun barrel pressed behind his left ear, the click of its hammer cocking.

"Oh, hell," he said, his own voice sounding distant and fuzzy to him. "Am I dead now?"

"That depends, Cal," said Douglas Gray. "Are you going to give up my Blue River shipment that you stole? If not, yeah, I guess I'll splatter you out right here." He nudged the gun barrel beneath Lindsey's ear.

"I hope you won't shoot me, Doc. I really do," Lindsey said in a quavering voice. "I didn't steal from you, and I didn't do nothing untoward to the woman. I admit I wanted to awful bad. So I left to keep myself from doing something bad to her! I knew if I stayed, I might. She was there, sleeping peaceful, when I cut out, though, I swear."

"To hell with the woman," said Gray. "Where's my Blue River?"

"All right," said Lindsey, "I have to admit I took a full bottle of it from your shipping crate. I wrapped it in a soft cloth, laid it down inside my saddlebags. It's still half full. You can have it if you want it. I want you to have it! Your crate of Blue River was in the wagon. I wasn't thinking straight or I would have took it all, but I didn't. See how tore up I am? I've become a filthy liar, a dope fiend — a craver of women! I even caught myself praying, all the time lying like a damn dog! I finally caught myself and stopped, 'cause I figured what good is it lying whilst I pray! I couldn't believe none of it! Why would I think God would? So I just shut up. Do you see what I mean?"

"Yeah, you're a mess, all right!" said Gray.

He grabbed Lindsey's rifle by its barrel and jerked it from his lap. "Stand up!" he said. "I hate talking to a man who's on his knees!"

"Are you not going to shoot me, then, Doc?" Lindsey asked, rising slowly, both hands in the air. "I know I done wrong, leaving in the night without telling you. Being around that woman got me so balled up inside, I didn't know whether to jump back or shave a chicken. But I'm coming around now, I swear I am! Some anyways."

"Okay, you left. I'm not going to shoot you for that." Gray shrugged. "Why were you following me, though?" he wondered. "What did you plan to do when you caught up with me?"

"Okay, can I tell you the truth?" Lindsey asked, almost pleaded.

"By all means, do," said Gray.

"I need Blue River," said Lindsey. "It's all

I've thought about. I've got some left, but when it runs out, I'm done for. I figured on taking whatever you have."

"Bad news," said Gray. "I'm out too. If you didn't take it, the woman did. Either way, it's gone."

He let down the gun hammer and stepped back.

Lindsey let out a sigh of relief. "I'm obliged for you not shooting me, Doc."

"Stop calling me Doc. I'm just a railroad gunman like everybody else. If I catch you dogging my trail again, I will kill you."

"If you're telling me to go, Doc," said Lindsey, "I'd sooner stay, if it's all the same."

Again with Doc. Douglas Gray told himself to be patient. It would take time to get rid of his former title, if he could get rid of it at all.

"You figure if you're with me, I'll conjure you up more laudanum somewhere?"

"I'll do better finding it with you than I will alone, Doc," said Lindsey. "I saw you slipping away from the wagon before it rolled into New Water Stop One. I was a scout, you know, so I'll inform you they left the wagon in town. They're mounted now. Hooves are harder to follow than the wagon."

"If you're asking to track them for me, be my guest, Cal. Sterns owes me money. If he thinks he's going to weasel out of paying me, he's in for a hard lesson. I'm still a gunman, don't forget." He hefted the Colt hanging in his right hand.

"I won't forget, Doc."

In a slim-quarter-moon darkness, C.C. Ellis, Bailey McCool and Jackson Hoyt silently walked their horses farther into the thick scrub. All of the riders now wore bandannas across their faces. C.C. and Jax handed their reins to one of the two men assigned to hold the mounts while the outlaws breached the fence with the help of large wire cutters.

With their horses in trusted hands, the three walked back to the edge of scrub brush and juniper and knelt alongside six other men. Now there were eight men and one woman waiting in silence, rifles in their hands. Bandoliers of extra ammunition crisscrossed their chests and hung from their shoulders. The only sound coming from the fence line in the darkness was the occasional muffled click of a wire cutter, its tempered steel jaws doing the job.

In the guard tower at the front of the Gadsen Mine complex, a young railroad security man, Reese Donovan, leaned on both palms and looked out the wide row of windows.

Delbert Rydell, the Gadsen Mine security chief, watched the young railroad guard staring out the front of the tower at the lumpy black hillside.

"Nothing," Rydell whispered almost to himself.

He looked to the left, then the right. Still nothing. He stood looking across the back of the one hundred forty acres, left to right, then back again. Delbert Rydell could not stand the silence any longer. He gave a little chuckle.

"If they come in from any of these three directions, they'll have to crawl on their side."

He chuckled a little louder, seeing if he would have any followers. He didn't. Two armed uniformed mine company guards only stared blankly at him. Donovan, the railroad security man, gave a critical chuff at such a childish remark.

"As wide as it is back there, I think we need two good men on horseback to go check things out."

"I don't know what things you think need to be checked out," Rydell said, "but I already sent two men to ride fence back there a half hour ago or thereabouts."

"So you don't remember exactly how long ago?" said Reese Donovan, the young railroad man.

"I said thereabouts," the mining guard said. "Did I whip my Ben Franklin from my watch pocket, look at it and write the time down? No, I did not. Heaven forgive me!" he added with heated sarcasm.

The two armed uniformed guards muffled a quiet laugh.

"Why not?" Donovan asked sharply.

The guards fell silent. Rydell took three hot angry breaths through thick hair-filled nostrils. Young Donovan only stared him up and down. He didn't care.

"Because, by hell, sir," said Rydell, taking a short step forward, "I do not announce my every movement to a damn time device! Do you?"

"Yes, I do, as a matter of fact," Donovan said coolly. "Not every second, but certainly every minute, when I am watching for a robbery." He lifted his chin slightly. "But then, I am not an idiot."

Before the heated exchange could get worse, the door opened and Assistant Railroad Security Chief Vincent Collins stepped inside.

"My goodness! What is all this loud bickering about?"

"Nothing, Mr. Collins," said Donovan. "With your permission, I feel I need to take a ride across the back fence line."

"Any particular reason, Mr. Donovan?" the security chief asked.

"Just to keep on top of things, sir," said Donovan. "Mr. Rydell sent out two riders. I think they have been too long."

"I appreciate your diligence, Reese," said Vincent Collins. "But let's not cast disapproval on Mr. Rydell's judgment. He's been security chief at Gadsen Mining far longer than you've been with us at the railroad. I'm sure young Reese here meant no offense, Chief Rydell."

Rydell gave Collins a sharp nod of approval. "No offense taken," he said. "I realize the boy is new at his job. Security and detection are not a business one learns overnight." He glared at Reese Donovan.

Collins smiled at each of them. "Good, then," he said. "Let us all be friendly. We need to trust one another more — like the good book tells us to do. Don't you agree, Mr. Donovan?"

"Oh, yes, I do agree, Mr. Collins," Donovan replied immediately, although no verse in the good book sprang to mind regarding whom to trust, whom not to trust.

Again, Collins smiled and said, beaming, "All right. I admit I felt an ugly air of disapproval when I came in here. I hope our little exchange has cleared it up?"

He rubbed his hands together as if he had wrestled some great obstacle to the ground.

"Yes, I think so," said Rydell grudgingly.

"Me too," young Donovan agreed.

Again the smile in the grainy darkness from Collins.

"I personally think we've been had once again by C.C. Ellis and his gang," he said. "It's not the first time. After these outlaws sent rumors flying in every direction, a reliable informant told us they would hit here. It appears our informant was either wrong or lying."

"Sorry to hear it, Mr. Collins," said Donovan.

"Eventually, we'll get them, and they know it," said Vincent Collins. "Until then we simply have to play along with whatever bull dip they throw at us. We had to spread out our manpower and resources, which is exactly what they intended."

"So should I forget about riding back there?" Donovan asked.

Collins gave another, this time more enduring, smile.

"Yes, stay here for now," he said. "You can

send riders back there after a while, maybe after daylight when this blasted drizzle has stopped, perhaps?"

"Yes, sir. Of course, Mr. Collins," said Donovan. "That is exactly what I'll do."

Chapter 9

Bailey McCool was the second of the riders to lead her horse easily and quietly through the cut fencing, after C.C. Ellis. Behind her, Jackson Hoyt walked along in the same manner. The resistant if not impenetrable fencing had been opened wide in three separate places.

This opening, in the center, was six feet wide and almost straight back from the facility's main gate. The two others were at either back corner in case they were needed for a fast fighting escape.

Each outlaw walked their horse a full thirty yards onto the Gadsen Mine's one-hundred-forty-acre property before climbing into their saddles and riding on. In the silent gray morning preceding dawn, the riders felt a cold mist touch their faces, the backs of their hands.

To their left, twenty yards away, Jax saw two dead men lying on a pile of rock, their horses stripped of saddles and tack and grazing calmly on sweet wild grass.

"What do you think?" Harvey Brewer had sidled up to Hoyt and, motioning toward the two dead men, asked in a whisper, "Should I?"

Jax whispered in reply, "I wouldn't."

"I just thought C.C. ought to know about them," said Brewer. "What's wrong with that?"

"Nothing," said Jax. "But he does know. He's seen them too." He looked at Brewer skeptically. "You're asking me? This your first job, is it, Harve?"

"Guess where you can go to for me, Jackson Hoyt!" Brewer said, getting a little put out by Jax's attitude.

Jax chuffed. "Go there? Ha! I keep a table there."

Staying off the path leading straight to the guard tower and the office building and guard barracks beneath it, C.C. and his riders turned left and continued on a shorter trail to another low-standing building thirty yards away. Dawn announced its arrival on a red-orange string stretched along the silvery eastern horizon.

C.C. watched his other men appear on foot as if out of nowhere, and slip into position surrounding the building, its barns, its corrals. He was almost troubled that they had gone so far without incident, without mistakes, with no close calls, but he had learned to never question good luck. *Take it, enjoy it, look for more,* he thought, dropping from his saddle and giving his reins to one of the two men who had ushered them in through the cut fence.

"There's a big guard dog here," he reminded Bailey and Jax over his shoulder.

At that very moment, they heard a dog growling, and looking around on their way to the side door, they saw Kid Santa Cruz patting the head of a huge mastiff who had been trained to guard and protect but was currently wolfing the chunks of jerked elk the Kid was feeding him.

C.C. stepped aside and let Bailey and Jax through the door ahead of him.

"D-d-don't worry," said Kid Santa Cruz. "He-he-he growls at everybody, but he won't bite."

"Good, keep him fed," said C.C., but he waited a few seconds longer.

When he heard a scuffle going on inside, he shouldered the door open and charged, his Colt coming out of its holster in spite of the rifle already in his hand.

On the floor, a money counter lay prone, his hands spread on the plank floor. Jax stood over him, his rifle butt raised above the man's head.

"Don't worry, boss!" Jax said to C.C. "I've got him."

Bailey held her rifle on three other money counters. "He tried to pull a gun on my friend. It got him butt smacked." She spoke with a huskiness in her voice, hoping to sound like one of the men.

C.C. looked at a hideout pistol lying on the floor a few feet away.

"I told you I've got him, boss," said Jax.

Without answering, C.C. stepped over and picked up the pistol the money counter had pulled.

"Mind your manners," C.C. said to the man on the floor. "Next time, this man will give you lots worse. That goes for all of you."

He looked all around the room. In addition to the men Bailey was covering, two more men were hurriedly filling canvas bank bags with cash, some of it banded, some of it loose. Several full bags stood near the door. Gesturing with her rifle, Bailey urged them to move faster.

"Everybody, do as you're told," said C.C. "This will all be over before you know it."

Two more full bags plopped onto the floor beside the others.

"Dang, son!" said Jax, sounding greatly

impressed behind his raised bandanna mask. "Looks like we are making us some money here."

In the watchtower, the two armed uniformed mine guards and their boss, Delbert Rydell, stood gazing out at the dark front trail. Looking out toward the rear fence line were the railroad security men Vincent Collins and Reese Donovan. Every lantern and candle in the tower had been turned off. Only a fine moonlight shone dimly through the large windows.

"As dark as we have it in here, Donovan," said Collins as if the shadowy black interior of the tower required a lowered voice, "let me remind you, it is next to impossible to see inside here from out there when we turn off the lanterns." He gestured with an unseen hand at the back of the mine property.

"Yes, I know, Mr. Collins," Donovan said, his voice equally low.

Before Collins could say more, a glaring lantern light swept into the tower from the stairway as a man carried it up quickly and banged on the door with his fist.

"Mr. Collins!" the man said excitedly, his voice far too loud.

"Damn it, you fool, shut up!" Collins

shouted. "Turn that lantern off! What the hell do you want?"

Reese Donovan hurried and opened the door and said, "Set the lantern down out there and get in here."

The man had not turned the lantern completely off; rather he had trimmed the wick so low, it was only a thin red line atop the fuel tank. Donovan motioned him inside anyway, knowing no one could see a lantern light trimmed so low.

"I said what the hell do you want?" Collins barked as the man stepped inside.

"We're being robbed, Collins!" the messenger said. He gestured at the rear window overlooking the back fence line. "They've come right through the security fence!"

"Where are they?" said Collins, trying to make sense of what the messenger said.

"Back there!" the man said, getting louder.

"Who saw them?" Collins asked.

"One of the counters went to the jakes. Coming back he saw men with rifles sneaking inside the counting building! One of them was feeding Killer something. Killer was wagging his tail!"

"They're poisoning our dog!" Collins shouted. "Those sumbitches!"

Delbert Rydell opened the door and brought in the lantern. He raised the glowing wick.

"The possibility of surprise is over, Collins!" he shouted.

He sat the glowing lantern on the long shelf beneath the large windows.

"You're damned right it is!" Collins shouted back.

He yanked a Smith & Wesson pistol from under his coat and shot Rydell in the face. The uniformed guard next to him jumped and ducked, but couldn't avoid the splatter of blood and brain matter as Rydell flew backward and slumped down the wall. Although half stunned, Reese Donovan managed to grab the gun at his side, but then, instead of drawing it, he simply held it there in his holster when he saw Collins let the big Smith & Wesson hang by his side.

"We found out Rydell has been an informant for these outlaws," he said to Donovan. "Tonight he proved it. The two riders he said he sent out to check the fence line were confederates of his. They rode to the rear fence to tell the outlaws we have an ambush waiting for them. I had the riders killed." He gestured down at Rydell. "That's why I killed him." He looked at the two uniformed guards. "Get out there and fight them! Show us you are with us!"

The two guards hurried out the door.

Donovan started to follow them, but Collins stopped him.

"No, Reese, you stay with me," said Collins. "I'll teach you how to handle these so-called long riders."

"Yes, sir!" Donovan said eagerly.

He watched Collins throw open a large back window. Grabbing a thin tin megaphone from the floor, Collins shouted out the window.

"This is Detective Collins with railroad security. This robbery is over. Our sharpshooters have you surrounded!"

The circle of light from the lantern on the windowsill glowed in the silvery rainy mist.

As Collins's amplified voice resounded across the large compound, glowing lanterns came alive in a wide circle encompassing the entire rear fence line and beyond.

"Let us see you walk into the light and throw down you weapons, or we will start killing you! You can't win!" Collins said.

Inside the countinghouse, C.C. Ellis cupped his bare hands around his lips and through an open window shouted a terse reply: "Want to bet?!"

Beside Ellis, Bailey McCool stuck her Colt out the window and fired two shots straight up. A few yards behind the lit-up circle of railroad sharpshooters, Ellis's riflemen had formed their own circle and lain in wait. At the sound of Bailey's signal, shots suddenly rang out and blossomed in the mist.

Raised lanterns exploded as well-placed shots screamed out of the darkness and blew the lantern fuel tanks into orange-red fireballs. Sharpshooters ran from under a falling shower of flame. Two men whose arms and backs caught fire fell to the ground and rolled in the wet grass while other men hurried over to help smother the flames licking their skin and clothing. Lanterns appeared to fly as sharpshooters scurried to any cover they could find. Bullets flew between the two groups.

"Have you had enough?" Collins shouted through the tin megaphone when a lull fell over the gunfire. "Now come out if you want to save yourselves."

Ellis cupped his hands again and called out through the window, "Collins, we are not coming out until you clear us a way to make a run to the trail. If not, we're staying right here until we're all dead."

"Don't be fools!" Collins shouted. "I told you, you can't win! We can sit here and wait you out!"

"Good luck!" said Ellis. "We're not coming out. We'll stay right here. We'll burn this building down around us. We ain't leaving!"

Ellis beckoned over Bailey, Jax and Harvey Brewer. Huddled near the window, he told them, "As soon as these money counters are finished bagging, take some rope, tie their hands. Cut a bag into strips and tie their mouths shut. Jax, you get our horses inside here. Tell our men out there to get reloaded and ready."

"What're we doing, C.C.?" Jax asked.

"We're riding out of here. What did you think?"

"Yeah, that's what I thought when you was telling him," said Jax. "Bet he's planning how to break our siege here."

As the outlaws spoke, gunfire erupted again from along the rear fence line, the sound of two heavily armed groups firing hard at one another. The money counters were still busily loading cash into the bank bags, only now they moved around cautiously, hunched over. With dawn trying to break free of the gloomy night, a silver-gray mist hung over the land.

"Suppose we've lost anybody?" Ellis asked.

"I doubt it," said Jax. "Maybe one of the riflemen surrounding the sharpshooters."

Bailey chuckled. "I think the sharpshooters were too busy hiding their asses to do any sharpshooting."

"I hope you're right," Ellis said. He hefted one of the bags, judging its weight.

"What do you think?" Brewer asked. "Will these piles of greenbacks stop a bullet?"

"We're going to find out," said C.C.

It was barely twelve hours since Assistant Railroad Security Chief Vincent Collins had pieced together with certainty that Gadsen Mining site security chief Delbert Rydell was the inside man feeding information to outlaw leader C.C. Ellis. All mines in the region paid their employees on the same day each month. But only the night before had Rydell realized that out of the four possible facilities, Gadsen Mining was the target of the upcoming robbery.

Collins hadn't particularly wanted to kill Rydell, but he knew he had to. Rydell knew that Collins himself had taken money from outlaws over the past few years. With Rydell out of the way, Collins had nothing to worry about. He would continue his rise with the railroad uninterrupted.

It's that simple, he told himself.

"Mr. Collins," Reese Donovan asked, standing beside him, gazing out at the drizzly morning, "does he mean it? Will they really try to hold out back there?"

Collins's hand was wrapped around the top of the megaphone, which he had set on the shelf in front of him.

Without turning to his companion, he said, "We shall see, Mr. Donovan." Collins watched the slow drizzle run down the window glass. "I think he is inviting me to play either poker or chess with him. I'm not sure which."

He tapped his fingers idly on the tall cone. "I'll let it be his choice. But rest assured, Mr. Donovan, whichever he chooses, I'm a fair hand at either."

Chapter 10

Near the breached rear fence, rifle shots rang out and echoed through the morning gloom. C.C. Ellis, Bailey McCool and Harvey Brewer leaned against a wooden table they had turned over in the middle of the floor. Kid Santa Cruz and Jackson Hoyt stood among the horses they and three other outlaws had brought indoors.

The money counters, finished with bagging the bundles and the loose piles of money, sat leaning against the far wall of the room. Their wrists were bound with a rope that then tied around their waist. Strips cut from a white canvas bank bag circled their necks, ready to be pulled up across their mouths and tightened when the time came for the robbers to leave.

"No more jerky for you, Kiler," Jax said to the big mastiff.

"His name is Killer, not Kiler," said one of the money counters.

"Yeah?" said Jax. "Why'd somebody carve *Kiler* on the board above his doghouse door?"

The money counter shrugged. "Probably couldn't spell *Killer,* is my guess."

"Well, I'll be damned." Jax grinned at the big dog leaning affectionately against Kid Santa Cruz's trouser leg. "I wondered why he ignored me when I called him Kiler."

"Of course," the man said. "If you say *kiler,* Killer doesn't know what you're talking about."

The big dog's ears perked up on hearing his name.

"See?"

"Yeah, I see," said Jax. He jerked his chin in the direction of the doghouse he'd seen outside. "One of you ought to fix that."

"Let it go, Jax," Ellis called out, "and join our conversation over here."

"Whatever you decide, I've got you covered, boss," said Jax, approaching. "These mining guards and railroad security men are busy trying to figure out what you're thinking. As long as they're doing that, whatever we do is going to catch them halfway by surprise."

"But they've had time to tighten their position around us," C.C. countered, making sure everyone understood. "They are out there right now trying to find better positions. That's why it's so quiet. Once they get resettled, all hell will break loose. Do we want to make a run for it now while it's calm or wait until there's bullets flying through here? It's fifty-fifty we can't make it out of here."

"So that means it's fifty-fifty *we can*," said Bailey.

"You're right," said Ellis. "I'm just trying to give everybody the truth."

The truth? Harvey Brewer looked from one rider to the next, noting that none of them looked greatly worried; they all looked ready, determined. As a lifelong bandit and outlaw, a former rider with the James-Younger Gang and Quantrill's guerrilla cavalry, Brewer reckoned there were much slimmer odds of any of them getting through this alive.

"To hell with the truth!" He spat tobacco into a brass spittoon he had found sitting beside an overturned desk. "Truth has never done a damn thing for me."

He glanced at the bags of cash sitting beside the door. "Daylight's upon us," he said, "so load my horse with my share of the loot, open the door and get out of my way. I'll wait for the rest of you in hell or in that general area." He gave a wide, devilish grin.

The others nodded while the tied-up money counters sat wide-eyed, afraid, as if they had known all along that the outlaws would take them as hostages when they left.

C.C. stood up and dusted the seat of his trousers. "All right," he said, walking to the horses. "We've been here long enough. Let's get the hell out."

"You got it, boss," said Jackson Hoyt. "I'll let our outside men know."

He hurried out the side door. Killer stood up, then lay back down.

The counters watched intently as C.C. and his riders gathered their horses.

"You are leaving us here, then?" one of the tied-up counters tentatively asked.

C.C. didn't reply.

Jackson Hoyt came back inside and said, "I told them. They're ready. They'll fall in with us when we ride out. They said they lost two men in that last big round of shooting."

"That's too bad," said C.C.

"Yeah," Jax agreed. "But losing only two men makes me wonder just how sharp these railroad sharpshooters are."

He strode over to the line of seated money counters.

One of them looked up at him and said, "You have our word we won't call out and tell anybody you're leaving."

"We appreciate that," Jax replied.

He reached down and pulled the canvas strip of cloth over the man's mouth and tightened it.

"You can trust us," said the next money counter.

"I know," said Jackson Hoyt. "I'll just tie these up in case any of you forget."

He went from one to the next, pulling up their gags, checking their tied hands. From the rear fence line, the sound of rifle fire, which had been almost silent for an hour, started back up with growing intensity.

Inside the watchtower, Vincent Collins gazed through the rain-streaked glass and listened to a low roar of horses' hooves begin to swell from the direction of the countinghouse. He and Reese Donovan looked at each other as if waiting for the other to comment. Rifle fire grew louder, fiercer.

Collins looked down at his armed men, railroad and mine security personnel alike staring out toward the sound. He grabbed the megaphone standing on the shelf beneath the window.

"Here they come! Spread out! Shoot early and fall back! Don't let them get in among you! You'll be shooting one another," he shouted down to the swell of men whose numbers had drawn closer during the past quiet hour. "Do not shoot at one another!"

Some of the men who had taken up safer positions for themselves, out of one another's line of fire, now hurried back to the original line beneath a building morning rain.

As the men below settled behind what cover they could find, Reese Donovan and Vincent Collins felt the rumble of hooves vibrating in the tower's timber framework. Donovan grabbed a rifle.

"My God!" said Collins. "Here they are!"

Over the crest of a low rise in the main trail that crossed the mining site end to end, a blackish roiling cloud made up of man, mud and horses surged forward. It broke through as if penetrating some thin ethereal membrane, and dispersed the rain and mist heretofore forming the patina of this desperate, despondent morning.

"Ah!" shouted Collins. "Our bold outlaw leader likes to command his troop from the front!"

He swung one of the railroad company's Winchester rifles up to his shoulder and aimed along the barrel at C.C. Ellis, who rode far enough ahead of his gang that he could fire to his left or right with no fear of hitting one of his own.

"Ahhhh, yes! Yes! Yes! Take that, Mr. Desperado! You worthless saddle trash!" Collins shouted.

"You got him, Mr. Collins!" Donovan exclaimed, having caught a glimpse of the outlaw leader swaying in his saddle as the shot rang out in the watchtower.

"Yes, Reese," said Collins, calmly. "I did, indeed, nail the scoundrel."

"My goodness! You hit him dead center!" said Donovan, almost jumping up and down.

"Precisely where I aimed," Collins replied, smoke curling up from his rifle barrel. "It is safe to say that shot alone will have a great influence on the outcome of this battle, I assure you." Collins grinned in conclusion.

"I agree, sir! Wholeheartedly!" said Donovan.

Collins glanced down and levered a fresh round into his rifle chamber. Yet when he looked back up, his smile vanished, replaced by a puzzled and disappointed expression as his eyes quickly searched the oncoming horde and found C.C. Ellis coming on, still firing.

"Something is wrong! He's still in his saddle! This is not right!"

As if by some dark twist of magic, C.C. Ellis still led the riders, his horse pounding ahead, water spraying up from around its hooves.

"No, it can't be right! I saw you hit him, Mr. Collins!" said Donovan, neither of them realizing that when the bullet struck C.C. Ellis dead center, it had had to spin and tear and bore its way through eight inches of cash pressed tight behind the buttons of his long trail duster.

The bullet couldn't hit its mark. Instead of staying dead center, the projectile's rounded nose had immediately begun to soften and veer left inside the crisp, newly printed cash. The bullet found C.C.'s right ribs and followed them around until it skipped off of them, exiting on his right side.

Jackson Hoyt was riding hard through the drizzle and spray of hooves, running flat out to get to Ellis's side. All the riders fought on the run, having seen Ellis jerk back in his saddle when the bullet hit him. Now they continued fighting with an eye to the blood spreading on the back of his trail duster.

"I'm with you, C.C.!" Jackson shouted.

"How bad are you hit?"

"I'm all right, Jax," Ellis shouted back. "It's just a graze! Stay close. We're going to take them for a ride."

"Okay, boss. Tell me what you want us to do!"

"Follow me straight ahead!" said Ellis.

"You're taking us out the front gates?" Jax shouted, sounding doubtful.

The front gates were closed, and workers crowded outside, waiting to get inside to work.

"No!" shouted Ellis. "Cut left before we get there! Let's make them mount up and chase us around this place. Keep them trying to defend both the front gates and the rear fence. We've got all kinds of cover in here and all kinds of ways out when we're ready to go."

"Whatever you say, boss!"

They were all still firing on the run, still dodging fire from three directions: front, left and right. Railroad and mine security gunmen had begun hounding their path, but Ellis's outlaw gunmen had taken a toll on them. Bodies lay wet, dead and bloody in shallow pools in which falling raindrops danced, a ghastly, cheerless waltz on the surface of red-streaked puddles.

■ ■ ■ ■

Two miles from the fighting, Doc Gray and Cal Lindsey heard the heavy gunfire and watched the mine yard's smaller than usual work engine pull an open flatbed railcar up the long grade to the mine gates. The flatbed, made to haul coal, tools and shoring timbers around the site, today carried a full load of armed railroad security men and their new leader, Colonel Randolph Doss. With Doss came his two recently promoted personal bodyguards, Billy Tobin and Andrew Maggen.

Gray turned to one of the two men leading the security men's horses away from the small loading dock.

"Pardon me, my good man," he said, touching his battered hat brim. "If you're readying yourselves to deliver these horses back to Colonel Doss at the Gadsen Mine facility, my scout and I will be happy to take them off your hands and deliver them for you."

"Nothing would please me more," the man said, " 'cause I have been paid in advance. But I won't pay someone else to deliver them for me."

"I'm not asking you to pay me, sir," said

Gray. "I happen to work for Colonel Doss. I'm Security Agent Douglas Gray. The men fondly call me Doc." He produced a small tin identification badge from his trouser pocket. "You have heard all the fighting going on up there? Had I arrived five minutes earlier, the colonel himself would have me bringing the horses up to them."

"The yard engineer just told me they've got a swarm of wild outlaws pinned down!"

"Yes, it is all true, sir," said Gray with an air of authority. "I have information the outlaws Doss is fighting are desperate for fresh horses. They have men out searching the hillsides for anything with four legs that can wear a saddle! They need to make a run for it. Every last one of them is a man-killer!"

He extended a hand for the lead rope the other man held. "We may well be saving your life by taking these horses to the colonel for you. We are armed and trained professionals. We know exactly what to do should these jakes try taking the horses or anything else from us. Do you?" Gray gave him a cold stare.

The man patted his trouser pocket.

"I do carry myself a little four-shot Mexican *gato* popper at all times." He started to raise the small pistol from his pocket.

Gray raised a hand, stopping him. "Please, sir, you look like an honorable man," Gray said, lowering his voice. "Don't bring shame on yourself, showing us a gun the size of a squirrel's fetch-it."

The man raised his empty hand from his trousers with an embarrassed look on his face. He handed the lead rope over to Gray.

"I hope I'm doing the right thing here," he said.

"You are, sir. Trust me, you are," said Gray.

"You sure are," said Cal Lindsey, suddenly deciding to be a part of this. "He's also a doctor. You can always trust a doctor."

"For the last time, I'm not a doctor!" Gray snapped, then said to the man, "I've showed you my railroad security badge, sir! Don't you think this is the right thing to do?"

CHAPTER 11

"What have we coming here, Donovan?" Collins asked, looking down from the watchtower through the pouring rain.

"Good Lord," said young Reese Donovan. "I believe the one center front is our new security chief, Randolph Doss."

"The colonel, for hell's sake?" said Collins. "He simply shows up unannounced, no telegram, no courier, nothing?" Collins smoothed a hand down his wet shirt and tie.

"Apparently so," said Donovan, "and those must be his personal bodyguards on either side."

The two watched the small yard engine struggle, its iron wheels slipping, losing ground in spite of a road crew shoveling sand onto the rails in its forward path. The men on board leaned forward in the downpour, holding on to each other for balance.

"Why in hell's blazes don't they get off

and walk?" said Collins. "Or better still, where the hell are their horses?"

"I would have no idea, sir."

Reese Donovan shook his head slowly, both of them watching a side gate open to the siding dock as the small yard engine arrived billowing steam. Now some of the men did jump down from the flatbed and push it the last yards up the final incline to the loading dock inside the Gadsen Mine complex.

"Sir, are we going to meet them down there or have them sent up here?"

"Damn it," Collins grumbled. He looked in the direction of heavy gunfire coming from somewhere back on the rocky hillside. He turned to two uniformed guards standing in long raincoats inside the tower door. "Go down and escort our leader up here."

"Shall I go with them, Mr. Collins?" Reese Donovan asked.

Collins looked him up and down.

"Yes, do that, Reese," he said. "You may want to mention to the colonel that we are heavily engaged at the moment. Because he's a military man, I'm sure he will take great interest."

Before Donovan could leave the tower and escort Doss and his men up the mud-slicked hill from the siding dock, he and

Collins saw two of Doss's men misjudge their step and slide off the thickly coated plank walk, necessitating three other men to help them back up.

"On second thought," said Collins, "let them come to us."

He stepped over to a tool closet, took out a thick rope, opened the door and tied it to a strong rail post. He heaved the large coil of rope and watched it uncurl through the pouring rain toward Doss himself.

"Grab it, Mr. Doss. It will help pull you out of the mud," he shouted through the loud rain. "Let us welcome you to Gadsen Mine —"

"Is this man daft?" he heard Doss ask one of his men as they stopped on the tower deck, eight feet from the open door.

Collins let his welcoming words go for now. "Get in here out of this weather, sir," he said instead. "Let me take your hat."

Collins reached out a hand, but Doss doffed his bowler hat and shook it, slinging water everywhere, then placed it back atop his wet head. He turned his attention to the growing gunfire past the large foggy windows.

"The hell is this?" Doss said.

"That is the gang of long-riding outlaws I've been telling our office about," said

Collins. "They have had themselves a free hand in these foothills for some time now. But it is all about to change — today in fact. They have relied heavily on recruited informants within both the railroad and the mining industry." He gave a smug grin. "We have exposed a good many of them. Today you'll see us topple these long riders and their leader, Christian Clayton Ellis, for good."

"That's good news, Collins," said Doss. "It's what I'm here to see. My men and I will ride out with you to deliver the death blow."

"Great, sir!" said Collins. He glanced down to where the yard engine sat against the dock, its flatbed empty, Doss's men having taken shelter wherever they could. "May I ask where your horses are?"

"I hired a fella down the rails to lead them here," said Doss. "Told him not to push them, let them take it easy along the way. He should be delivering them in a few more minutes."

Collins and Donovan gave each other a skeptical look while rumbling toward them came cannon fire and a promise of more rain.

On a lap around the one-hundred-forty-acre

mining facility, C.C. Ellis had made up his mind it was time to get out of there. In the corner of the property was an escape route hidden by a rugged upturn of stone some eighty feet high. Heavy rain had opened dry rock beds into rushing streams down the hillsides. New rivulets had cut meandering silty paths of their own.

For anyone in their right mind, traipsing out into the weather at a time like this was madness. For an outlaw and his gang of like-minded — that is to say, desperate, wild-minded — riders, a time like this was ideal. It crossed Ellis's mind that the definition of a bold and daring outlaw was to create the worst possible life-or-death situation you could, then figure a way to come out of it alive, hopefully with a large cache of money buried somewhere awaiting your return.

"What next, C.C.?" Bailey McCool said through the blowing rain, a high wind having swept in to join the rest of the day's foul prospects.

Ellis glanced behind their men at the railroad gunmen still in pursuit, and shook his head.

"Keep riding, Bailey!" he said. "I think they have gained on us. We need to keep them out of range."

"Damn it!" Bailey said. "How does the same wind that's blowing us back seem to be blowing them closer?"

"Soon as I figure it out, I'm going to let you know!" Ellis shouted above a hard peal of rolling thunder, following a sharp stab of lightning.

He took another quick look behind them. The railroad gunmen were getting closer to them. A riderless horse splashed past them, its loose reins and stirrups waving at its sides.

Bailey laughed out loud and started to say something. But her words didn't make it past her lips. She rocked forward in her saddle, then back. Ellis saw the bullet hole in her back and grabbed her as she swayed. So did Hoyt, who was riding at her other side. The sound of the long-rifle shot caught up to them, causing the five men behind them to turn in their saddles and return fire, kicking up mud and water ten yards in front of the railroad gunmen.

"I've got her, Jax!" shouted Ellis, raising Bailey from her saddle as her horse raced ahead from under her.

Jax helped to keep her from falling, then turned her loose when Ellis had swung her over his lap, blood running freely down his thigh, his calf, his boot.

"Pin them down!" Ellis shouted to the riders behind him as he veered off the muddy trail into a tumbled pile of boulders.

Jax turned his horse around and pounded through the mud and groundwater to join the five outlaws who had turned off the trail and spread out among the same long pile of boulders. The six laid down a relentless barrage of rifle fire at the pursuing gunmen.

"Bailey, listen to me," C.C. said loudly.

He took off his wet trail duster and spread it on the mud and laid her on it, facedown. Bailey turned her head sideways and looked up at him.

"Don't shout, C.C. I'm not deaf."

"I know," said C.C., trying not to appear worried. He saw confusion in her eyes. "You took a bullet. Lie still. Let me see what I can do."

"I didn't take a bullet, C.C. It was forced on me, just like last time." She offered a faint smile. "It made its way through all that money padding and went through me."

"Take it easy, Bailey," said C.C. He reached a small cloth up to cover the exit hole in the top of her breastbone. "Keep your hand pressed here," he said, guiding her wet hand over the wet cloth and pressing it there firmly.

"What now, Dr. Ellis?" she said, trying to

be flippant about everything.

"Right now?" said Ellis. He showed her another cloth he held cupped in his left hand. "I'm going to get you in my saddle, on my lap, and hold this against the wound in front. Then we'll get you to a doctor somewhere. You're going to have to quit getting shot so damn much." He'd seen how close this wound was to the last one.

"I'll stop, I promise," she said weakly, seeing the look of concern in his face. "Jesse James was shot twice in the chest in the same spot."

"You're not Jesse James."

"Thanks for noticing," she said, her voice even softer.

"You're tougher than him," Ellis added. "Now lie still. Let me do what I need to."

"I've heard that before," she said, drifting a little.

To their right, rifle fire still roared, most of it pouring toward the railroad gunmen, only a little coming back at C.C.'s men. At the sound of splashing, he turned and saw Jackson Hoyt leading his horse and Bailey's.

"Just want you to know we've put some rabbit in them. They're running in every direction. Bad thing is, there're more of their men riding our way." He gestured toward where distant riders were splashing hard in their direction. "We can hold them here and clip a few more of them down or leave them sitting in the mud. What do you say?"

"She dozed off for now, but she needs help, or she's going to bleed out," said Ellis. "I would leave her here if I thought they would take good care of her. But they won't. They'll kill her."

"Yeah, and if we do leave her here, I'm staying with her," said Jax. "So that's that."

"Yeah, I know," said Ellis. "Get the men ready. We're cutting out of here now while we're close enough to get out through the rear fence."

"They're keeping their eyes on us, ready when we are," said Jax. "What about our men guarding the rear fence?"

"They'll hear us coming soon enough," said C.C. "I'll fire three signal shots. They'll let us through and stop anybody following us."

He stooped and picked up Bailey, who to his surprise had managed to get a bottle of Blue River from her pocket and take a swig.

"Don't let go of my horse, Jax," she said in a strained voice.

"I've got him," said Jax.

He and Ellis raised the wounded woman up into C.C.'s saddle. They leaned her forward against the pommel of the saddle, and Jax steadied her until C.C. climbed up behind her.

C.C. pressed Bailey firmly against his wet chest. He reached his left hand up under her arm and pressed it against the exit wound high on her left shoulder.

"Are you comfortable enough?" he asked.

"I'm good," said Bailey. "Get going while my Blue River is doing its job."

Jax swung up into his saddle, Bailey's horse right beside him.

"Stick close, Jax," said Ellis. Before going forward, he looked back though the downpour, water running from his wide hat brim. "Damn," he whispered under his breath. "We're leaving a lot of our men laying dead behind us."

"Not as many as these buzzards are," said Jackson Hoyt. He sighed. "Still, I know how you feel about it."

Ellis adjusted the wet packs of money and loose bills he'd stuffed inside his shirt when they'd stopped long enough to bury most of their bags of money.

"Watch your ears, Bailey," Ellis said. He raised his Colt, fired three shots straight up and batted his dripping wet boots to his horse's sides.

■ ■ ■ ■

Douglas "Doc" Gray, Cal Lindsey, Menard Baggs and Ave Pettigo led the string of railroad gunmen's horses through the growling storm, upward toward the sound of gunfire. They hadn't followed the rails up the steeper incline to the main gate, because the rain, groundwater and rushing mudslides had forced them up the narrow trail toward the rear of the property. Halfway up, a stranger appeared and set his horse on the trail before them. He was leading a horse with a body lying across its saddle.

"Watch this one close," Doc said quietly to the three men riding with him.

"You got it, Doc," said Cal Lindsey.

"What do you want?" Doc called out to the man through the pouring rain. "If you're looking for horses, these are not for sale. Or are you wanting to ride this storm out with us?"

The man didn't answer, just stared at them from the darkness beneath his drooping wet hat brim. With a yank on the lead rope in his hand, the body fell from the saddle of the other horse and landed with a splash on the muddy wet ground. Gray's hand went instinctively to the butt of his holstered Colt.

"What the hell?" he said.

The stranger motioned down at the body and waved Doc forward.

"Yeah, watch him real close," Doc whispered to Lindsey and the others as he tapped his horse forward.

He made sure the stranger saw him slip the Colt from its holster and hold it across his lap. Wind whipped beneath a grumble of thunder.

"Watch yourself, Doc," Lindsey cautioned him.

The stranger sat still and nodded down at the body.

Doc looked down . . . and was taken aback to see the dead pale face and wide-open eyes of Lawrence Sterns.

"If you're asking if I know this man," said Gray, "yes, I do, or I did." He raised his eyes from the body. "What happened to him?"

The man's quiet voice sounded rough, gravelly. *The voice of a man in bad health? Maybe . . .* Gray thought.

"Killed him," the man said.

"You killed him?" Gray asked.

The stranger gave a slight nod.

Gray beckoned his three men forward. "Look at this," he said, jutting his chin down at the body.

"Whoa!" said Cal Lindsey. He started to ask what had happened to Sterns, but seeing the bullet hole in his bloody chest, he instead asked, "Who shot him?"

"He says he killed him," said Gray.

"By God, then!" said Lindsey. "If I had a medal, I'd pin it on your chest and buy you a beer."

"Don't drink," the man said, his face in complete shadow beneath the hat brim.

"Oh," said Lindsey, "in that case, I'd even drink it for you." He grinned. "Why'd you kill him?"

"Accident," the man said, sounding as if it hurt him to talk.

Lindsey looked sorry he'd opened his mouth. "An accident?" he asked in a more serious tone.

"A mistake," the stranger said.

"Well, he's dead as I ever hoped him to be," said Lindsey with a short laugh. "I can understand killing a man by accident. You're cleaning your gun and it goes off or something. But I don't know how you shoot somebody by mistake, unless you made a mistake and shot the wrong man. Is that what you're saying you done?"

The stranger sat silent.

"Lindsey," said Doc Gray, "why don't you

shut up? He says he killed Sterns. That's good enough for me."

"By mistake," the stranger said again. His voice sounded worse the longer he tried to talk. "I meant to kill the colonel."

"The colonel? Dang, stranger," Baggs cut in, "you carry some mighty high sights. Any special reason you want to kill Colonel Randolph Doss, or did you just not like his face?" Baggs grinned.

The stranger raised only a finger as if Baggs had guessed his answer.

"Damn, sure enough?" said Baggs. "You killed him because you didn't like his face?"

Gray cleared his throat. "I hope you'll excuse my men. You can see I have a hard time getting them to keep their mouths shut." He stared coldly at Baggs and Lindsey. "Let me ask you, are you headed to the same place we are?"

The man tipped his head toward the gunfire coming from inside the Gadsen Mining Company's fence, up on their right.

"You're still wanting to kill the colonel?" Gray asked.

"Yes," the man said in his terrible croak.

"Well, hell, then, mister," said Gray, "we both want to kill the same rotten pig!"

He looked the man up and down: the wide-brimmed slouch hat dripping water;

ornately tooled but well-worn Mexican boots; a long, soaking-wet trail duster.

"You're one of C.C. Ellis's long riders, aren't you?"

No reply.

"All right, I can see you are," said Doc Gray. "That's your business. You want to ride up with us, you're welcome. I like riding with a man who knows when to keep his mouth shut."

He shot Lindsey a glance, then turned his horse back to the wet muddy trail. "Lindsey, roll Sterns off into the rocks. Ride up front with me, long rider. We'll talk about killing Colonel Randolph Doss. If you're wondering why I have his men's horses, I hope when he sees I have them, it will draw him out to me and I can kill him on the spot."

The stranger sidled his horse closer to Gray as they rode up the slick trail in the hard-blowing rain.

"I'm Douglas Gray. They call me Doc. I took care of injuries and illnesses for the railroad. I was fired, but the *doc* still sticks."

"I'm Sven," the stranger said.

Lightning twisted and curled, followed by thunder, above the rifle fire from the hillside to their right.

Sven. Doc Gray ran the name through his mind. Sven Handley was the only Sven he

166

could come up with. If this was Handley, Doc reminded himself, he was riding side by side with one of the deadliest gunmen to ever have come out west since Wild Bill Hickok.

Damn . . .

He cut a glance at Sven, eyed him up and down, then looked away. Yep, now it started coming together for him. It made sense that a man like Sven Handley would be one of Ellis's long riders. The man might have come west for other reasons, but before long, the appeal of quick money would have gotten to him as it did so many others, men with quick and steady gun hands who didn't live by other men's rules. He wasn't going to ask if this was Sven Handley, not now anyway. Had the man wanted Gray to know his last name, he would have said it. He'd find out though. Hell, with a few men like Sven Handley, Gray thought, he might start his own gang.

Chapter 12

When the railroad and mine guards realized Ellis and his riders were heading to the rear fence line, they concentrated on stopping them. Knowing the gang had lost a lot of men in the fighting, it was the aim of the railroad and mining company to put them out of business once and for all. Knowing this, Ellis and his riders intended the same fate for the detectives.

"Listen back there, C.C.," Jackson Hoyt said, regarding the earth-trembling roar of hooves far behind them. Far behind yet gaining. "Maybe I should drop back and join them. Every gun helps."

Glancing back now, Ellis saw only six of his men left fighting on the run. Mounted detectives had moved in on the rocky hillsides on either side of their trail. Farther back an even larger group followed, gaining ground.

"No, stay with me. The men knew they

were giving us three a getaway. They want to get Bailey out of here as much as we do."

"Yeah, but damn it," said Jax, "they're getting picked off and slaughtered one at a time!"

"We're leading them out of here if they can make it."

"Yeah, and if we can make it!" said Jax. "How is Bailey doing?"

"Not good," said Ellis, "but she's not bleeding as bad as before." He still held her pressed to him. "The fence is close ahead. Those who can, will follow us."

Without another word, he turned his horse and pounded on through the storm, mud splashing high around him.

"Here come C.C. and Hoyt now," said one of Ellis's long riders spread along the hillside facing the breached rear fence.

He looked through a telescope lens blurred by the steady downpour. A rifleman beside him squinted with his naked eyes beneath the shelter of his hat brim.

"What's that across his lap?" he asked.

The one with the telescope looked again. "He's carrying somebody. I see boots sticking out."

He looked around at a dozen expert riflemen in position on either side of the trail coming from the facility, some with brass long-distance scopes.

"Claggett said they've damn near wiped out the railroad and the mine security forces."

"That's good to hear. When did Claggett come out?"

"An hour ago," said the first rifleman. "He's shot all to hell, though. They laid him under the ledge back there out of the weather. If he owes you any money, you need to go see him 'fore it's too late."

"I hate hearing that," the second man replied. "I always liked Claggett."

"Well, he's leaving in good company," the first man said. "We've lost a whole lot of our bunch."

"Let's hear what C.C. has to say —"

A huge explosion roared on the hillside above them. A ragged gunman flew ten feet up in the air and bounced broken and limp on the rugged rocks.

"Dynamite!" the first man shouted. "They've slipped in behind us."

Another blast sprang up forty yards below them. They ducked against the ground.

Inside the mine site, Ellis and Hoyt came almost to a halt.

"They're hitting our fence guard with

dynamite, Jax!" Ellis shouted, holding Bailey against his chest.

Rifle fire zipped past them like angry hornets. Another blast erupted on the trail just on the other side of the breached fence. Their horses reared in terror, but the two outlaws held them in place and took off as the nervous animals' hooves touched down.

On their left, more bullets spun through the rain. Up ahead, eight railroad men came charging down the slick, wet hillside. Two of their horses fell, sliding, causing more horses to fall around them. C.C. and Jackson Hoyt didn't waste any time watching. They booted their horses out through the breached fence, much of it had been hard to see for the roiling smoke, falling debris and blowing rain. More bullets zinged past, a lot of them coming from their own men trying to give them cover.

Bailey stirred and called out in a weak voice.

"Am I — Am I there?" She either couldn't get her words to come out or to make sense.

"Yes, you are," Ellis soothed.

"Where is he?" she asked.

"Shut up, Bailey. Jax is right behind us," said Ellis. "Listen to me. If I go down, get yourself off this trail into all these rocks. We're taking a beating!"

A dynamite blast went off right behind them. Ellis heard his men riding into the rocks, firing back through the metal mesh fencing.

Kid Santa Cruz shouted, "G-g-get ow — ow —"

"Get out of here!" Harvey Brewer shouted.

Within minutes the firing from the fence line had diminished to almost nothing, the skilled shooting of Ellis's men taking its toll on the railroad detectives. Brewer and Kid Santa Cruz fell in on either side of Jackson Hoyt behind Ellis.

"Clear the way," shouted Hoyt.

A man waved them to a cliff overhang farther back, away from the fighting. They could see through the rain where wounded men sat leaning against the stone-and-shale walls, patched with bloodstained bandannas and wet cloth torn from shirts taken from the backs of the dead.

"Whoa, C.C.!" said the aging gunman Willie Town, who had ridden with the gang since Holden Ryan was the leader, back when both Sonny and C.C. were no more than kids. "Is that Bailey McCool you're carrying?"

"It is," said C.C. "I'm afraid she's losing ground. I've got to ride to New Water Stop

One, see if they've got a doctor yet."

"Wait a minute," said Willie Town. "I've been treating the wounded, such as I can."

He gestured back under the overhang with a blood-crusted hand and called out to the man named Sven, who sat there alone. "Hey you, quiet stranger," he said. "Go get your friend Doc Gray. Get him up here quick-like. We need him!"

Sven lowered his hat brim and walked past them, not fast, not slow, and Willie Town said, "Don't get in too big a hurry. We've still got Christmas to look forward to."

The stranger eyed him and walked on, speeding up just a little after looking at the wounded woman in Ellis's arms.

"There goes one that seems as strange as he looks," said Willie. "He rode in with some men who left the railroad security force and stole everybody's horses, including the new security chief's, Randolph Doss."

Ellis looked at him expectantly, Bailey still in his arms.

"The thing is," said Willie Town, "one of Doss's deserters is a man they call Doc. Says he was a hole patcher back in the Civil War. We took him right in. If he's what the men call him, Doc, he can do her more good than I can."

Ellis gave a slight sigh.

"Here," said Willie, "give her to me. I'll carry her back beside the fire. The way you look, you're apt to drop her in it."

"Obliged, Willie," said Ellis. "I've got wounded myself. Not too bad, but it could use a bandage maybe."

"Let me lay her down and I'll take a look at you myself. I'll pour a tall tin cup of whiskey if you need one," said Willie.

"I need one," said Ellis. "So does Jax when he gets here. He took our horses over to another overhang, out of the rain. We've got to be ready to run if these railroad buzzards hit us too hard. I would think they want to stop fighting as bad as we do."

"I bet they do," said Willie. "From what we saw from here, it looks like you've beaten the hell out of them."

"It's hard to see who's winning when the fighting's going on. We've taken a hard licking ourselves," said Ellis. "Where's that whiskey?" he asked.

As he helped Willie Town lay Bailey on a pallet near a small fire, he saw Brewer and Kid Santa Cruz ride by in the pouring rain, followed by two other men he didn't recognize.

Sven, the quiet stranger, returned with Doc

Gray, but hung back while Gray, Ellis and Jackson Hoyt stood in the firelight near the sleeping woman and talked about the new bullet hole in her back and the one still healing only a few inches from it.

"I have to make it clear," said Gray. "I'm not a doctor. I'm a security agent with some battlefield nursing experience."

"Nurse, doctor or blacksmith," said Jackson Hoyt, "the question is, can you treat our friend and keep her alive?"

"I can do that," said Gray. He looked down at the sleeping woman. "The fact is, I have treated her before. I recently dressed this other wound, cleaned it and put those stiches there."

He pointed as he spoke toward the stitches, the entrance wound, the exit. "I need to take the stitches out, but not just now." As he leaned over her, she stirred but only a little. "She told me her name. I forgot it. What is it?" he asked."

Jax and Ellis exchanged glances.

"We forget too," said Ellis.

Doc Gray smiled slightly. "That was foolish of me, wasn't it?" he said.

"Yep, it was," Ellis agreed. "You know we've been fighting the railroad and mine security agents."

"Because they think we robbed them,"

said Jax.

"So I heard," said Doc Gray. He had taken off his jacket and started rolling up his sleeves. "I stole the horses the chief of security and his men rode up on. It was too slick to ride them up, so I took them off their hands."

"If you left them afoot, we're obliged," Ellis said. "They teach you how to steal horses when you became a nurse?"

"I became a nurse when someone handed me a saw, gave me a stiff shot of rye and told me to cut off a man's foot."

The three fell silent.

"But nothing that drastic is going on here so far," Gray said. He cupped Bailey's forehead. "Doesn't have any fever. That's always good."

He turned when Willie Town arrived with a pan of steamy water and set it beside Bailey's pallet. "Now, if you two will excuse us, I'm going to undress her enough to bathe her clean, front and back. Then I'll inspect the new wound and check the other one."

"Can we help?" Ellis asked.

"I've got Willie Town helping me," said Doc Gray. He tilted his head toward the front of the deep overhang. "They've got a coffeepot boiling up front there. Get yourselves some and rest."

Ellis looked at Willie Town, who gave him a nod of approval on Doc Gray.

"Let's go, Jax."

When they arrived at a low fire with a coffeepot hanging above it, Ellis said, "Lucky for us these men of ours let Doc Gray in."

They filled two tin cups with steaming coffee and stood under the front edge of the stone overhang.

"Leading that many stolen horses was a good calling card," Hoyt replied. "Doc told Willie Town the men riding with him are runaways of the colonel's, except for the quiet stranger. They met him along the trail."

"There's something a little off-center about the lot of them," said Ellis. "I've heard of a hired gunman named Sven. Can't recall his last name. Stands to reason he might've come here looking for work and something turned him against the colonel. Who knows?"

"I'll take my coffee back there and watch things," Jax said.

"Good," said Ellis. "We'll just keep a close eye on all these men."

"You figure this Doc Gray is all right? He did a good job dressing Bailey's other wound?" Jackson Hoyt asked.

"Likely he is," said Ellis. "But stick close anyway while he's tending to her. We'll hear what she's got to say about him once she wakes up."

When Ellis had finished checking on his riflemen spread out across both hillsides, he walked back to the coffeepot, where he found both Jackson Hoyt and Sven, the quiet stranger. As soon as he arrived, Sven stepped back.

"She's awake," Jax said. "I came to get you."

As they walked back under the overhang, Jackson Hoyt glanced over his shoulder. "That's an odd one," he said, regarding the stranger they'd left standing near the hanging coffeepot.

"Doesn't talk much, I take it," said Ellis.

"Right, and I found out why," said Jax. "He was a security detective for a big coal mine operation in Kentucky. The miners rebelled, hung him from a rafter and set him on fire."

Ellis shot him a look.

"He told you all this while the two of you were standing there just now?"

Jax gave a thin smile.

"Must've figured I was a good listener," he said. "Anyway, Randolph Doss — the

178

colonel — was commander of the soldiers sent to put down the miners' rebellion. Says he wants to kill Randolph Doss so bad, he can't stand it."

Ellis shook his head.

"If Doss caused what happened to him, I guess I can't blame him. Did you find out his name?"

"Yep, it's Sven, all right. Sven Handley."

"Okay," said Ellis, recognizing the name right away. "It's been nagging me, trying to remember his last name."

"Now that you remember," said Jax, "what do you know about him?"

"Just what I've heard," said Ellis. "He's a serious gunman, for sure. Did he say what he did to the men running the mine?"

"No," said Jax, "but I figured he wouldn't. Whatever he did, he must've left it behind in a hurry. Nobody wants to talk about killing when there might still be law looking for them."

"You're right," Ellis said bluntly, cutting the conversation off as they stopped and stood over Bailey's pallet.

"Here she is," said Doc Gray, "almost as good as new. No damage done to anything that won't heal or will kill her." As if an afterthought, he said, "The older stitches have been removed and no need for any new ones. No redness, no swelling. Everything's as it should be."

He took Bailey's hand and said to her, "You have no fever, which is always good news."

Bailey lay on her side to keep pressure off the wounds, both new and older.

"Obliged, Doctor," Ellis said for her, seeing that Bailey was looking away. "How long before she'll be able to ride?"

"Under the circumstances," said Doc Gray, "she can ride as soon as she's had some hot food and rested a couple of hours to let her blood replenish itself."

"I'm getting up," Bailey said. "I can ride right now."

Ellis pressed her back down gently.

"Listen to what Doc is saying. You rest a couple hours. We'll be back for you."

Bailey looked at the doctor and saw him offer a slight smile.

This sumbitch, she thought. *If I get a chance, I will kill him.*

She felt for the holstered Colt on her hip, but it was gone, her whole gun belt was gone. She let her hand down on the pallet in front of her. She would bide her time; she would get her chance. He was dead right now; he just didn't know it yet.

Chapter 13

When Ellis and Jackson Hoyt left, Doc Gray stooped over beside Bailey's pallet and handed her a shot of Blue River in a small tin medicine cup. "I know you need this," he said. Bailey hesitated. "Don't worry. It's from a bottle I had hidden away from Cal Lindsey."

She considered it, but only for a moment longer, then sipped it as he held it to her lips.

"My first hunch about you was right. Turns out, you are one of the long rider gang." He smiled the same warm friendly smile she remembered. "And now here we are. We meet again. Although I still don't know your name. Apparently neither do your friends, or if they do, they don't like revealing it."

The laudanum felt smooth and good going down, like warm fingers caressing her insides, calming, leaving sweet and peaceful feelings in their path. *Back home on the farm . . .* she thought. She had to remind herself to pay attention.

"We don't say each other's names around strangers," she said, "and you were right. I am one of them."

There was a slight note of warning for him there if he was listening for it. She couldn't tell if he was.

"You know, I had no idea you were cutting out that night or why. You stole all the horses, all the Blue River."

Again the smile, this time with a little chuckle behind it.

"I wasn't stealing the horses or the laudanum," she said. "I was just leaving. The horses' lead rope was loose. They decided to take off with me, and there we went."

Gray laughed under his breath.

"And the Blue River?" he asked. "Is it all gone?"

"No, I have some left," she said. "Why? Do you need some here?"

"No, I think we're about finished here," Doc Gray said. "But Cal Lindsey would sure welcome some extra."

"He's here with you?" she said.

"He is," said Gray. "It broke his heart when you cut out on us. I realize now why you did, though. You had to meet up with your gang."

"I know what you did," she said suddenly.

"What I did?" he said puzzledly.

"You had your hands all over me," she said. "Don't try to deny it. I was awake the whole time."

"All right then, I won't try," he said. He gave a little shrug. "I did have my hands on you. I had to examine you to detect any fever on or around your wound, your legs, stomach. I'm sorry if it bothered you. I ordinarily have a light touch. People have commented on it."

"I'm not talking about my gunshot wound or my legs! I mean touching me all over in places where you had no right or reason to put your hands. I know the difference between checking someone for fever and touching me to suit your pleasure."

"I see," Gray said, his voice going lower. "You think I did something untoward to you while you were asleep?"

"No," Bailey said. "I just told you I was awake through the whole thing."

"Yes, you did tell me that," said Doc Gray. "You were awake and sky-high on Blue River."

"Blue River that you made sure I had plenty of, not realizing I had used plenty of it in the past."

"You're right," said Doc Gray. "I didn't know you had used laudanum, apparently many times before. You never mentioned it." He paused, then said, "Why was it so important you keep that a secret?"

"No reason," said Bailey. "I just saw no need to tell you my personal business."

"I see," the doctor said. "Let me ask you, though, if you were awake through all of what you say happened, why didn't you say something, do something, anything to stop me?"

"I was half knocked out, and I wasn't thinking clear. But I knew something was going on that shouldn't be."

Doc Gray looked down and shook his head.

"I swear to you, I was doing nothing other than what I've been trained to do. Had I thought I was guilty of anything, I would not have told your friend that I'd treated your other wound. I would have waited to see whether or not you recognized me!"

She ignored his answer.

"You wanted to know why I left. That's why. I didn't know what would be coming next from you, maybe even from you and your friend Cal Lindsey."

"Wait a minute," Gray said. "Lindsey and I are nothing alike. You saw how I got rid of him while I undressed you. I would never have thought of doing something like what you're saying. You must have formed some deep, dark opinion of men from somewhere."

"I'm no prude," Bailey said, "and I have no dark opinion of men. I am a free woman. Maybe had you shown some manners, not been such a sleazy —"

"Wait a minute," said Doc. "It looks like nothing I can say is going to matter or change what you think happened to you. I can only tell you, my intentions were nothing less than honorable."

"Let's get finished up here," she said. "I don't want to see your face!"

"Wait," he said. "I need to tell you my men and I are traveling with you. We're bringing the string of railroad men's horses with us."

"We'll see about that," Bailey said. "Take your men and horses and get away from me."

"How will I explain it to Ellis and Hoyt?" he asked. "They've asked me to ride with them, partly in order to keep an eye on you."

"That's your problem," she said, feeling the laudanum, wishing she didn't. "If they find out what I can tell them about you, they'll kill you like a bug on the ground."

"Then don't tell them please. Miss —"

"Bailey," she said. "My name's Bailey. Don't worry," she added, backing off. "I won't tell anybody anything. I handle my own trouble unless I see I can't manage it."

"The only way they'll ever know about any of this is if you tell them," Doc Gray said. "I hope you will take some time and think this through. If you tell either of them, you'll be causing the death of an innocent man. I swear you will!"

She calmed down. Had she misread him, his intentions that day? She didn't think so, but she had to put it away for now. She didn't want Ellis or Jax or any of her friends knowing about it. She knew any one of the riders would kill Doc Gray if they knew. That wasn't what she wanted. What did she want? She thought about it, the laudanum dulling her senses. She wasn't sure what she wanted, but having someone killed was one of her choices, not now anyway. She took a deep breath.

Okay, she'd told him she knew what he had done. She'd warned him to keep away from her. If he and his men were traveling with her and Ellis's riders, she was counting on him having enough good sense to leave her alone.

We'll see how it goes . . . she told herself.

She watched Doc Gray move off a few feet as Ellis and Jackson Hoyt walked toward her from the front of the overhang.

"How's our friend doing, Doctor," Ellis asked.

"Miss Bailey's coming around nicely," the doctor said.

"I see she's told you her name," said Ellis. "It's unusual for her to reveal anything about herself this soon."

"I suppose having met before, the last time she was shot, gave us a familiarity of sorts," Doc Gray said.

He offered a smile to Bailey, but she curtly looked away.

"If you're here to find out if I'm able to ride, C.C.," she said, "I am."

She forced herself up enough to sit leaning back against a pillow.

"Oh?" Ellis looked at Doc Gray. "Is she that strong already, Doctor? You said she needed a few hours' rest."

Doc Gray sighed, considering it. "I know what I said. The weather is terrible. Miss Bailey has been shot twice in as many weeks. . . . I would ordinarily say no, she badly needs to rest. But with the railroad and the mine company trying to kill you, maybe it would be best if you get out of here."

As he spoke, he stepped over and placed a hand on Bailey's forehead, as if checking for fever. She sat perfectly still.

"After all, I'll be on hand if she needs me along the way."

Bailey looked up at Ellis.

"Where are we going, if I may ask?" she said.

"First place we're going is to New Water Stop One," said Ellis, lowering his voice a little. "Maybe by then the weather will clear up, and we can all go our own separate ways." To Doc Gray he said, "Are you going to have trouble over all those horses?"

"No," said Doc. "Chances are, nobody will ever ask. But the truth is, I took the horses from the man Doss paid to bring them up to the mine. The storm got too bad for me to proceed and I had to take them all the way to New Water Stop One to shelter them." He smiled and said, "It might be interesting to hear where some of those horses came from anyway. The railroads are not particular when it comes to procuring good horseflesh."

"So I've heard," said Ellis.

Jackson Hoyt and Bailey McCool raised their eyes just enough to give each other a knowing look.

"The good thing about this bad weather,"

Ellis said, "is that an hour after it stops, you'll never see where we were or which way we headed."

The four looked out at the hard rain spilling down off the hillside like a waterfall.

New Water Stop One
Two days later

The rain had diminished only a little every few miles along the hillside trails and game paths leading away from the Gadsen Mine. Lightning had knocked down telegraph poles and lines all across the rugged foothills. The men at the mine, already suffering a bad shortage of horses, had no means to reach out for help, except to dispatch scouts and other riders to the nearest surrounding towns.

Those riders, once they'd managed to get a decent horse under themselves, took off in every direction with no intention of ever returning.

With the herd of wet, mud-splattered horses trailing closely in their wake, C.C. Ellis, Jackson Hoyt and Bailey McCool rode out of the foothills surrounding the Gadsen Mine. Much of the money from the robbery had been lost to the storm as men fell dead in the mud and rushing water inside the complex.

"We've lost a lot of our riders," C.C. Ellis said to Jackson Hoyt as they stopped atop a muddy trail and looked out at the storm-ravaged land.

"The railroad and the Gadsen Mine lost more," Hoyt said. "People die. It's the business we're in."

Ellis let it go and said, "I put the word out for everybody to break up and go home. Everybody's gotten a share."

"With more to come," said Jax, "the rest of it buried under some rocks. I'm sorry we lost men, but I'll drink to them and remember them well. That's the best I can do."

"I know," said Ellis. "I just hope we don't lose any others now that it's over. I figure the railroad and the mine have already upped any bounty they have on us."

"They haven't had time to do it legally yet," Jax said. "They have to show proof it was us who did the robbing. They have to take it before a judge, get a ruling —"

"Since when does doing something legally matter?" said Ellis, cutting him off. "If the railroad security leaders tell their men our bounty has jumped from five thousand to ten, they'll be out sniffing for us now before the rain stops — the greedy ones anyway."

They rode on.

Bailey was already looking better, her

strength coming back. With them were Harvey Brewer and Kid Santa Cruz. With Doc Gray rode his two men, Menard Baggs and Ave Pettigo, and now Sven Handley.

When they were less than five miles out of New Water Stop One, three men carrying rifles stepped off the steep rocky hillside above them, their three horses tied to a scraggly deadfall pine.

"Hands up," shouted one, his rifle already pressed against his shoulder. His eyes widened at the sight of Ellis and Hoyt. "Blast a wild hog! Boys, we've done caught the leader himself!"

He saw that Ellis and Jackson had not raised their hands an inch. "Don't test me, damn you!" he shouted. "Get them hands up!"

Along the trail, Bailey and the other riders had heard the voice and stopped. The horses on a lead rope stopped with them.

"All right, you heard him. Let's raise our hands," Ellis said.

The man speaking gave a stiff grin.

Ellis's and Jax's hands rose, but not empty. Ellis came up cocking his big Colt. Jax brought up the shiny Remington from across his belly. Both guns fired at once. Two of the three gunmen fell dead on the ground. The third fired wildly and tried to climb back up the rocky hillside like some reptile.

Shots from Bailey, Brewer and Kid Santa Cruz rang out almost as one. The quiet stranger had also drawn his big revolver, but seeing his help wasn't needed, he held the big gun hanging down at his side as the third man staggered and twisted and jerked and fell from the impact of the bullets. Everyone stopped at the direction of Ellis's raised hand.

A cloud of smoke loomed over the trail. Rain fell hard, yet not as hard as before. The herd of horses grew nervous from the gunfire, but Bailey settled them. Up on the hillside, one of the ambusher's horses whinnied.

Stepping over to the downed riflemen, his gun still covering them, Ellis called, "Somebody get their horses and bring them down. Strip their saddles and harnesses."

Sven Handley carried his gun covering the hillside as he walked up to where the horses stood. Ellis stepped over and stood above the man who had been the spokesman for the other two.

"Damn . . . this wouldn't have happened . . . if you'd just done like I told you," the fallen man said in a pained whisper.

"I don't take orders well," Ellis said.

"I can . . . see that," the badly wounded man replied.

"You followed us from the mine?" Ellis asked.

"No. We . . . followed you up there, saw what you . . . was fixin' to do." He waited a few seconds to gather his breath. "But the word is out now. Everybody knows . . . with all that shooting . . . dynamiting."

"It couldn't be helped," Ellis said.

He bent and slipped a Colt from the man's holster and shoved it down behind his gun belt.

"I reckon . . . not," the man said in reflection.

As they spoke Doc Gray approached.

"Who's the monkey sumbitch?" the man said.

"He's a doctor," said Ellis.

"A doctor," the man chuffed. "I'm sliding . . . down a rough road. I see hell winking at me. You show up . . . with a doctor?"

"In case I could help, I'm here," said Doc Gray, his hand still holding his Colt at his side. He picked up the man's cocked rifle.

"Then help, by Gawd, or shut up," the man said.

"Watch your face," Doc said to Ellis.

Ellis ducked his head to the side just as Doc pulled the rifle's trigger and shot the man through the forehead.

"And that's that!" said Jackson Hoyt, who had started walking up but stopped when he saw the rifle jump in Doc's hands.

"Sometimes that's the only help you can give a man," Doc said, the rifle smoking in his hands.

Part 3

Chapter 14

The streets in New Water Stop One had become a pasty mud. Debris rushed down narrow streams running on either edge of plank boardwalks. The heaviest part of the storm had come and gone, but rain still fell from a swollen gray sky, sheets of it bending and whipping on sporadic winds. When Ellis and his straggling company rode up the middle of the muddy street, a big hound barked and bounded off the boardwalk toward them, forgetting the rain and the condition of the main thoroughfare.

After a few struggling steps, the dog turned around and pressed back. Wading across the narrow rushing stream, the hound climbed onto the boardwalk, shook himself off and flopped down.

"I don't blame you, pal," Jax said quietly.

Hearing the hound and seeing riders come into view, an elderly man stood up from a chair in front of the jail and looked down the street.

"Uh-oh!" he said, and he called over his shoulder through the partly open window, "Deputies! You two had best get out here. We've got a tough-looking bunch coming our way."

Instead of Deputies Wade Parnell and Robert Flitz, Sheriff Max Boyd himself stepped from the jail office onto the boardwalk and looked up the street.

"Damn," he said under his breath, "one storm blows out, another one blows in."

Through the door the two deputies stepped out behind him. Wade Parnell held his Colt open in his hand, replacing rounds he had spent a couple of days earlier. The sheriff watched him slip the sixth round into the cylinder and close it. He slid the gun back into its holster and adjusted his gun belt in place.

"You'll blow a toe off one of these days, loading that sixth shot," said the sheriff.

"But I'll have it there, just waiting, if I ever need it," said the deputy. "That's the whole purpose in having bullets, ain't it?"

"Have it your way," said the sheriff. "I'd hate to see you drop it and blow your damn head off."

The other deputy, Robert Flitz, had grabbed a shotgun from the rack. He checked it, loaded it and looked off toward the riders as he clicked it shut.

"These saddle jakes couldn't even wait for the rain to stop all the way," Sheriff Boyd said.

"Think this is just the start of them?" asked Deputy Parnell.

"Why?" said the sheriff. "You got somewhere you need to be?"

"Just curious, is all," said Parnell.

"I figure there's a bunch of them coming," said the sheriff. He looked closely at the riders. "Looks like that's Miss Violet riding with them."

His hand went to his hat brim instinctively, adjusted it and smoothed his hand back along its edge.

The nine riders stopped in the falling rain in the middle of the muddy street. They sat their horses there where the elevation was higher by inches than along the edges by the boardwalks and streams of runoff water. On their way into town, they had corralled the railroad men's horses at a secluded ranch in a deep valley where one of their men, Stoy Meachum, had lived. After his death, his mate, Rena Deceno, had stayed on, and the place was ideal for hiding horses or anything else, Ellis reminded himself, water running down from his tilted hat brim. He watched the sheriff step out onto the boardwalk, unbuttoning his coat, pulling the right front of it back behind his Colt.

"Good day to you, Sheriff Boyd," C.C. Ellis called out while the others watched rooflines and alleyways for gunmen.

The big hound still lay watching them, but showed no further desire to relocate.

"Same to you, Ellis," Sheriff Max Boyd replied, tight jawed. "Got word you might be coming this way." He touched his hat brim to Bailey with a warm smile. "Good day to you, Miss Violet."

Bailey returned his smile.

"Oh?" Ellis cocked his head slightly and waited until the two greeted each other. "Where might you have gotten such word as that?"

"There was a robbery over at the Gadsen Mine," Sheriff Boyd said with a touch of sarcasm. "Maybe you haven't heard about it."

"Not a word, Sheriff," Ellis said. "Where did you hear about it?"

"There've been three separate railroad security agents through here, proving none of them has sense enough to get in out of the rain. They say a gang slipped in, cut their fencing, robbed their safe, lit out with their payroll money and whatever other cash was there."

"This world has gone crazy, sure enough, Sheriff," Ellis said. "Worse every day —"

"That's enough, Ellis," said the sheriff. "We both know who robbed the Gadsen Mine. There's just no proof. The thieves wore masks. They even talked a man out of half the riding stock! Said they would deliver them up the hill for him."

"Whoa, Sheriff," said Ellis, "you lost me there."

"The new security chief, Randolph Doss, paid a deliveryman to lead their horses up the muddy hill to the mine. But one of the thieves offered to deliver the horses for him. They stole the horses — and now the deliveryman himself has disappeared!"

"It sounds like you've got a lot on your mind, Sheriff Boyd," said Ellis. "I won't keep you any longer. Is the big tent saloon open for business?"

"I just want you to know," Sheriff Boyd said, "I will not allow my town to be shot up by anybody — bandits or security agents either one. Step out of line in my town, C.C. Ellis, you'll answer to me! I don't play favorites! I've told the other side the same thing."

Ellis and his riders sat quietly until the sheriff finished ranting and stopped to take a breath.

"Well, is it?" Ellis asked.

"Is it what, Ellis?" the sheriff barked.

"Is the tent saloon open?" Ellis asked again.

Sheriff Boyd stared at him for a moment.

"Of course! It is open for business as usual," he said. His fiery demeanor settled. "For your own good, I'm warning you, Ellis. There might be more railroad men coming there. They've all got their bark on."

He studied the soaked, mud-streaked riders. "Now, all of you get out of here before we all drown!"

"We're gone, Sheriff Boyd," said Ellis, turning his tired horse in the falling rain on the slick, muddy street.

Out front of the big ragged tent saloon, thick pine walk planks lay sunk flat in the mud on the street side of fast runoff water. Two thick posts had been driven deep and strung with a rope four feet high on which to tie horses' reins. Thick walk planks had also been laid from the mud street into the open front fly of the tent. Horses could be seen through the rear fly, standing in water to their knees, grazing on tall stands of wild grass.

Inside the damp, leaking tent saloon, Ellis

and his long riders moved two wooden tables together and ordered whiskey and tall wooden tumblers of draft beer. Ellis took a seat offering a view out both ends of the big tent.

"Remind me again why we come to this little whistle-stop so much," Jax said privately.

"I wanted everybody to come here after the job so I could see who's dead and who's alive," said Ellis, "but with all these railroad men around, I doubt if most of our men will show."

"Now I remember," Jax said. "We came here to tease the railroad."

Halfway through the first tumbler of beer, Ave Pettigo stood up and quietly slipped away toward the rear fly of the tent. When Pettigo walked away from the table, Cal Lindsey took his place, keeping himself a safe distance from Bailey McCool and the killing stare she gave him at every opportunity.

As soon as Pettigo was outside, Ellis issued an order to everyone at the tables: "Get ready! The fight's coming."

Without questioning him, everybody laid rifles across their laps beneath the tabletops or drew sidearms and held them out of sight, prepared, cocked and ready.

Coming down the middle of the muddy street, four of the Lory brothers and two other members of their gang walked six abreast, their wide batwing chaps slinging water with each step. The lapels of the Lorys' trail dusters were pulled back behind their side holsters in spite of the rain. Water ran from the tapered brims of their black Montana hats. They looked at the tired, wet horses tied to the hitch line out of the stream of runoff water.

"I'm killing C.C. Ellis myself first thing," said Brady Lory in passing.

"Yeah? I've heard he's real tough," said Adam Lory in a mocking manner, walking beside him.

"Just so's you understand he's mine," Brady said.

Adam Lory shrugged. "Give him hell far as I care," he said. "It all pays the same." He looked to his left and said, "Right, Peyton?"

Scarface Peyton Lory looked straight ahead.

"I don't care who you kill or how you kill them. Let's get done here and drink some whiskey."

Next to him, Billy Lory walked along with little to say. But he did manage to ask, "How do we know we can take the railroad man's word for the reward money?"

"He'll pay up. They always do," Adam Lory said with confidence.

Two new members of the Lory Brothers Gang kept quiet, but each wondered if joining this Lory Gang might have been a mistake.

"But what if this time he won't?" Billy asked. Rain ran down inside his boot wells. "What if this time he decides he'll just —"

"You ever heard how a railroad man squeals when you cut open his trousers and he sees you're fixin' to nut him, Billy boy?" said Adam.

"No," said Billy, getting a dark, terrible image.

Adam chuckled and added, "It's a sound you're not likely to forget."

"He'll pay us what he says he will," said Brady. "The railroad's got all the money in the world. Everybody, shut up and get ready."

He looked at the two new men, Jason and Simpson Smith, two cousins out of Kansas. They both nodded they were ready.

Looking the big tent over, Adam Lory said, "What a dung-hole dump this place is. This would gag a privy rat."

Brady laughed. "So are you saying you won't drink here?"

"I never said that at all," Adam Lory replied. "I've drunk in worse."

They walked on toward the open fly.

"Go in shooting?" Adam asked.

"How else?" said Brady.

He grabbed the fly and yanked it farther open. Dashing inside, the brothers spread apart, guns drawn, cocked and aimed. The bar stood empty. They looked at the two tables in the rear corner. But Ellis and his riders weren't calmly enjoying their beers and whiskey. The two tables had been moved again, ten feet apart, and turned up onto their sides, their thick board tops facing the Lory brothers.

"Oh, hell!" said Brady Lory.

Before the six gunmen had time to think or react, a wall of red-orange gunfire erupted along the tables' upturned edges.

The Lory brothers managed to return fire, but they did so while bullets from Ellis and his gang behind the tables cut, nipped, grazed and sliced through them, badly throwing off their aim. In the midst of the gunfire, Sven Handley stood up, took a long-armed aim and sent a bullet slamming through one of the new men's foreheads.

"It must certainly be over and done," said Randolph Doss.

He and four men in suits sat on their horses in the windy rain. He checked his gold railroad watch, closed it and stuck it down in his vest pocket.

"The shooting has stopped," he said. "Would you not expect to hear a little cheering or something?" He gave a puzzled half smile.

Almost before he'd finished his words, he saw two Lory brothers rush out of the saloon, clearly wounded and helping each other limp into the rain. The other two Lorys came next, dragging the two new men flat on their backs, one shouting in pain, the other dead, his head leaking brain matter into the mud like a busted melon.

"I have to say, this comes as quite a shock," said Doss.

He booted his horse forward a couple of steps in front of the other four men. For their benefit, he sat for a silent moment, considering what to say.

Then he called out in a loud voice, "You in there, come out with your hands raised."

Jackson Hoyt called out in reply, "They are raised already. Now what?"

"I warn you, sir, don't be obstinate. I still command enough men to come drag you out."

Inside the tent saloon, Jax looked at Ellis

and Bailey and said, "See? I told you we've been coming here too much."

He stepped back from the fly and Bailey McCool took his place. She stood with her rifle butt propped on her jutted hip. A tall beer tumbler was in her other hand, foam drooping over its edge. She sipped beer and stared at Doss, making him feel uncomfortable.

"I think the young lady is flirting," one of the men with Doss whispered to another.

The four muffled their laughter.

Feeling increasingly uncomfortable, Doss fumed and shouted to one of the men he'd posted along the muddy boardwalk.

"You there," he said. "I believe those are their horses at the hitch line. Go get them! Bring them to me!"

Bailey stood watching until the man got to the hitch line and reached a hand out to a horse's muzzle.

"If you touch one of those horses, you will die touching one of those horses," she called out calmly.

The man jerked his hand back.

"I'm only doing what the colonel told me to do, ma'am," he said.

"I don't know if I can get all that carved on your grave marker," she said. "I'll try, though, if you touch those horses."

"Everybody, stay where you are!" shouted Sheriff Max Boyd, running, slipping, sliding up the middle of the mud bog of a street.

The big hound tried loping along behind him, but stopped after a few slippery attempts, slogged carefully back onto the boardwalk and plopped down to watch.

"Colonel Doss, I warned you not to go starting trouble here! I warned this bunch the same way! If I have to, I'll arrest you and make the railroad come get you out! You had your fight up at the mine. Let that be the end of it until the law takes it up!"

"Sheriff, these outlaws robbed a payroll that was under my railroad's protection!"

"Show me some proof. Name me one face inside this tent right now that you saw at the mine the day of the robbery," the sheriff said.

"Proof? Damn it! This is not a court of law, Sheriff!" shouted Doss. "The law doesn't work with these outlaws! I work for the railroad. We are the law — the real law! Not this system that just gets in the way and lets criminals go free!"

"That does it! Get out of my town, Doss! I won't have that kind of talk here, you railroad-loving son of a bitch," shouted Max Boyd.

"Uh-oh!" said Jackson Hoyt, who had

walked to the front tent fly with a tall tumbler of beer in his left hand, his shiny Remington in his right. "They're getting ready to lift each other's scalp. Time for us to go, C.C."

He looked around at C.C. Ellis, Cal Lindsey, at Baggs and Sven Handley, at Kid Santa Cruz and Harvey Brewer.

To hell with it, he thought. Go or stay, he was with the right crowd.

He heard Doss out on the street say, "Who the hell are you?"

Jax looked out of the tent and saw Doc Gray walking away from his horse on the hitch line, where he'd taken down his medical bag and draped it over his shoulder. He walked on through the sucking mud and the falling rain, toward Doss and his men, his hand away from his gun.

"I'm Dr. Douglas Gray," Doc said. "I work for you, for the railroad."

"Well said, Dr. Douglas Gray," said Doss. "If you work for me, you, indeed, work for the railroad." He thumbed himself on the chest. "I am the railroad!" He looked around quickly to see whether anyone would contest his claim.

"Take it easy, Doc," Ellis said barely above a whisper.

"Yeah, Doc, real easy," Jax whispered, his

big shiny Remington in hand.

"Yes, Colonel!" Doc Gray smiled. "That's why I chose my words with such care. You, indeed, are the railroad, most certainly to those of us familiar with your renowned military career."

"Good job, Doc," Jax whispered to himself. "Now get out of there."

Doss stared at Gray for a moment.

"What may I, and the railroad, do for you?"

"Take a gun out and shoot him, Doc," Jax whispered.

"Shut up, Jax!" whispered Ellis.

"Why," said Doc Gray, "as you can see, I'm returning to work."

He patted the bag on his shoulder. Seeing Doss shoot Pettigo a concerned look, Doc added quickly, "And I bring with me Ave Pettigo and Menard Baggs, both of whom conducted themselves heroically when we were separated from our group during the Gadsen Mine robbery."

"Heroes, huh? Pettigo and Baggs?"

Doss looked back at Ave Pettigo on the boardwalk, and at Menard Baggs, who had slipped out the rear of the tent, circled behind the buildings and now, on the boardwalk, inched in beside them.

"How is it I find you traveling with outlaws, Dr. Gray?" he asked bluntly.

"If I might say, Colonel, we men of science are much like men of the cloth. We go wherever we are needed. We save lives. The world needs us here today, Colonel Doss! I see you have men in need of my care right now." He gestured at the wounded from the shootout in the tent saloon, who lay in the thick mud like pigs. "With your permission, Colonel, I am officially reporting back for duty this minute."

"With my permission, go to it, Doctor," said Doss. "We might be bringing you more wounded souls any minute."

Chapter 15

While Doc Gray and his two nurse helpers, Ave Pettigo and Menard Baggs, shoved the wounded up onto saddles, the rest of Doss's men readied themselves for the muddy trail. Standing around the upturned tables, Ellis and the rest of the gang speculated on what caliber bullets had made the various bullet holes, as they reloaded and checked out their shooting gear.

"Do you think he'll be coming back?" Bailey asked Ellis.

"Who, the colonel?" Ellis replied.

Jax grinned to himself.

"No, not the colonel," Bailey said. "Dr. Gray."

"He told me earlier he might try to stay here and take up doctoring again," Ellis said. "Now it looks like he's back working for the railroad."

He studied Bailey closely. "Why? Are you interested in the doctor?"

"No," said Bailey. "That is, yes, but not in the way you're thinking."

Sven Handley stood at the other end of the table, staring out through the open front fly at the dismal rain. But he was listening.

"I've got a score to settle, is all," she said. She saw Sven Handley glance at her with interest, then look away.

"Anything I hear about him, I'll let you know," said Ellis, knowing she was not one to discuss any unfinished business brewing between her and Doc Gray.

Bailey nodded and stepped back as the bartender came around the makeshift bar with two tall bottles of whiskey in his hands and held them out to Ellis.

Ellis took them and asked, "What are these for?"

"For the trail," the bartender said, smiling stiffly. "Call them tokens of peace!"

"Peace, huh?" Ellis looked the two bottles over. "I didn't know you and I are mad at each other, Frank."

"Oh, no! We are not, Ellis," said Frank Merrick. "It's from them."

He jerked his head toward the open fly and lowered his voice. "Some of the colonel's men. He okayed them to get some whiskey for the trail, but they're just a wee little hesitant to come inside."

"I see," said Ellis. "Tell them we've got our bark off — for now anyway."

He held the bottles toward the open fly and said, "Obliged," to the faces gathered out front. The faces looked relieved and backed away. As the bartender set more bottles on the bar for the railroad security men, one of them walked in with a large canvas carry bag. Behind him came Sheriff Max Boyd and Deputy Wade Parnell.

"What's this," the sheriff asked, "somebody's birthday?"

"No," said Ellis. He motioned for Jax and Kid Santa Cruz to carry the bottles. "Those men peeping through the fly offered these bottles as a show of peace."

"And you trust them?"

"No, Sheriff, but I trust everybody when I drink," Jax cut in.

Beside him, Kid Santa Cruz said, "I d-d-do —"

"All right, so do you, Santa Cruz. I got it," said the sheriff. "So you are leaving?" he said to Ellis.

"Yes, as soon as everybody's finished saying goodbye, Sheriff."

"I hate seeing all of you ride off in this blasted rain. Could be more storms coming."

"We can tell you're broken up over it,"

Jackson Hoyt cut in.

Sheriff Boyd gave him a dark, sharp look, and whispered, "Lunatic," under his breath. To Ellis he said, "I get a feeling this is a checkpoint for you and your bunch, so if it'll keep you away, I'm going to make a list of any of your riders who happen by here the next couple of weeks."

"Sheriff, I'll appreciate hearing if anything has happened to any one of them. Not on account of them being a party to robbing the Gadsen Mine, of course, but from being such a high-spirited bunch. I never know when one might try to pet a rattlesnake or ride straight off a cliff, shooting at the moon."

Boyd gave Ellis a startled look.

"I've seen them both occur, Sheriff."

"Really?"

"High-spirited, like I said."

The sheriff shook his head a little as if to clear it. "Well, all right." He gestured out front and said, "Deputy Flitz gathered your horses. He's holding them in an alley across the street. If you'll send a pickup man every few days, I'll let him know what I've heard."

"I appreciate it, Sheriff," said Ellis. "If the colonel or his bunch start imposing on you too strong, holler out. Or get word to me by one of the pickup men. We'll be here quick with our bark on."

"Obliged," said Boyd, "but this doesn't make us friends, Ellis."

"It doesn't make us enemies either, Sheriff," said Ellis.

"We'll just have to wait and see about that!" said the sheriff.

Ellis and his four remaining riders stopped atop the same wet, muddy hill they had ridden down with the string of railroad security men's horses, plus the three horses whose riders had been shot down following their failed hillside ambush.

"It's a fine-looking spot even in all this rain," C.C. Ellis said of Stoy Meachum's ranch some three hundred yards below.

From the rear of the house, a short trail reached up a shorter hill and joined a long game path. This path, well traveled and less steep, was an easier route, a little shorter, but ran past a neighboring ranch. The fewer eyes on their comings and goings, the better.

Ellis sat his horse between Jackson Hoyt and Bailey McCool. On the other side of Bailey, Harvey Brewer and Kid Santa Cruz kept half a horse length back. Out of sight of the house below, rifles on their laps, eyes scanning the silver-gray gloom surrounding them.

After no more than two minutes, they saw Rena Deceno step out of the house and give them a long wave back and forth, a faded red kitchen cloth in her hand.

What's going on? thought Ellis. *She always gives a long wave, like a railroad switchman. But never with a red cloth in her hand.*

"Harvey, you and Santa Cruz stay out of sight and circle around behind the house."

Neither Kid Santa Cruz nor Harvey Brewer asked why. Without a word they stepped their horses back, farther out of sight, and in seconds seemed to have disappeared.

"Why the red flag, you think?" Jackson Hoyt asked as the three rode down toward the house in the stinging rain.

Just then they saw four saddled horses standing under a lean-to in the side yard.

"There's your answer, Jax. Looks like she's got company and wanted to let us know before we got here."

"That's Rena, all right," said Jax, "considerate to a fault." He nodded at an outhouse sitting a few feet from the house. "You two can go on without me. I'm going to visit the jakes."

Ellis and Bailey kept their horses moving

forward at a walk.

When they dismounted at the hitch rail out front, Rena stepped out onto the porch before they could even spin their reins.

"C.C. and Bailey!" she said. "My goodness! It seems like forever since I've seen you."

Okay, something's up! thought Ellis. *We brought the string of horses here not a week since.*

"Yes, it's been too long!"

He took a step up onto the porch. Bailey stayed beside her horse, one hand slipping over the handle of her Colt.

Behind Rena a hand reached out from the open doorway and wrapped around the woman's neck. A gun came up fast and pointed against the side of her head.

"All right, outlaw, freeze up," a voice said quietly. "You two ain't fooling me!"

Another gunman had stepped into sight around the corner of the house. The hand with the gun in it motioned the other man toward the outhouse.

"Get that one, Fess," he whispered, "and we've got them all!"

The other man hastened forward in the rain and mud, and when he got to within ten feet, he aimed his sidearm at the outhouse door. Before he could fire, four bullets ripped through the weathered plank door, spitting splinters. The gunman jump in place with each fiery blast and landed squirming in the mud, blood spewing and flying from the gaping holes in his chest.

The gunman holding Rena squeezed her tighter. He tried to pull her back inside the house, but turned her loose with a terrible scream when her hand snatched a long hatpin from her pocket, reached back over her shoulder and buried it in his eye.

Before Ellis could step inside to finish the man off, he heard three shots explode and saw Kid Santa Cruz striding through the room, having entered from the back. The man lay dead on an Indian rug.

"Got him, C.C.!" Santa Cruz said, his gun smoking in his hand.

"You sure did, Kid."

Ellis walked back out on the front porch and saw Brewer, Bailey and Hoyt taking aim at two men hurrying from the lean-to on horseback. One of them fell sideways from his saddle and landed dead in the mud, splashing groundwater all around. The other turned in his saddle and fired two shots toward the outlaws. Brewer's hat spun in the air.

"His hat? His damned hat?" the man cursed the smoking gun in his hand and continued to rant. "I didn't want his damn hat! What am I going to do with it?" He shook the gun as he unleashed another round of harsh curses.

His words stopped as a bullet from Santa Cruz's gun hit him squarely in the side of his head. Another shot, this one from Bailey's gun, nailed him in his heart. He splashed flat on his back in the mud so deep, it all but covered him.

"There's a man who's angry with his gun. Not me, though," Jax said, and blew away the smoke rising from his shiny Remington.

Seeing the bloody fight was over, Rena ran to the corpse on the floor, her long hatpin pushed so deep into his wide-open eye, he seemed to be balancing a pearl there.

"Oh, God!" she gasped. With a deep breath she circled her thumb and finger around his punctured eye and, with her other hand, slid the pin out, wiped it on his shirt and ran out front into C.C. Ellis's arms.

"Oh, C.C., hold me!" Rena said tearfully, clutching her breasts.

Pressing her to his chest, C.C. gave Jax a bemused look. Jax and Bailey exchanged smiles.

"There now, Rena, they're dead. You're all right."

"I know, I know!" she sobbed against his throat. "But I'm shaking all over. Hold me tight!"

He did, saying, "You're all right. We're with you now. Try to put all this ugliness out of your mind."

"I will! I will!" she said, turning bolder, her hands moving all over him, pulling him against her even tighter.

"Holy Moses and John!" Jax muttered to Bailey. "He didn't even shoot anybody and she's going to do him on the porch."

"Easy, Rena," Ellis whispered near her ear, "you've got to settle down. They're all dead."

"I know!" she said. "I will!"

But as Ellis tried to set her away from him, her lips stayed warm and wet on his throat. Her hatpin fell to the porch, and her fingers trembled as she tried to unbutton his shirt.

"Rena!"

Ellis took both of her hands, held them and stepped away from her. He beckoned for Bailey to step in.

"Now, now," Bailey said soothingly, her arm going around Rena's shoulders, drawing her farther back from Ellis, "let's go inside and boil some coffee. Let the menfolk get rid of these dead rats. You'll feel better."

"I'm all right now," said Rena.

She took a deep breath and stepped back from Bailey. "I'm — I'm sorry," she said. "When I get so scared, I just grab whoever is closest."

To Ellis she said, "Sometimes the fear turns me into a cowering child. I can't calm myself down! Other times I become some insatiable harlot, some sexual creature who can't seem to get enough and has to —"

"We understand, Rena," said C.C. before she could finish. "We're your friends."

"Thank you for understanding, C.C., and thank you too, Bailey. I might have done something I would be sorry for." She looked back at C.C. "Or at least embarrassed by."

"Think nothing of it, Rena," said C.C.

"The hell was going on here?" Harvey Brewer asked.

He and Santa Cruz had come back with their horses, catching only the sight of Bailey guiding Rena back out of Ellis's arms.

"Nothing, Harve," said Jackson Hoyt quietly. "Just C.C. Ellis winning a lady's heart by the feat of showing up."

CHAPTER 16

The torrential rain had slowed Poker Joe Elliot down. He'd meant to be in New Water Stop One to see Ellis and Sonny Ryan first thing before cutting out for Mexico. The sudden storms that descended on the foothills had changed everything. Along his way he'd met Willie Town driving a wagonload of supplies from a slipshod Comanchero trading post almost too remote for a wagon to reach.

"Sonny's lit one way, Ellis the other," said Town as the two sat atop a hill trail in the rain, looking in the direction of town. "It sounds like you fellas took a hard beating from the railroad jakes."

"Yeah, we did, I hate to say," said Poker Joe. "It's knocked everybody's plans off the edge." He nodded at a bundle wrapped in a yellow slicker and tied behind his saddle. "I've got a bunch of money there. It's not marked, but I was told to get it to Ellis or

Sonny, and I haven't been able to."

"If I were you, I'd roll a rock over it until these storms go back to hell."

"I'm glad I come upon you, Willie. Now if something happens to me, at least you've heard from me."

"Nobody will doubt you, Joe," said Willie. "Take what you need, which you've got coming anyway, and leave the rest up here. Hills always keep secrets."

"I could give this to you, Willie. You'll likely see Sonny or Ellis before I do."

"Yep, I might," said Willie Town, "and if these Comancheros I deal with decide to waylay me, you'll always be in suspicion."

"Damn it," said Poker Joe. "See why I don't like having money on me for long? It's just an infirmament, a punishment for things you've done that you don't even know you did!"

"If you're getting religious on me," said Willie Town, "I will take my leave. Give me a few minutes' start before you hide the money so we can stay friends if something happens to it."

"That's wise thinking, Willie."

Poker Joe watched the muddy wagon roll out of sight, then rode down the trail in a different direction. He found a deep overhang where he led his horse out of the rain, duckwalked the money thirty feet inside, buried it and brushed his hands back and forth to get rid of any signs. He kept a thousand dollars in his saddlebags and fifty dollars folded and stuck inside his shirt. *For the game,* he thought, smiling to himself.

Outside the overhang, thunder crashed hard, jarring the row of hills. The rain, which had nearly stopped, started again, only this time harder. Lightning twisted and licked down like some terrible serpent.

Hang it all to hell! Well, he didn't care. He did a little jig. "New Water Stop One, here I come!" he shouted.

His horse drew its head back and gave him a studious look as if knowing he'd lost his mind.

In the rear of the tent saloon, Poker Joe sat at one of the long benches built onto either side of the table. There were bullet holes in the thick plank top, but any splinters had been picked loose or hammered down flat and the holes filled with sawdust putty and smoothed out. The patch job fooled no one, yet served as a good topic of conversation between hands. During a lull, two men had managed to lay three sheets of corrugated tin over a tear above the rear fly and tie them down. Their efforts turned the sound of splattering rain into the rat-tat-tat of a slow snare drum.

After two hours of serious play, Poker Joe noticed without counting that his cash had almost doubled in size. Sipping rye whiskey, he flipped the piano player a coin and requested he play "Sweet Betsy from Pike."

"Not that damn song again," one of the other three players groaned.

Joe grinned, raking in the pot from the previous hand.

"Yep, I'm afraid so," he said. "You know what they say. Losers carp and complain. Winners tell jokes and enjoy the music."

"I never heard that," said the complainer, Red Stoffer, who hadn't won a hand since Joe sat in.

"I've heard it different times," said a player named Ted Roberts.

Red Stoffer glared at him and said, "I get the feeling you agreed with him just to keep down trouble."

"Hold it," Poker Joe said to Red curiously. "What trouble is he keeping down?"

"The trouble over you listening to that yowling you seem to relish so. This infernal rain is bad enough. We don't need some dirge about the struggles of starving fools who bounded off in search of gold!"

Poker Joe gave a little chuckle.

"Yeah, I admit, I do carry a sentimental hankering for that song," he explained while sorting and stacking the cash he'd just won. "My ma used to sing it when I was knee-high. You see, her and my pa trekked to Californy in forty-eight, all us children with them. They commenced panning streams running down to American River —"

"Are we going to play poker," Red Stoffer said, "or listen at you jawbone about your ma and pa?"

"I happen to like hearing about his family," Ted Roberts put in. "Please continue, Mr. Elliot."

"No, no, he's right," said Poker Joe. "I apologize for my lack of manners."

He shoved his chair back a foot, folded his stack of cash and shoved it inside his shirt. "If you'll all excuse me, I'll go out back and add what I can to the water level."

The other three rested their cards atop the table. He stepped over to the coatrack, took down his drying coat and put it on. Raising his damp hat, he sat it atop his head.

"Wish me luck I don't drown," he said.

Two of the others nodded to him. Red Stoffer only chuffed. As Poker Joe walked around the table and passed behind Stoffer, he quickly grabbed him by both ears and slammed his face straight down hard three times. Blood flew. When he turned Stoffer loose, his face rolled over on its side in a bloody pool that contained shards of front teeth. Sawdust plugs in the bullet holes had leaped in the air and fallen to the wet, muddy floor. Out back, thunder slammed like cannon fire behind a boldly crackling streak of lightning.

Poker Joe slipped his coat off and hung it back on the peg. He hung his hat above it and pulled his cash from inside his shirt. "On second thought, it's too damn awful to be going out back."

The poker players sat staring. Red Stoffer, still out cold, gurgled blood and otherwise lay perfectly still. The bartender, who had observed the entire incident, came over with a bar towel. He raised Stoffer's head by a handful of red beard, spread the bar towel in the blood beneath Stoffer's blood-soaked beard and dropped his head back in place. The players nodded their thanks.

Joe gave the bartender a coin and flipped another one to the piano player. "You know what I want to hear. Play it as long as you like." He looked at the other players and said, "That is if there's no objections?"

"No objections here!" Ted Roberts said quickly.

"Huh-uh! Not from me!" said the other

player, "I've always loved that song."

Overhead, rain began pelting harder and faster on the tin roof, the slow snare drum becoming a horde of mad, dancing squirrels.

The three players continued their game hand after hand while Red Stoffer lay cheek down on the tabletop. When Sheriff Max Boyd and his deputies came through the front fly and stood looking around at the small crowd, the piano player stopped and directed Poker Joe's attention toward the three lawmen, each of them carrying a shotgun.

Sheriff Boyd saw Red Stoffer and walked over in no hurry. The piano player went back to playing "Sweet Betsy from Pike," delivering the song with a lighter touch and softer lyrics.

"Evening, Sheriff," said Ted Roberts.

"Evening, Ted," said the sheriff. He looked at Poker Joe Elliot. "Evening, Poker Joe."

"Evening, Sheriff," Joe said without looking at him. Instead, he looked at Roberts and slid seven dollars into the middle of the table. "I call you."

Roberts laid his cards down. "Nines over fives, Joe," he said. "I expect you've got it beat?"

"Naw, it's yours, Ted."

Roberts looked surprised. "It's about time!" he said.

Poker Joe sighed and turned to the sheriff. "I haven't lost a hand, five in a row," he said. "You and your deputies walk in, I lose one right off."

"That's too bad," Sheriff Boyd said. He nodded toward Red Stoffer. "Is he only there until he finds a place to live? Or just taking a break?"

"Taking a break," said Joe, "in a manner of speaking."

"What manner of speaking?" the sheriff asked.

"The manner of him speaking ill of my sainted ma and her taste in music. I had to thump him some. He's quieted right down. When he wakes up, we're going to keep him here until he can walk straight. I know what a head thumping can do to a man's balance and judgment."

As they spoke, Red Stoffer made a low, painful-sounding groan.

The sheriff asked Ted Roberts, "Are you going to be here a while, make sure Red Stoffer doesn't stagger out in the rain and get himself drowned?"

"I will, Sheriff," said Roberts. "We all will," he added, taking in the bar and the few customers there.

"Poker Joe, I don't want to hear of any more trouble tonight with your name on it," the sheriff warned. "Can I count on that?"

"You've got my word, Sheriff," Joe said. "And I'm obliged for not having to go to jail in this terrible weather."

"Mind what we've both said, Poker Joe, and we'll get along just fine. At least until this rain's out of here."

"I know, Sheriff," said Poker Joe, attending to the cards in his hand. "It's got everybody cockeyed crazy."

Everyone at the table looked at the front fly as it swung open and the colonel's security men stepped inside, hurling curses at the night. They slopped in from the mud, rifles in hand, and stood looking all around.

"Where is the sumbitch that got his face busted?" asked the one in front.

The bartender pointed at Red Stoffer, who had raised his swollen face and held it between his hands.

"Hellfire, man! Who did this to you?"

Red Stoffer only shrugged.

"Hold your nuts, Burns! I'm handling this," said Sheriff Boyd. "I've talked to Red about what happened. Everything's under control."

All four men took a step toward the sheriff

and Deputy Wade Parnell.

"Don't tell me to hold my nuts," said Curly Burns. "The colonel sent me here because we heard a man got his face beat in!"

"That would be me," Red Stoffer said through thick purple lips.

"Who did it?" demanded Burns.

"Don't answer him, Red!" said Sheriff Boyd. "I told you, Burns, I've already talked to him. You need to take your play lawmen out of here. You're close to upturning my supper. I'll blow your toes off!" He stepped closer, the sawed-off shotgun aimed at Burns's boot.

Burns bristled. "You might bluff your way with these little town rubes. But you won't bulldog me and —"

The shotgun erupted in the sheriff's hands. Burns screamed and the front two inches of his left foot disappeared into the churned red mud beneath it. Smoke curled up.

Boyd grabbed the man's rifle and pitched it to the side. The other security men stood stunned, unable to respond thanks to the deputies covering them with their cocked shotguns.

"Anybody else wants to shorten their boot size, talk to my deputies. Anybody wanting to walk out of here all parts in place, pitch those rifles down."

The bartender came around from behind the makeshift bar carrying a big Starr pistol, a large oaken bat standing up from his hip pocket. The piano player picked up a large steel spike he kept at his feet.

"We're sending Doc Gray for you, Burns! You sit tight. He'll be here," called one of the railroad men, who was hurrying out of the tent.

The other two walked across the soggy ground and left through a gauntlet of guns, clubs and threatening looks, leaving their maimed companion sitting at the large table with towels wrapped around his bleeding foot. Two customers gathered the railroad men's rifles from the mud and laid them on the bar top. The bartender would give them to four men he felt would use them well, should relations between the town, the colonel and the Colorado Western Express Railroad ever split apart with a call to arms.

In the night, the rain and wind slowed and settled for a while. The moon even showed its three-quarter face in a gray-streaked black sky.

"Do you think they're over, C.C.?" the woman asked quietly, even though there was no one in the darkened house or nearby to hear them.

"What? The storms?" he said, propped up on a feather pillow beside her, their naked bodies warm against each other.

"Yes, the storms," she said. She reached up and brushed a strand of hair from his forehead. "What else would I be asking about being over?"

C.C. let that part go.

"No, the storms are not gone yet," he said. "But I'm obliged we were given some time tonight," he addressed the window, the moonlight, as if something way up there might hear and appreciate a kind word.

She relaxed against him, her leg resting over his, a hand on his flat stomach. "You're so warm," she whispered, snuggling even closer. "In case you still wonder, I like having you here with me."

"In case you still wonder," he whispered, "I like being here with you, all day, all night and most of tomorrow."

She turned silent for a moment, then said, "Did I do wrong on the porch, throwing myself against you that way?"

"Rena," C.C. said, "I think you can do no wrong." His hand drifted up to her breast and stayed there.

"Be serious, C.C.," she said, laying a hand

atop his, feeling herself grow even warmer.

"All right, I will," he said. "My riders see a lot of things out of a lot of people. What you did on the front porch has already been forgotten, unless it keeps being brought up."

"I won't mention it again," she said.

"And neither will they," C.C. said. "They have lots of respect for you. Anyway, it was nothing."

She smiled, believing him. This was the same sort of thing she had heard Stoy Meachum say at times when such truths and loyalties came into question. They were all outlaws, every last one of them, but in a sense they were her outlaws.

After Stoy Meachum's death, they had come forward as true friends do. They had looked out for her. None of them ever said, *If you need anything, let us know.* If she needed anything, it was simply done, often by parties unknown, and it was never mentioned again.

"C.C.," she said, "I feel so good, the two of us here together alone."

The other riders had headed off to the Nacanely Ranch over the hills "to get one of those big jugs of whiskey he makes." At C.C.'s hint, they were gone in moments.

"This whole night to ourselves." Rena stretched, luxuriating. "Should I not say how badly I've wanted to see you?"

"I have felt the same way, Rena," C.C. replied, turning on his side to take her in his arms.

"Will you ever leave the long rider life behind you?" she asked, the two now pressed front to front, the pleasant aching for each other coming back, not allowing them to lie still for long.

"I ask myself that a lot," C.C. said quietly to her warm breasts, her hand on his neck holding him there.

She forgot what she'd asked him, looking at the pale golden moonlight through the window. "My God," she whispered. "I am so happy right now, I could run into the yard and dance the night away. If it wasn't for the wet ground, of course."

"You wouldn't want to do that, Rena."

"Oh? Why not?"

"Because even though I sent everybody to get the whiskey, there's at least one up on the hillside. To keep an eye on things here."

"Really?" said Rena. "Without even saying it, someone stays in case railroad security or bounty hunters show up in the night?"

"All the time, no," said C.C. "The way things are right now, yes. Everybody is screwed down tight to the wood, with big shots from the railroad's home office here, bounty money getting raised. It'll lighten up and get better after a while, but right now it's bad. Outside of our own circle, none of us knows who to trust."

"All right, that does it, C.C. Ellis," said Rena, only half joking. "We're getting out of here."

"Oh? Going where?" C.C. was happy to go along with whatever she said here in the dark of night, knowing it was just playacting.

"I don't know," said Rena, "San Francisco — London, maybe?" She pulled him down atop her and wrapped a leg around his waist. "We both have money. We can go anywhere we choose. You've been the man in charge for a while. Stoy once told me how well Old Man Ryan lives on the cut he still gets."

"Stoy told you that?"

"Yes, why? Should I not have mentioned it?"

"It's not that you shouldn't have," said C.C. "It's Stoy who shouldn't have said anything."

"I never told anybody," said Rena, "except now telling you."

"I understand," said C.C., seeing this could go a lot of ways if he didn't head it off. He sat up at the side of the bed. "Stoy

Meachum is gone," he said, "so it doesn't matter. Now, you and I, the way things are with us, let's not say anything to anybody about something like that. Okay?"

She looked at him curiously in the moonlight shining through the window.

"What does that mean, 'the way things are with us'?" she asked. "How are things with us?"

"I'm thinking we're sort of close, Rena. Do you?"

"No, C.C.," she said, "I don't think we're sort of close. I think we are very close. I think we are together, the two of us, like a married couple who doesn't live together, of course."

She straddled his lap, a knee on either side of him. He felt her warm and damp against him down there. She nuzzled his neck and said, "I think we've been together like this for some time now."

"Wait," C.C. said.

He leaned them both toward the pillow and slid a hand under it, bringing something out in his closed fist. Then he leaned them over to the nightstand and lit a lamp. Rena giggled slightly as he sat them both back up, and he handed her a small gold box.

"Just so you don't think I'm talking off the top of my head," he said. "Open it."

She did. She gasped at the diamond ring inside.

"Oh, my goodness, Christian Clayton Ellis, what have you done?"

C.C. smiled, seeing her eyes fill. "It's a betrothed ring, Rena," he said.

"A promised ring," she said, turning it in her fingertips.

"So you'll know you've been on my mind, look inside," he said.

"It's engraved?"

Turning the ring in the lamplight until she saw the letters, her eyes welled again. " 'Rena, always my love,' " she read in a whisper. "You're right. This was not something off the top of your head. This took some doing."

"Just so you know," he said.

The two leaned again, switched off the lamp and this time fell over onto the bed together.

"I've never done this with someone I'm promised to marry," she said, admiring the ring on her finger in the pale moonlight.

"Neither have I."

"I won't be able to wear white at our wedding."

"Neither will I," C.C. whispered.

Chapter 17

Doc Gray and Cal Lindsey headed toward the tent saloon, along the way taking in the big finely trimmed private Pullman car sitting alongside the long platform.

"Well, well," said Lindsey, "that must be the private car the company had built for Colonel Doss. It looks like a dandy, don't it, Doc?"

"Yes, it does. It is a splendid-looking rig," said Doc.

"How long will it be before they build you one of those?" Lindsey asked.

"I will never get one of those, Cal," Doc Gray said. "Had I finished medical school and created a cure for some terrible disease, then I might someday have had my own Pullman car. As it is, I'm one of the ones who will always be asked to get off and walk when the railcar is too full."

Cal Lindsey gave a dark little chuckle.

"What about your Blue River, Doc?"

Lindsey asked. "I bet if you got your hands on enough of it, you'd make a million."

"I didn't invent it, Cal. I only distributed it here and there. To make a million on that, I would have to have half a million invested in it to begin with. That's not a way for someone like me to get rich. That's a way for big money to make bigger money. Meanwhile, I'll keep plugging bullet holes and make a dollar or two on laudanum by the bottle."

"Dang, Doc," said Lindsey. "You sound bitter about it."

"Anytime I see a mindless fool like the colonel celebrated and rewarded for killing off whole tribes of Indians and slaughtering whole herds of buffalo, yes, I get a little put off." They stopped at the tent flap and Doc ushered the other man inside. "After you, Cal. And pay me no mind tonight. I'm trying to decide what to do with the rest of this miserable life I got stuck into."

"I understand, Doc."

Inside the tent they saw Doc's patient, Burns, sitting with his wounded foot propped up on a barstool. Sheriff Boyd's deputies, Parnell and Flitz, sat lounging nearby, their shotguns at their sides.

"So there, Curly, let me ask you," said Poker Joe, "when you lose a mess of toes that way, I've heard you keep thinking they're still there for a year or more. Any truth to it?"

He stood pouring a tall water glass full of rye and brought it over to Burns's table. He took a long swig and let out a whiskey hiss.

"I don't know what to think," Burns said. "I didn't plan on coming here tonight to get my toes shot off! I might be bleeding to death. I can tell you how that feels."

"If you want to save them toes," Deputy Wade Parnell called out, "you'd better leave the whiskey alone. Whiskey makes your blood thinner than cat piss. You'll bleed out faster."

"Hear that?" Burns said to Poker Joe. "He waits until I throw down on half a water glass of rye, then tells me not to drink!"

"Save them how, Deputy," said Poker Joe, "in a pickle jar? On a pegboard? What . . . ?"

"Here comes the doctor," said Parnell. "Ask him. I'm tired of fooling with you."

"Security Officer Curly Burns, what happened here?" said Doc Gray, already starting to unwrap the maimed and bloody foot.

"Damned Sheriff Max Boyd blew my foot off, Doctor!" said Burns. "No warning, nothing!"

"Hold it, Burns," said Deputy Parnell. "In all fairness, he did warn you."

"Like hell he did!" said Burns.

"Both of you, shut up," Doc Gray demanded. "I'll get it cleaned and dressed, get the bleeding to stop. That's the best we can do for now."

"What about saving my toes, Doctor?" Burns asked, his voice quavering a little.

Doc Gray looked down at the hole in the soggy ground left by the shotgun blast. He saw blood and bits of bone, tendons and meat ground to a texture of sausage. "I can't save them, Curly. I can't even recognize them."

Curly gasped.

"Here," said Doc Gray. He took a small tin cup of laudanum that Cal Lindsey handed him and held it to Curly Burns's trembling lips. "Drink this, Curly. It will help you calm down. That'll help slow the bleeding."

Burns swallowed the laudanum.

"My damn toes!" he sobbed. "Son of a bitch blew my toes off!"

Colonel Randolph Doss entered the saloon and went to the table where Curly Burns sat behind the glass of rye.

"Word of this terrible, cowardly act just reached me, Officer Burns," he said. "As soon as you are up and around, I want you by my side as we take our vengeance on these scoundrels with their badges."

He looked questioningly at Doc Gray.

"It's going to take a few days, Colonel," said Doc Gray. "We shouldn't try to rush it."

"Of course not, Doctor," said the colonel. "I want some of my top professional men handling this. Unless Colorado Western Express Railroad takes over local law and order, there will soon be nothing here. It's time New Water Stop One learns what law really is! Starting with this foot-shooting sheriff!"

Poker Joe, who had eased over to the bar when the colonel walked in, decided this was a good time to leave.

But as he sidled along the bar, someone called out, "There goes the sumbitch who caused all this! He's one of C.C. Ellis's long riders! Somebody kill him!"

Colt out and cocked, Poker Joe ran out of the tent and tried to make it to his horse at a hitch line along the edge of the street. Yet once he was off the plank walk, trying to run was like running in a bad dream. No matter how hard he tried, he was putting no distance between himself and the men chasing him. He went down to his knee. When he stood back up, his gun stayed down, stuck out of sight in the deep mud. In seconds he was swarmed by men pounding him with their fists.

"Everybody, get back. I've got him!" a man shouted, aiming his gun at Poker Joe, who wobbled to get to his feet.

A loud shot from out front of the tent saloon brought everything to a sudden halt. All eyes turned toward the tent, where the colonel held his smoking Colt high.

"Don't kill this wretched miscreant," the colonel roared. "Bring him with me to the town jail. Before we hang him in a properly officiated manner, I will have gotten from him everything he knows about C.C. Ellis and his long riders!"

"Then we'll hang him," a man called out. "My son, Thomas, has never seen a hanging!"

"Then he is in for a treat and an education," said the colonel, "compliments of the Colorado Western Express Railroad!"

"Hang me for what?" Poker Joe shouted, still searching the mud for his vanished Colt. "Don't I get charged with something, get a trial and all like that?"

"Shut up!" shouted the colonel. "We'll figure that out as we go." He shouted to the four men holding Poker Joe's mud-slicked arms, "Come, men, to the jail with this outlaw!"

"Colonel, there might be deputies at the jail!" a man called out. "They are shotgun sumbitches, the two of them, not to mention the sheriff!"

"Yes, and I am counting on you civil-minded fellows to send them both packing. If the sheriff is there and gives us any guff, shoot him! When we get things settled here, I'll appoint us a sheriff we can count on!"

The men standing in the deep mud raised a loud cheer and applauded the colonel.

While they clapped and hooted, Poker Joe saw that ten feet behind him on a drier patch of street stood Sheriff Max Boyd, a shotgun already raised to his shoulder. The cheers died down.

Five feet from Max Boyd stood Deputy Wade Parnell, also with a raised shotgun. Twenty feet behind them, Deputy Robert Flitz stood leaning against a mud-stuck buckboard, a Winchester resting on the wagon's wheel, a bandolier of ammunition draped over his shoulder. Seeing the shotguns and the Winchester backing them, the men raised their hands. Out of habit, Poker Joe raised his muddy hands too.

Speaking slowly and clearly, the sheriff said, "Poker Joe, put your hands down, get on your cayuse and get the hell out of my town."

"No, Sheriff!" said Joe. "I'm staying to help!"

After all the searching, he'd finally seen the handle of his Colt barely protruding from the mud. He reached for it, pulled it up and tried to adjust its mud-packed handle in his hand. But Sheriff Boyd saw that while Joe's Colt was cocked, the barrel was full of mud.

"Joe," he warned, "if you pull that trigger and it fires at all, you will likely blow your head off. Get in the saddle. Get out of my town! Don't make me say it again."

Joe slogged to his horse and tried to get into his saddle, but kept slipping from his stirrup.

"Damn it," the sheriff grumbled.

He stepped over and shoved Joe up with his free hand. When Joe reached down for the reins, Sheriff Boyd murmured, "Tell C.C. Ellis I'm hollering out. He'll know what I mean."

Without another word, Poker Joe turned his horse to the driest center of the wet street and left, kicking up mud and sloppy water in his wake.

The colonel gave three of his men a guarded look that said, *Follow Poker Joe. Kill him!*

Sheriff Boyd didn't see the look pass

between them. Instead, he heard a hard clap of thunder as a fresh fine rain set in around the town. After a moment, the sheriff motioned for the men to lower their hands.

As they did so, Colonel Doss shouted, "I hope you are satisfied, usurping the railroad's power. I won't forget it, Sheriff by God Bensen!"

"It's not Bensen. I'm Boyd. Max Boyd," the sheriff said quietly.

"I don't give a damn if you're Wild Bill flipping Hickok!" the colonel shouted in a rage. "You are interfering with railroad law here. We won't stand for it, will we, men?"

The men gave a weak response, at which Colonel Doss looked shocked.

"Let me make it clear," said the sheriff. "You can leave here now upright under your own steam. Or keep testing me, and leave here being carried, the last taste in your dead mouth that of horse piss and street mud."

Chapter 18

Daylight broke with a spread of dim silver-gray light and a wind full of cold peppering rain. It was the chilled rain that woke him, Poker Joe Elliot thought. Then amid the beads of rain came a warm, wet upward swipe on his cheek accompanied by a rancid smell as could often be found around dead creatures before the buzzards touched down. He felt that same warm lick again, this time with something rising and falling rapidly against his cocked leg.

A coyote? he wondered, letting his knee down. *Humped by a coyote? Hell no!*

That had to be some crazy dream he'd been having before daylight tapped him on the shoulder. He opened his eyes slowly . . . and saw a young coyote leaning over him. Another coyote flipped away, now that his knee wasn't cocked.

Stop! he either shouted or thought he shouted. Either way, sleep left him. So did the two young male coyotes, the one licking blood from his face. The other? He wasn't sure what that was about. But he saw them race away off the trail into the rugged hills.

"Holy cats!" he said, thinking right away how pained his voice sounded.

He thought hard. Had it been his face that took the slamming on the tabletop instead of Curly Burns's? He put the pieces of last night's events together in his mind as they came to him, like a man piecing together a puzzle suitable for framing.

While his head cleared, he drew his muddy gun from its holster and cleaned off as much drying mud as he could. When he got back to his horse, he saw a three-foot-long branch lying across the saddle; a short broken fork held it hooked in place. The horse sputtered and tried to shake the branch loose.

"Easy, boy."

Poker Joe pitched the branch to the ground. *Okay, that means something,* he decided. He touched his fingers to a stiffness on his cheek. Feeling something stuck there, he peeled it off and looked at it. *Tree bark? Yep,* he told himself, *that's what it is.*

He had been riding pretty fast, in case anybody tried to follow him. He led his horse back along the trail, looking up.

What a rotten piece of luck. He saw more

pieces of broken limb strewn across and along the trail. Damn, he must've been flying — caught the limb right across his face. Knocked him stone-cold. He looked his horse over good, making sure there were no injuries after such a slam.

"Nothing ever hurts you," he said to the horse, almost grudgingly.

At a stream alongside the trail, he stooped and got the remaining mud off of his gun, while his horse drew water. He holstered the wet gun and climbed into the saddle, which wasn't easy, given his clothes were thickly crusted with dried mud.

Wait a minute. . . . Searching inside his shirt, he was surprised and relieved to find that his winnings were still there. *What a night!*

He laughed to himself, tapped his boots to the horse's sides and rode away, his neck, his back and the whole side of his head throbbing in pain.

As soon as Poker Joe reached the Stoy Meachum Ranch, he told C.C. Ellis what had happened in town the night before, and what Sheriff Max Boyd said: *Tell C.C. Ellis I'm hollering out.*

Ellis understood. He looked out through the falling rain for a moment.

"I swear, C.C.," said Poker Joe, "I only meant to thump Red Stoffer's head a little, for bad-mouthing my ma. It all just got out of hand after that."

"You had a gun?" Ellis asked.

"Yep."

"A knife?"

"Oh, yeah."

"But instead of shooting him, which you could have, or stabbing him in the heart, as some men might have been prone to do, all you did was slam his head on the table, right?"

"That's all, just three times," said Poker Joe. "Then I turned him loose, let him lay there and sleep. Had the bartender bring him a towel to lay his face on."

"All right, what happened after that wasn't your fault, Joe, so forget it. The sheriff shot the railroad officer's toes off in an act of upholding the law."

"I agree," said Poker Joe.

They were on the porch, waiting for Jackson Hoyt, Bailey McCool, Kid Santa Cruz and Harvey Brewer to bring out their mounts, including one of the railroad men's unbranded horses, which had come up in the herd from the Gadsen Mine, to swap for Joe's tired nag.

Behind Ellis, the door opened and closed.

Rena leaned into his side and murmured, "Anything I can do to make you stay here with me . . . anything at all?"

"It's business, Rena," said Ellis. "As soon as it's over, I'll be right back here. You're going to see a lot more of me from now."

"Oh? I should certainly hope so," she whispered. She drew his attention down to her folded hands. She moved her right hand from atop her left hand just enough to reveal the ring on her third finger. "I want us to get used to feeling our arms around each other."

"So do I," Ellis whispered, leaning his face close to her cheek.

They turned away just enough to kiss discreetly, then turned back to the riders who had stopped at the edge of the porch.

"We saw that," said Jackson Hoyt. "You can't be doing that until you make an honest women of her."

"That's right, Ellis," said Bailey McCool. "Rena, make him state his intentions and stick to them."

"I will, Bailey," Rena said.

She raised her folded hands to her face, covering the ring, and gave Ellis a soft little smile. He gave her a wink as he mounted his horse and took a lead.

He smiled to himself, thinking of Jax and

Bailey as he'd seen them in the bunkhouse this morning at dawn, covered by a blanket, their clothes on a chairback, a jug of whiskey on the floor beside them.

"What's going on with you, boss?" Jackson Hoyt asked, riding up.

"Nothing, Jax. Why do you ask?"

"You seem to be in a much better mood than in a long while," said Jax.

"Is that a bad thing?" said Ellis, keeping his eyes on the trail ahead.

"No," said Jax, "but it's noticeable as hell. What's the good mood all about? I might want one myself."

"Money, Jax. In spite of some of the trouble it's caused and might yet cause, we've made ourselves a fortune the past few months. We could fold it all up now and not do anything that doesn't suit us."

"You don't mean stop robbing mines, railroads and such?" said Jax.

"Just thinking out loud," said Ellis. "But yes, if we wanted to, we could pull back out of this business, go somewhere far away and live well from now on." He looked at Jax. "We might could both think on it."

"To be honest," said Jax, "I was thinking about it last night in the bunkhouse. I wondered where I'd rather be, who I'd rather be with and what I'd rather be doing." He smiled. "Hell, I couldn't come up with nothing. So I gave up. I drank a bunch of whiskey and kept doing what I was doing."

"What you were doing must've suited you," said Ellis.

"Oh, for sure. If it hadn't, I would have stopped," said Jax.

At an upward turn onto the trail leading up to New Water Stop One, a dark figure in a black hat and a long trail duster sat in the rain, gazing down. Hoyt sidled his horse over closer to Ellis. The others began putting more room between them, not knowing how many other riders might be waiting up along the rocky hillside. Hoyt was the first to speak.

"I believe that's Sven Handley," he said quietly.

"I think you're right," Ellis replied. But he didn't bring his riders any closer together just yet. He had early on pegged Sven Handley as a gunman with scores to settle, yet he knew of no trouble brewing, past or present, between Sven Handley and any of his riders.

As they got nearer, Ellis gestured for Handley to ride beside him and Handley did — so smoothly that it was as if he'd been riding beside him all morning.

"Something I want to show you up ahead, Ellis," he said in a gruff, gravelly voice.

About twenty feet farther on, Handley pointed at two horses standing off the trail, hitched to a downfallen pine.

"Well, well," Ellis said calmly, bringing the group to a halt.

Three bodies were tied to the backs of the two horses. Rain had washed away much of the blood that had covered them; one lay with a bloodless purple wound in the back of his bald head. Ellis didn't look for any other wounds, but he knew there were more. He turned questioning eyes to Handley.

"I followed them last night out of town. They'd been sent out to kill this one."

Handley tilted his head toward Poker Joe Elliot. Joe straightened in his saddle.

"Colonel Doss sent them?" said Ellis.

"Yep." Eyeing Poker Joe, Handley said, "It looks like he ran into them or into somebody wanting to kill him."

"He hit a tree," said Ellis.

"Yeah, that'll do it," said Handley. "Funny but it might have kept him alive."

"Hey, listen, both of yas," said Poker Joe. "No offense, but I'm sitting right here. You can both talk to me, instead of about me."

"The tree could have killed you," said Handley. "It might also have saved your life. I followed these three. They rode out ahead of you to spring an ambush, maybe find the long riders' hideout. I watched them wait and wait till finally they either got tired of waiting or realized they were looking too close for something they never wanted to find. I saw they were leaving, so I went ahead and killed them. I've got their tin security badges in my pocket, in case they become useful."

"Obliged," Ellis said with a nod.

Poker Joe sat in silence, contemplating the irony as rain had his hat brim sagging down around his face.

"So the tree limb might have killed me, but more likely might have saved my life," he said. "No matter which, you saved my life, killing these jakes before they killed me."

"Maybe all of that," said Handley. "Maybe none of it at all. Fate brings its own irony with it."

He turned to Ellis and said, "I know you're headed for some hard settling with Colorado Western Express Railroad. I want to be there for it."

"All right." Ellis waited, knowing more was coming.

"When the time comes, I want to kill the colonel myself."

"I know," said Ellis. "You said so before, but you never said why."

"Do I need to," said Handley, "between men like you and me?"

"No, you don't need to," said Ellis. "But it makes me think you need to get something clearer in your head."

"Maybe."

Handley dismounted and stepped over to the bodies, waving the riders past him. Ellis gave his riders an okay nod. They moved on slowly. He stepped down from his saddle and joined Sven Handley.

"Sounds right," Handley said, his voice still gruff, but not as bad as it had been. It didn't sound as painful for him to talk. He reached down and pulled a knife from his boot well.

Ellis watched him cut the ropes holding the dead men to the saddles. He cut the horses' cinches and shoved saddles, bodies and all off to the wet, soggy ground. Two of the bodies appeared to have died fighting over the saddle.

Handley wiped his knife blade across the wet ground out of habit and shoved it back down in his boot well.

"I want to kill him because he had his men

beat me almost to death," he added. "They buried me while I was still alive. Days later, a band of Comanchero traders came through and heard me screaming my head off under the dirt and rock."

"I think I heard about this," said Ellis.

"Yes. And I was there as a new official of Colorado Western Express Railroad. I'm married to Preston Horn's daughter. He knew I'm a hired gun. That's why he hired me. A gunman is a murderer if he works for himself, but he's a hero if he works for the railroad."

"The Preston Horn, owner of Colorado Western Express Railroad." Ellis whistled. "And the railroad men beat you, thinking you were Sonny Ryan?"

"Yes, Sonny's men switched clothes on me when they came and set Sonny free. That's why when I take off this duster, I'm still dressed like one of your long riders. At first, I wanted to kill Sonny Ryan, but I've had lots of time to think about things since then. Sonny Ryan didn't bury me alive. The colonel and three of his men did that. I've got all three of their names up here." He tapped his forehead.

Ellis sat quiet and listened.

"Yes, in a crazy way they saved my life when they buried me. Had they shot me in the head, I would have been dead and gone now. Do you see what I mean? Their terrible act saved my life."

Handley sounded worn out with the matter. As they continued talking, they shooed the unsaddled horses away and went back to their own horses.

"When something keeps coming to your mind that riles you, that you can't seem to get rid of, what do you do?" Handley asked.

"The best you can," said Ellis, "and hope one day those thoughts forget where you live."

The two swung up in their saddles and caught up with the others.

Riding ahead of the others, Ellis saw Sven Handley ride his horse up into the rocky hillside and disappear in the lingering mist.

Can we count on him? Ellis asked himself. *Yes, I believe we can.*

He smiled to himself, picturing Rena lying on her back in the big feather bed, holding her hand above her, watching her ring glitter from various directions. For a moment he fought the urge to turn the horse around and ride back to the ranch. Instead, he forced himself to put the feeling away. He settled his thoughts on staying alive, and rode ahead of his riders, leading them on toward New Water Stop One.

■ ■ ■ ■

The colonel and Doc Gray stepped out of the new Pullman car onto the platform in a cold windblown drizzle.

Security officers stood on each side of the car door, wearing black bowler hats and long raincoats that covered them from their boots to their ears. Under their raincoats they carried big Colts in shoulder rigs.

"What do you say, Doctor? Is she a beauty or what?" The colonel swept his arm to take in the shiny car. "Could you see yourself practicing medicine out of a rig like this?"

"I would be humbled and, frankly, stunned," said Gray, feeling the effects of the quick dose of Blue River moving through his chest.

The colonel had also taken a drink, for the sake of the nagging pain in his lower right side.

"Well, Doctor," said the colonel, "get yourself humbled, and commence being stunned. I'm putting you and your assistant, Lindsey, in this, our new traveling medical car." He smiled broadly. "I have ordered another private security car for myself. It has already been approved by Mr. Horn himself."

"My, my," said Doc Gray, looking more closely at the glistening Pullman car. "This will take some getting used to."

"Get used to it, Douglas," said the colonel. "Having seen how you conduct yourself and the splendid way in which you have won the hearts and minds of my security force, I want you at my side. Be my right-hand man, as they say! Together we are going to whip this small railroad company into something the nation can be proud of."

"Nothing could please me more than that, Colonel."

"And that is exactly why I was brought in, you know: to present a face of stability and dare I say class to this entire operation."

The colonel stepped closer, bringing the conversation to just the two of them. "By the way, my good doctor, I want to start bringing you in on the current situation. It's important that you are up-to-date."

"Yes. Thank you, Colonel," said the doctor. "I'll try to keep up with you."

"For instance, if my ranks appear somewhat sparse right now, it's because I have sent twenty of my best men out in two separate commands."

"Oh?" Doc Gray waited for the rest of it.

"Yes," said the colonel. "They are out patrolling in the rain right now, as we speak.

I think it's time we take down the welcome signs C.C. Ellis and his gang of thugs feel this town has extended to them."

"Oh?" Doc Gray repeated. "Where are all the security men?"

"I sent them out in three patrols: two all along the trails up to here and another along the trail where the Gadsen Mine is, along with other important companies who use our valuable rail services. After all, we must keep our valuable customers safe and happy. They are what keep the railroad running."

"I understand, Colonel," said Doc, not understanding at all.

Splitting one's forces had become greatly unpopular ever since General Custer tried it as a tactic at the Little Bighorn. What he did understand, though, was that the colonel seemed to be poking at C.C. Ellis's men, like poking at a hornet's nest with a stick.

Before drawing any conclusions based on what the colonel had told him, he decided it was time he called on Scotty Dowell, the colonel's longtime trail scout, to look around and see what was going on out there.

As soon as the colonel was finished talking to him, Dr. Gray left the loading platform and trudged away through the rain toward the tent saloon to find Scotty Dowell, whose loyalty had gradually been swaying of late from the colonel to the doctor, as Scotty was realizing Colonel Randolph Doss had lost his mind. Hearing his new plans would only confirm it for him, Doc was certain.

Scotty was on his horse just outside the tent saloon.

"Thank goodness I found you!" Gray cried.

"Whoa!" said Scotty to both his horse and to Doc Gray standing in the mud. "I'm on my way out. I've had enough of this flooded dung hole to last me a lifetime."

Doc stepped closer to the horse's side and spoke to Scotty in a low voice.

"The colonel wants you to do some scouting out there, see what's going on," he lied.

He had considered being honest that it was he who wanted to know, not the colonel, but this was no time to chance Scotty turning him down.

Scotty slipped down from his saddle and gave Doc a firm look.

"I can likely tell him what's going on without riding out in this blasted rain," he said. "We've got railroad security men laying along a ridge seven miles out, waiting to ambush C.C. Ellis's long riders. We've got bounty hunters sliding in from all over hell to collect bounty that's just been bumped up on the long riders. Hell, we've even got a new sheriff here shooting toes off!"

"Have you been drinking, Scotty?" Doc asked.

"No, but I should have been," he said. "I took my first shot of rye whiskey and laudanum earlier today. I regret not drinking it years back when I was scouting for the army."

He muffled a laugh and said, "I've seen lots of fighting and lots of killing. It always started in places like this, under circumstances like these. We've got too much scheming and brewing going on right here. Lives are going to end for it."

"All the more reason we need somebody with experience like you have —"

"Save your breath, Dr. Gray," Scotty said. "Hell, I'm going. I always go. I just need a good bottle of rye to help shake off this cold rain."

"One minute," said Gray.

He hurried in and out of the saloon and handed Scotty a tall bottle of rye.

Scotty chuckled. "The colonel knew I'd go before he even asked you to tell me."

"I bet he did, Scotty," said Doc Gray, feeling bad about lying to him. "Say, Scotty, what if I ride along with you?"

"Naw," said the old trail scout. "I know

you're a good man, Doctor, giving out Blue River medicine to the wounded and all, but on horseback, up in these steep hills, I fear you'd only get in my way."

Chapter 19

C.C. Ellis looked up at the hand signal from Jackson Hoyt more than a hundred feet up the rocky hillside. Ellis brought the riders around him to a halt and said quietly, "Rider coming."

He looked back up and saw Jackson sink out of sight, while his riders were disappearing on either side of the trail. Ellis took a position just off the trail and climbed down from his saddle.

A single rider came into sight around the turn in the trail ahead.

"It's Scotty Dowell, the colonel's scout," Ellis announced. "I've seen them together."

In a moment, Scotty came riding in, one hand holding his hat on. "Hoss," he said to Ellis, "I'm damn glad it's you!"

He stopped his horse and sat catching his breath. Then he leaned forward with both hands on his saddle pommel. "Colonel Doss had Doc Gray send me to tell you there're ten railroad security men up ahead fixin' to ambush you."

"That makes no sense," said Ellis. "The security men are the colonel's men. If he had them all set to ambush us, why would he send you to tip us off?"

"Hmm, I don't know," said Scotty. "Doc sent me, said the colonel wanted me to warn you . . . which I did just now as you heard."

He looked all around with a rye-whiskey-lit smile. "If you won't listen to me, ride on ahead. Maybe when they start shooting —"

"Wait. I get it," Ellis said. "Where do you think they are up ahead?"

"Oh, I can show you," said Scotty. "I saw them not higher up than that one." He pointed at Hoyt, who was coming down the hillside, feeling his way among the rocks.

"Did they see you?" Ellis asked the old trail scout.

"No, I don't get seen very often," said Scotty. "If they saw me, they didn't let on."

He paused as Jackson Hoyt made his way to them, taking the reins of his horse from Bailey.

"I'll tell you something about the colonel," said Scotty. "He is known as the ambush master. He's got an ambush they put in one of their military books!"

"Yeah?" Hoyt asked. "Where?"

"Up there at West Point," said Scotty. "It's in one of their warfare journals. I once saw a copy of it. It's called the Captain R. Doss double-back ambush, him being a young captain at the time he invented it."

Ellis looked around. "Anybody ever hear of it?"

"I have," said Jackson Hoyt. "It's a fake ambush. A line of shooters lies watching the trail. But they are only there to fool you. Thirty or forty yards away, more men are waiting on horseback. They wait for the men in front to attack the small number of men already settled in the rocks. Then they ride in behind them, shooting the hell out of them from both sides."

"That's it?" said Ellis. "It sounds like a sucker's bet to me." He looked almost disappointed. "One more simple-minded way to bait us into a one-sided fight."

"It's not perfect," Hoyt said with a shrug, "but if you're the attacker, thinking you've got the upper hand, and all of a sudden now you're hit from behind and in front, it can ruin your day. Maybe your whole week."

"Like I said," Ellis repeated, "a sucker's bet."

He looked at Scotty, who had turned up a swig of rye. "Take us closer to them," he said.

Scotty corked his bottle. "I can do that," he said. "But if they see us . . ." He trailed off.

"They won't," said Ellis. "We're invisible. Take us up higher first thing. There's track up there." He looked at Hoyt. "Can we see down this hillside without being seen from up there?"

"You bet," said Jax.

"Then we're good," said Scotty. "I'll ride up there with you and help set it up."

Jax look at Ellis for his approval.

Ellis said, "Doc Gray tells me Scotty Dowell is the best trail scout for miles around."

"I do like riding with the best," Jax said. He eyed the bottle of rye in Scotty's hand.

"You need a little taste to steady your hand, young fella?" asked Scotty.

"Obliged," said Jax, "but my hands stay steady. I'm going to wait until we've thinned the security force out some."

"I understand," said Scotty. "It'll be right here when you want it."

"Sounds good to me," said Jax.

Thirty feet away, Ellis called, "Jax, come over here for a minute."

"Be right back, Scotty." Jax turned his horse and rode over to Ellis. "What is it, boss?"

"After you and the others get to the top

of this hill and look at the railroad men where they are waiting and how many there are, I want you to change plans at the last minute."

"What?" said Jax. "You don't want us to charge them?" He looked very surprised.

"No," said Ellis, "once you're up there on the rail tracks, I want you to gather everybody toward New Water Stop One and ride on."

"Ellis, why? This is a fight we can win!" Jax said.

"We didn't come looking for a fight we can win or lose," said Ellis. "We're headed out to help Sheriff Max Boyd like he asked us to."

"Yeah," said Jax, "but this ambush was practically dropped in our laps with a big ol' ribbon tied around it, you know?"

"I know," said Ellis. "And how many times in your life or mine has somebody been that good to us?"

"You mean . . . ?" Jax let his words trail.

"Listen to me, Jax," Ellis said. "I've never won a battle by fighting the way my enemy wants me to. Have you?"

Jax thought about the question for only a second.

"Hell no!" he said. "Never have, never will. Wait a minute. Is Scotty in on this?"

"Scotty has been with the colonel a long time. He's never going to cross him. But the colonel didn't actually send him. He said the colonel told Doc Gray he wanted him to do this."

"You're right," said Jax, starting to get it.

"That's how some people lead. They pass along just enough to keep their orders traveling from one to another. If it all works out well, of course that's what they wanted, and everybody involved was just a part of their plan. If it all goes to hell, they had nothing to do with it. Orders must've gotten misunderstood somehow."

Jackson Hoyt relaxed with a deep sigh and adjusted his hat brim.

"How come I didn't see all of this right off like you did?" he asked.

"That would take more explaining than we've got time for, Jackson Hoyt," said C.C. Ellis. "Gather up and go while the rain has slackened down some. We've got an ambush we're going to slip past."

In a fine mist, young Reese Donovan led sixteen well-armed Western Express security men through a rail tunnel that had years ago been blasted and bored through a wall of solid stone too thick and deeply embedded to be blown up and hauled by wagon down the high trails.

At the far end of the eighty-foot-long tunnel, they bunched their horses up and gazed back into the dark. The length of the tunnel and the grayness of the day kept the light at the other end obscured.

"I can see a man getting the willies in a place like this," said one of the riders to another, keeping his voice low.

"Nothing to worry about," the second man replied. "If we can't hear a train coming two miles away in here, we might deserve to get run over by it."

A third man chuckled. "You got that right," he said. "If you ask me —"

"Everybody, listen close," said Reese Donovan, getting the men's attention. "Up ahead, if you look on this hillside, you'll see our men spread out along the rocks thirty yards up."

He paused and let the men take in what he'd said. "The reason you can't see them better is because we don't want you to," he continued. "We have it from a reliable source that Sheriff Max Boyd has gotten word to C.C. Ellis that he needs his help in town."

The man who had chuckled did it again, saying, "What kind of world are we in, sheriffs and outlaws walking hand in hand!"

"If I tell you again to shut up and listen, I'll take your security badge and send you back to town. From there you can go home. Do you understand?"

"I do understand, sir," the man said. "Sorry."

Donovan continued. "The reason we don't want them to be completely invisible is so when C.C. Ellis's men spot them, they'll realize we are about to ambush his outlaws — at which point they will want to take the upper hand and ambush our men first."

The riders fell silent.

"Here's where you and I come in," said Donovan. "When Ellis's men drop down and try to ambush us first, all of us lying low here in the tunnel and farther up the trail are going to hit them hard from both sides and behind."

The men remained silent.

"Any questions?" Donovan asked.

"You've made it very clear, sir," said one of the men. "I can't wait to get my sights on these saddle bums!"

But the way he said it made some men think he was only razzing their young leader.

"I feel the same," said Donovan. "I also want to tell you that when we get this cleaned up, and I know we will, Colonel

Doss will make arrangements with the Gadsen Mine to use their yard switch engine to bring him out here in what is now his medical treatment and supply car."

A couple of men applauded, but the others showed little interest.

As Reese Donovan rode his horse away at a walk, the man with the sense of humor said guardedly, "Hear that, fellas. Once we bait these outlaws into a fight and get the hell beat out of us, the colonel will come out and show us his new medical car! Oh, boy!"

"Yeah," said another, "let's hope he don't have to show the inside first. The cutting board, the leg saw!"

The men gave a dark laugh and formed up in a column of twos.

Sven Handley searched for an hour until he found a brushy game path that led up to the less steep side of a wet hill of broken rock overlooking several wider trails. The first level below him, some seventy or so feet down, supported a rail track meandering through, in and around the foothills, north and northeast of him. He was as near unapproachable as a man could be. He'd known he would be, coming here.

From the tracks below, he had estimated

the game path to be a good three-mile ride over tumbled rocky hillside and loose gravel. From there he had rounded to this side of the hill and ridden up to where he now sat, his long-range rifle across his lap. Overall, he told himself, anyone on the tracks below would have to ride no less than eight miles from that spot to this. Their only other option besides riding the rugged wet distance would be to climb straight up by rope hand over hand while he was up here killing them as quick as he could lever a fresh round and fire it.

He had tied his horse's reins to a jut of rock sticking out from under an ingrown skeleton of an ancient juniper bush that stood high enough to provide the animal some protection from the cold, windblown mist. No such provision for himself, though, he realized. He sat with a blanket wrapped around him and a large green rain slicker pulled down over it. He looked at five different positions of cover available to him along the ridgeline. Every one of the positions seemed to beckon him like a child with a hand raised, eager to be called on.

For two hours his long brass scope searched the distant ridgelines, game paths and rock draws on the wet land stretched out below him. He saw elk and deer herds.

He saw a wily panther dogging their trails. For a moment he treated himself to the thought of returning here someday to hunt. But he dismissed the thought, knowing how foolish it was to think he'd ever come back here for any reason. Time and again he would look in the direction of New Water Stop One.

Come out, come out, Colonel Randolph Doss.

He walked back over to the wet horse and took a sip of water from the canteen hanging from its saddle horn. Moving back to the edge, crouching the last few steps to avoid being skylighted, he saw the small horses and their even smaller riders come silent into sight way down below. He looked back along the tracks toward town, hoping to see Colonel Doss's Pullman car roll into sight. But no such luck.

All right, he told himself.

He wanted the colonel so bad, it was hard to turn the idea loose. Yet he knew he had to. The fates were having none of that today. He crouched and backed away before standing. He looked from one possible firing position to the next.

Next time, Colonel . . . next time, he thought.

Chapter 20

Andrew Maggen and Billy Tobin rode up from a path down below the rail tracks to join Reese Donovan and his men, bringing news that Ellis and the long riders had been spotted.

"Any minute now they'll see our decoys waiting to ambush them," Maggen said. "Then the fun will begin."

"For God sakes, man!" said Reese Donovan from the edge of the long tunnel. "This is not a laughing matter! Men are going to be dying here most any minute now!"

"They are outlaws, Mr. Donovan," said Andrew Maggen. "Ain't killing these jakes why we're out here?"

He looked back over his shoulder at Tobin, chuckling as he spoke.

"Get yourselves in here, damn it!" Donovan tried to shout quietly. "One glance at you two and Ellis's men will cut out of here.

This entire operation will all be for nothing!"

Still five feet from entering the tunnel, Maggen half rose in his saddle as if to say more on the matter, but a glob of thick blood erupted from his open mouth and sprayed horses and riders alike. A powerful crack of rifle fire caught up to the bullet, resounding from the high ridgeline above them. Pieces of Maggen's forehead fell to the tracks and wooden rail ties beneath them while his Colt flew from his holster and rang out on the steel track. Though safely inside the tunnel, the railroad men hunkered down in their saddles and crowded farther back.

"Who the hell shoots like that?" shouted Reese Donovan.

"I don't know," said Tobin. "Let me in before he gets reloaded and shoots at me—"

His words choked in his throat. He had turned his back on the high ridgeline. Now his chest puffed out and exploded from his shirt. Fragments of his heart and lungs peppered the men and their horses. The bullet came out of his chest and buried itself in Donovan's saddle pommel.

The men cursed and spit warm blood. The horses whinnied and reared and romped madly in the dark confines of the tunnel, their riders struggling to hold them in place.

Enraged, Reese Donovan showed more guts than good sense. He jumped his horse right to the opening of the tunnel and shouted wildly as he emptied his Colt into the hillside, the shots going no more than halfway up the steep rocky hillside.

"C.C. Ellis! You rotten son of a bitch! Come down here and fight like a man, you thieving, craven, murderous coward! You hear me? Fight me like a man!"

"Mr. Donovan, please come inside here," one of the men coaxed. "You're our leader! Don't act like this! C.C. Ellis is a cold-blooded killer! Get the hell in here before he kills you!"

Up on the ridgeline, at one of the five positions he had scouted earlier, Sven Handley peered through his scope and listened to Reese Donovan hurl insults up at him. He didn't know C.C. Ellis very well, so he wasn't sure the long rider would appreciate the railroad security men thinking he was up here splattering their ranks all over the tunnel entrance with such ease. They had no idea in the world who Handley really was, alone up here like a voracious bird of prey, ruling his portion of these rugged hills with talons of iron and fire.

"I know you hear me, C.C. Ellis," Reese Donovan called up the hill, sounding calmer, more in control of himself. "There is no reason you can't come down here and talk, see if we can't reach some kind of gentleman's truce. What say you, C.C.?" he asked as cordially as he could.

Handley raised his rifle butt to his shoulder and looked down through the scope. He saw the men lurking at the tunnel's edge, Colts drawn, raised and ready, searching futilely for his position. This was too good a chance to let pass him by.

His right eye focused on the young man with his sopping-wet but very new-looking bowler hat tilted up for a better view. *Cock hammer, aim well, deep breath in and hold. . . .* He squeezed the trigger ever so easily. When the shot went off, it came as a surprise to him.

Perfect, he thought before he felt even the faintest jab of the big rifle's recoil.

The bullet touched the thin edge of the man's hat brim, enough to send it spinning up and out over the hillside below the long stone tunnel.

From his towering perch, Handley backed away in a crouch with only a quick glance down that showed the bareheaded Mr. Donovan on his horse moving inside the dark tunnel with caution.

"Damn you, Ellis!" Reese Donovan shouted. "Damn you to hell, sir. Damn you and all of your worthless outlaws!"

Handley wiped the rifle down, disassembled it and slipped both pieces into a sheepskin-lined sleeve. Closing the sleeve, he folded one end over, tied it down and walked to his wet horse and untied its reins.

Two down and two to go.

The two to go were the colonel and his trail scout, Scotty Dowell. And that would be the end of it. He slipped the rifle case under his saddle and snapped it in place. Mounting, he heard no gunfire; Ellis and his men would by then be slipping along the trail, still headed for New Water Stop One.

Twenty minutes further along, he saw a large number of men on a lower trail coming in the same direction, all of them wearing brown bowler hats. They looked like nothing so much as a parade of brown balloons bobbing in the rainy mist.

From the size of the group, their hats and their black raincoats, he had no doubt they were the railroad men waiting out of sight to ambush Ellis's men from behind. Giving up on the plan that his two shots had foiled, they had apparently decided to try to catch the long riders on the trail and take them on without benefit of the ambush. There were certainly enough of them to handle Ellis's few riders.

Handley stepped down from his saddle, took the scoped rifle from its case and walked the horse over to the edge of the trail, where he tied it to a downfallen scrub oak.

The small, toylike figures on horseback grew larger when he raised the long brass scope to his eye. He wouldn't have to kill anybody down there, he decided. He needed only to stick a couple of bullets in close to the front horses' hooves, enough to get them lying behind cover for the next few minutes, slow their pace for the next few miles. The shots would also tell Ellis approximately how far behind him the railroad men were.

You're welcome, Ellis.

The first shot did exactly what Handley had expected. It stopped the riders cold, the front horses rearing high and pulling back as they touched down. The men spread out, grabbing for cover in every direction. The second shot appeared to strengthen their commitment to getting out of sight. They moved faster. Those who had found cover after the first shot jerked down behind it.

All right, two's plenty, Handley told himself. He levered a fresh round out of habit and half turned before a voice stopped him.

"Well, well, Dan, look here," the voice said. "We've flushed out the long-shooting jake who killed Tobin and Maggen."

Handley looked them up and down in their wet bowlers, their shiny wet raincoats, all the while maintaining his two-handed grip. *What a terrible habit, this yammering right away,* Sven Handley thought. A sort of self-congratulatory ritual most often expressed between fools.

"Yep, they sent us up here to get him," said Dan, "and by Gawd, we got him!"

"All right, back shooter," said the other, "ease the rifle down on the rocks — careful you don't scratch it. I always wanted me one of them with the big looking glass."

Handley turned slowly to his right, making a show of how carefully he handled the rifle. He resisted the urge to ask if there was anything else either of them needed to say, something they might want to recite maybe. Halfway around to the rock, the rifle recoiled in Sven Handley hands. It could have claimed itself a misfire, had the high grain bullet not sliced through Dan's heart and triggered a fountain of blood.

Dan remained in his saddle, jerking back

and forth, staring wide-eyed at his gushing blood, his hands spread as if afraid to touch anything.

Handley kept his rifle in his left hand while his right hand went down and up in one fast move. Empty going down and cocking his Colt coming up.

The other man was quick, his gun already out of its holster. It barked in his hand, but at the same second Handley's Colt sent a bullet into his chest. Handley saw the other man's Colt fall to the muddy trail, and the man bowed forward, swayed in his saddle . . . and remained there.

Of all the luck! Handley grabbed at the pain in his left side, his Colt still in hand, pressing against warm, spreading blood. Limping, he made his way to the horses and without breaking down the wet rifle, he climbed into the saddle and laid it across his lap.

He rode away in the direction he knew Ellis and his riders would be taking to town, the coolness of the Colt pressed against the bleeding wound seeming to help some. He looked back once. The two men he'd just shot were both dead, he was certain, but the way they were slumped in their saddles, they could have been men dozing in the lobby of a hotel who at any moment might sit up and ask for a glance at your newspaper.

He stopped his horse, looking back in pain. He realized this was what had happened to him. He too had been left for dead. His killers had buried him alive with no thought or the slightest concern that he might be lingering among the living.

He thought about raising his Colt and shooting each of the men one more time to make sure they were dead. Yet, testing his grip on the Colt, he decided it would be too slick and heavy for his weakened hand to hold. And now . . .

He realized his mind was slipping a little, the loss of blood, the pain. Deep, dark, unreal thoughts were seeping in, spinning even deeper, darker, more unreal thoughts. He stared at the two men he'd shot, saw the world around them tilt and fade. He wouldn't shoot them. Hell, he couldn't shoot them. He called out to them inside his head, *See you both in hell. . . .*

He felt himself fading and whispered, "If not before . . ."

"Sven, Sven Handley, drink this. For your blood, drink it," the voice insisted.

He drank another hot spoonful, as if he had any choice. Antelope broth. At first he had tried to refuse it, thinking there was no way something that tasted this good could exist in the world he knew. And he was sure that when he'd finished it, he would never taste anything like it again. He felt the metal spoon warm against his tongue.

"That's it. Drink it down. We've got plenty more for you now that we know you're going to make it."

The voice gave a little chuckle and Sven could also hear rain peppering a canvas wagon top above him.

He opened his eyes into thin slits and looked around the small interior of the supply wagon. Opened them a little more and saw the weathered face of Scotty Dowell, one of the two men left for him to kill. He looked around a little more, testing reality, seeing if the colonel's face would also appear over him. When it didn't, he sighed and relaxed. Maybe this was real after all. The spoon returned. He drank from it. The broth was still delicious — not as heavenly as he thought it might have been a moment ago, but pretty good all the same.

"Where . . . ?"

"Where are you?" Scotty asked, finishing Handley's words for him.

Dr. Douglas Gray answered, "This is our medical supply wagon, Sven. She took a hard spill recently, but as you see, she's fine once again." He stepped closer and said, "What are you doing out here, or should I not ask?"

"Don't ask," said Sven. "I thought you were bringing the new Pullman car out along the rails today? It is still today, I hope."

Scotty excused himself, took the bowl and spoon and stepped out into the rain.

"Yes, it is still today," said Doc. "Only a few hours since I heard your big rifle out along the ridgeline. As to the new Pullman car, Colonel Doss changed his mind, didn't want to see mud tracked all over the floor, I suppose. Can't say that I blame him. I'm not going to ask you what the rifle shots were about."

Handley offered no answer. He touched his fingertips to a soft white bandage on his left side and followed the edge to where it stopped. "It didn't go through?"

"No, it didn't," said Doc. "Luckily, the bullet wasn't very deep. I lifted it, cleaned the wound, bandaged it. It had almost stopped bleeding when your horse carried you right up here, almost to the wagon gate."

"That's good. . . ." Handley's eyes closed. "I'm weak," he said. "I didn't think I lost that much blood."

"You didn't lose a dangerous amount, but you would have in another few minutes. Go on to sleep. We're headed back to town. It looks like yours is the only life we've saved today. The ambush must've gotten canceled by the rain." He chuckled. "You might find lots to do in town, though. I was told by a railroad man that the colonel has taken over the town, arrested Sheriff Boyd and his deputies."

"I need to get out of here," Handley said.

"Nothing doing. You're too weak," said Doc.

"I can ride weak."

Handley started pushing himself up, but Doc stepped in, lest he strain the stitches and get the wound bleeding again. He helped Handley sit up on the cot and put on one of a few clean, dry shirts Doc kept for just such occasions.

"All right, Sven," Doc Gray said. "I think you're crazy but I have somebody here as crazy as you are! Scotty!"

Scotty Dowell opened the rear canvas flap and stuck his head inside.

"Yeah, Doc?"

"Handley insists on riding to town in this rain. If he falls off his horse, he'll never get back on it."

Scotty looked Handley up and down.

"You want to know if I'll go along 'case he needs me for anything?"

"That's the size of it," said Doc. "If you say no, nobody is going to blame you —"

"I'm going anyway," Handley cut in.

"And I'll go too," said Scotty. "A man's this determined to do something, you can't let him do it alone."

"Obliged," said Handley, buttoning the bib of the clean shirt. This might be a good piece of luck coming to him.

"I'll get the horses," said Scotty, just as a long twist of lightning licked down, followed by a clap of thunder that sounded as if it had split the earth.

"Whoa!" said Doc Gray. "Maybe I should hitch the mules and go with you."

"Are you talking about hitching the mules I hear over there braying their heads off?" Handley asked.

"Yep, those would be the ones."

"No, thank you all the same, Doc," said Handley. "We'd be getting the wagon unstuck ever' other mile. If you sit here until the next time the rain slackens, some of this water will be gone on down to the river. Stay here in the wagon and stay dry. Scotty and I will do well enough by ourselves."

Chapter 21

Things had already been getting awfully sharp and touchy in New Water Stop One, thought Ellis. When Sheriff Max Boyd shot the toes off of one of the colonel's gunmen, Water Stop, as some of his riders had started calling the town, started drawing up like a cinch.

Everybody had begun picking a side to be on: the railroad's, the colonel's or the law's, meaning the sheriff and his deputies.

This terrible weather wasn't helping anyone's mood, Ellis realized as rain poured from the front funneled tip of his hat brim. But if there was anything good about bad weather, it was that it kept everybody indoors, off the muddy street.

He was glad of that today, he thought, barely looking from under his hat.

Before entering the town moments ago, his riders — Jackson Hoyt, Bailey McCool, Harvey Brewer, Kid Santa Cruz and Poker

Joe Elliot — had broken off and ridden away, swinging wide of the main streets, Poker Joe leading three horses, soaking wet but saddled and ready to ride. At last there was only C.C. Ellis left, riding alone. His outlaws had taken partly flooded alleyways behind the front street, then climbed onto the roofline and spread out.

Ellis caught glimpses of them moving along the town's long, adjoined roofs and facades, keeping up with him riding below. More than once he caught an ever-so-slight glint of a rifle barrel appear and disappear in the swirly gray overhead.

And now his turn. Two blocks from the jail he turned and rode into an alley. At the rear of the jail, he hitched his horse to a telegraph pole and waded through mud to the barred window, picking up an empty wooden crate on his way.

Then Ellis set the crate steadily on the wet ground, stepped up on it and found himself looking right into the shadowy face of Sheriff Max Boyd.

"Obliged you came, Ellis," Boyd said, speaking low, even though there was nobody inside guarding him and his deputies. "You said if I need anything, just holler. So I hollered."

"And here I am," said Ellis. "I'm not

alone. I've got five of my best riders, and we brought you getaway horses. Ready to go when you are, Sheriff." He held up a Colt and slipped it through the bars.

"Thank you, Ellis!" Boyd said. He took the gun eagerly and handed it down to Deputy Wade Parnell. "I'll be ready as soon as you do me one more thing."

Ellis nodded.

"Out front, facing the door, look down on your right at the bottom stone in the front wall? Pull on the stone and it will come out. Behind it are two keys on a small ring. One key is to the side door. The other is to this cell. Will you get them now while this bunch is over in the Pullman car doing whatever idiots do?"

"I'm on my way."

Out in front of the jail, Ellis tied his horse at the hitch rail right in line with the front door, blocking the view. He worked quickly in the wind-tilted rain. The loose mortar joint around the stone was just wide enough for him to work his wet fingers in to wiggle and inch the stone forward until it came loose. Once it was out, there was nothing to do but grab the key ring and slide the stone back in place. Done! He straightened and looked around the empty street. A block away he saw a Western Express steam engine chug slowly alongside the loading platform. With a blast of steam, it screeched to a halt as it bumped and coupled itself to the Pullman car. A switchman jumped down from the Pullman in the rain, checked the coupling and trotted away, giving a hand signal above his head to the watching engineer.

Just in time, Ellis thought, seeing a large number of the colonel's security men running to the platform in the rain, their rifles in hand. Among them, Curly Burns limped and wobbled along, using his rifle butt as a walking stick. A long, wet, soiled tail of bandage slopped along behind him. Even from a block away, Ellis thought Burns looked like a man afloat on a stiff dose of Blue River.

Poor sumbitch!

Carrying the two keys in his closed fist, Ellis unhitched his horse and led it into the alley before stepping up into the saddle.

At the rear of the alley, Poker Joe rode up to him, leading the three getaway horses. Motioning for Joe to follow him, Ellis took him around to the side door, stepped down, unlocked it and walked inside, his wet Colt out and ready.

"Any trouble?" Sheriff Boyd asked while Ellis unlocked the cell.

295

"Nope."

Boyd stepped out of the cell and walked straight to the gun cabinet.

"Help yourselves, Deputies!" Boyd said. "Damned neighborly of the colonel," he said, swinging open the unlocked doors.

Then he pulled out the long drawer beneath the cabinet, which held ammunition of all popular calibers, including lead balls and firing caps. "In case anybody's carrying a black-powder wad chopper," said the sheriff.

Parnell and Flitz commenced loading up everything they could carry.

"Let's get going, Sheriff Boyd," C.C. Ellis coaxed, "before the rain slows and they decide to walk here from the platform."

"What's your hurry, Ellis?" said Max Boyd, grinning. "I have half a notion to sit right down and arrest all of these bastards as they walk through the door."

"Or blow their by-Gawd heads off!" said Deputy Parnell.

"We came to get you three out of this place, and now you don't want to go?" said Ellis.

"What? You expected me to low-tail it out of here?"

"Well, that is why we brought horses for you, Sheriff," said Ellis, staying respectful.

"But this is my office, don't forget," said the sheriff. "I've got every damned right to kill them like garden snakes!"

Poker Joe Elliot and C.C. Ellis exchanged glances.

"What about the horses outside? As soon as the colonel's men see them —"

"Bring them inside," said the sheriff, extending his hand toward the open side door, "and put them in the other cell." With a more serious expression he looked at Ellis. "I'm obliged for all you and your outlaws have done for us. Now you can hightail it out of here, let me and my deputies earn our pay."

Deputy Flitz had hurriedly walked the horses around and brought them inside the jail. Now the horses blew and snorted and shook themselves off, leaving a trail of mud and water behind them.

"I'll stay," said Ellis. "But with a fight this big coming, I won't speak for my riders. I've got to leave it up to them —"

"You're taking votes? That's mighty democratic of you, Ellis," said Boyd. "Where you think we are, the Alamo? The colonel sure ain't letting anybody leave, vote or no vote!"

"They've seen us!" Deputy Flitz said, looking out through a cross-shaped gunport in a closed window shutter.

No sooner had he spoken than a bullet from the roofline across the street thumped hard into the thick shutter. The shot called in a thunderous reply from the roofline on the jail side of the street, where Ellis's riders were covering the next two blocks of the mud-stuck town.

"Sounds like the ayes have it!" Boyd said.

He cackled and shouted as rifle fire ripped back and forth above them. He sprang over to the other front window, closed the thick shutter and shoved a rifle through the cross-shaped gunport.

"Looks like we've got ourselves in a siege," said Parnell, firing his rifle. "I've never seen anything happen so fast. They just climbed up and took us over."

"That they did, Wade," said Sheriff Boyd. "That's what you can do when you have this many men backing you up."

Suddenly Ellis noticed blood on Poker Joe's forearm and asked, "Are you hit bad, Joe?"

"I'm okay," said Joe.

"What do you want to do?"

"We'll never make it out of here on these cayuses at a run. This mud will get all of us killed."

"I know," said Ellis. "Cover me!"

"Cover you? What the hell, jefe! Wait!" Joe

shouted.

But Ellis was already out the front door, looking down the street at the big engine idling at the platform. Bullets whizzed past him and thumped the front of the jail. Yet the rifle fire lessened and lost accuracy as the long riders poured rifle fire back at the roofline across the street. The railroad men there ducked down behind the facade and fired back blindly, unable to take good aim under the intense fusillade.

"Okay, the train engine is still running!" Ellis shouted at Joe as he jumped back inside the jail and slammed the door shut behind him.

"Sure it is," said Poker Joe. "You can't just start and stop one of those big steamers all day long!"

Flitz and Parnell had scooted the sheriff's desk across the floor and up against the side door; then they'd closed the shutters on each cell window. A bullet pinged off iron.

"What's that noise?" Ellis asked.

"A bullet hit the window bar!" shouted Flitz.

"No, the other noise!"

Ellis gestured toward the side door, where they could hear scraping and pounding, then Bailey McCool's voice shouting. Bullets thumped out in the alleyway.

"It's Bailey! Let her in!" shouted Ellis, even as he hurried to the desk and started to pull it away from the door by himself. Flitz and Parnell joined in to help.

"What the hell is this? Help me get him inside!" Bailey said as the side door opened.

Harvey Brewer was leaning against her side, his arm across her shoulders, with blood running down his chest.

"Is there a . . . doctor in the house?" he asked with a crooked, pained grin.

Sheriff Boyd swung the side door shut while rifle fire roared back and forth above them.

Ellis helped Bailey seat Harvey in a wooden desk chair, throw open his long duster and unbutton his short.

"Hang on, Harvey," he said. "We do have a doctor headed this way."

"Yeah?" Harvey looked at him quizzically.

"Yeah," said Ellis, "he's in the ol' supply wagon. If this round of rain has let up below us, he'll be getting here before you know it."

Harvey gave him a dubious look. Then he said, "Bailey, did the bullet go through or not?"

Bailey ran her hand down his back and brought it out covered with blood. "It went all the way through, Harvey," she said.

"Good," said Harvey. "Have you got any whiskey on hand, Sheriff?"

Without answering, Max Boyd produced a half-full bottle of rye and handed it to Brewer, who pulled the cork from it with his teeth. He swallowed a large swig and handed the bottle to Bailey.

Bailey took a swig of her own and corked the bottle. "Okay," she said, "now what?"

Harvey withdrew a knife from his boot well and stabbed it into the sheriff's desktop, eliciting a sharp look from the sheriff.

"Now," Harvey said to Bailey, his voice a bit stronger, "I'm going to cut two large strips of cloth out of your bloomers, and—"

"Like hell you are!" said Bailey, shoving his hand away.

"No, wait. Listen," said Brewer. "We'll roll the two strips into points, douse them in rye and plug these bullet holes until Doc Gray gets here. Understand?"

"Oh, yeah, I understand," said Bailey, "all except the part about ruining my undergarments! Why not a shirtsleeve, a pair of socks?"

"I suppose one of those might do," said Brewer. "I'm just going with what I know works."

"Not this time," said Bailey. "Use your

long johns."

She looked at Poker Joe, whose shirt was already bloody and ruined by the earlier bullet graze. "Give us your shirtsleeve, Joe, please!"

Outside, bullets slammed, ripped and thumped all along both sides of the street.

"Never mind, Poker Joe," said Harvey Brewer. "I've got my own danged shirt here. We can use it, I reckon, unless Dr. Gray gets here and says otherwise."

"I doubt if the colonel is going to allow him to come here and treat any of us," said Ellis, "unless we give ourselves up first."

He looked around, already knowing the response his next words were going to get. "Anybody here think we should give up? They still don't have nothing on us that a St. Louis lawyer can't talk them out of."

"That's true — you didn't even break me out of jail," said Boyd. "Nothing's been broken. You came to visit me, and a bunch of railroad security men got full of themselves and started shooting at you. Red-blooded men — and woman — that you are, all of you fired back!"

"That is how the law would likely look at it," said Brewer, taking another drink of rye. "Say what you will about lawyers, they kept the James brothers out of jail for a long time. Only way they nailed the Youngers was catching them red-handed in the act of bank robbery."

"All right," said C.C. Ellis, "getting back to us. Who's for giving up?"

"Not me," said Poker Joe. "Every time I've given myself up, I've landed in more trouble than I would have been in had I'd stayed on the run."

"Anybody else?" asked Ellis. After a few seconds, he said, "I already know what Jackson Hoyt will say."

"Kid Santa Cruz too," Brewer said, rolling one of the two pieces of his shirtsleeve into a point and dousing it with rye.

Outside, gunfire continued; in the jail office, voices fell quiet.

"All right, it's decided," Ellis said matter-of-factly. "We wait for a break in the firing, then steal the engine and the Pullman car and roll on out of here."

Chapter 22

Inside the livery barn, the Lory brothers, two of them wounded from their previous encounter with C.C. Ellis and his long riders, stood in a tight circle, checking their rifles and holstered sidearms. Rain pounded hard on the leaky tin roof.

"Lousy-ass rain," growled Adam Lory, one of the unscathed brothers, glancing up at the roof.

Brady, the other Lory who had not taken a bullet the day of their gunfight in the tent saloon, spit a stream of tobacco juice and ran a hand across his mouth, eyeing the corpse of his cousin Simpson Smith, who'd had his brains blown out that day.

"I got something to say before we kill C.C. Ellis and his bunch, so listen to me."

Adam Lory paid him no attention, continuing to check his guns, his foot-long boot knife. The other three watched and listened closely.

"First of all, Jason," he said to Simpson's brother, "I feel bad, stepping in your brother's brains the way I did to get away from the bullets flying."

Jason nodded and said, "I understand." He didn't want to hear anything more about it.

Brady looked at him expectantly, waiting for more of a response. "You understand?" he said. "That's all you've got to say about me stepping in a nasty pile of you brother's brains?"

"Turn it loose, Brady," Adam cut in. "Our cousin does not want to hear it, and neither do I."

"Neither do I like saying it," said Brady, "and I'm the one who spent half the night picking flakes of Simpson's brains off my britches leg!"

Adam Lory smoldered and gave his brother a cold stare, while Billy Lory tried to change the subject. He slapped himself on the hip.

"I'll say one thing about Doc Gray. He got me fixed up pretty quick. I might still limp a little, but it's going away."

The barn grew quiet. Billy stopped smiling.

"Are you waiting to hear us all shout amen to that, Billy?" said Brady.

"Shut up, Brady!" said Peyton, who had stood quietly listening. "The guns are quieting down. Can we get on out there?"

The five gunmen were just about to leave the livery barn when the loud blast of the engine's steam whistle stopped them in their tracks.

"Damn it, what a racket!" shouted Adam. "When did Colonel Doss decide to start blasting us with that thing?"

"Hell, just now, I reckon," said Brady.

"It's louder than cannon fire!" said Adam Lory. "Let's go kill these sumbitches and get on over to the saloon. I'm going to need a lot of good rye whiskey to wash that damn whistle out of my head."

"Are you planning for us to jump out there like something crazy the way we did last time, or pull back and wait to strike when the time is right?" Brady asked.

"First thing, we're finding us some good cover," said Adam. "When the time is right, we'll strike and not a minute before."

Along the roofline where the colonel's men had taken up positions, seven of them had stopped to reload while the rest of the men kept shooting, but the firepower wasn't the same. A man who had hunkered down to reload as quickly as he could, straightened up long enough to get off two shots, and saw C.C. Ellis, his three long riders and Sheriff Boyd and his two deputies step out of the alley beside the jail and walk out onto the muddy street.

"Look at this!" he said to the others on the roof. "Are you tough long riders giving up?" he shouted down, standing tall and chuckling at the outlaws plodding slowly through the thick mud toward the rail station a block away.

In a sort of answer, a silent rifle slug struck him full in the chest, followed by the sound of the shot trailing a second behind.

The men around him ducked down instinctively, as men do when a shot suddenly flies in out of nowhere. They watched their wounded companion fall backward on the flat roof, blood spewing from his upper body, front and back.

On the street, Ellis and his long riders glanced around in surprise.

Hoyt and Santa Cruz had come down from the roof and joined Ellis and the rest as they walked along the muddy street.

"Who was that shooting?" Jackson Hoyt said.

"I don't know," Ellis replied, "but I've got a good notion. Keep walking." He looked at those walking abreast of him on each side.

"Hold your fire!"

"Hold our f-f-fire?" said Kid Santa Cruz.

"Yes, Kid, if you can," said Ellis.

No sooner had he spoken than three men sprang up on the roofline, aiming their rifles, but their shots went wild and thumped into the mud when the man in the middle fell dead. His blood sprayed the shooters on either side of him and they ducked down.

"Keep walking!" said Ellis. "Hurry! While they're trying to figure what's going on! Keep walking!"

"What is g-going on?" Kid Santa Cruz asked.

"I don't know, Kid," said Ellis. "Keep walking!"

Four riflemen in dusters and bowler hats appeared in the street ahead, coming toward Ellis and the others. They had heard the distant shots but had no idea a long shooter had moved onto a distant hillside and taken the long riders' side. Ellis's gang had quickly turned steely, unrattled by the rifles above them, grateful for the shooter on the hill.

Seeing the four men coming toward them starting to spread out as they walked, Boyd said to Ellis, "What say I take my two shotgun-wielding deputies into that alley right behind them and let them see us coming at them?"

"That's good," said Ellis. "We'll cover you till you get behind cover of your own."

As he spoke, one of the four riflemen fell sideways, his bowler hat landing upside down in the mud. The railroad men on the roofline got off shots.

"Get going," Ellis said.

"We're gone," said Sheriff Boyd. "We want our chance before this long shooter kills them all!"

Ellis and his long riders walked on, not having fired a shot since they took to the street, and moved toward the rail station. Every step they took made them less of a target, moving at an angle to the colonel's rooftop gunmen instead of directly below the rifle fire.

Ahead of them, the three men stopped abruptly. They had clearly seen the sheriff, his deputies and their now infamous double-barreled shotguns.

"How the hell did this happen to us?" one of the three men asked the other two. "We've got enough men to overthrow the government of a small country. Yet here we are surrounded by a handful of outlaws and three lawmen?" He looked stunned. "Did either of you see this coming?"

The other two men both shook their heads

nervously, trying to keep an eye on every person who now seemed close to being able to kill them.

At the head of the alleyway, Deputy Parnell said, "What are you fixin' to do, Sheriff?"

"Keep me covered," said the sheriff. "While this is going our way, I thought I'd go ahead and arrest them both."

"Oh, hell no!" whispered Parnell. "Wait!" But he was too late.

"Good day, gentlemen," the sheriff called out cordially, taking a few steps toward the three men.

They didn't reply, but one of them tilted his head toward the men in bowler hats standing on the platform and muttered to his companions, "What the hell is the colonel doing about this? He's our security leader. Why ain't he leading?"

"I see the three of you have found yourselves in a bad spot here," said Sheriff Boyd.

He saw them looking over at C.C. Ellis, who was wading toward them from the other direction.

"Don't worry about him," said the sheriff. "He's with me."

"What do you want, Sheriff?" one of the men asked.

Boyd's gaze narrowed, his shotgun cocked

and aimed at the man's chest.

"What I want is to keep you three alive," he said in a firm voice. "So stick your rifle butts down in the mud and drop your pistols bedside them."

The three looked at him, then at the two deputies and their shotguns, then back at him. One started to speak.

"Naw, don't start arguing with me," said the sheriff. "You've seen Curly Burns and his new walk. If you don't get to doing what I told you to, I won't talk about it. I'll count to one and clip your toes off."

"Whoa! Wait, Sheriff!" one man shouted. With a hand raised, he jammed his rifle butt down in the mud, raised his new Colt with two fingers and dropped it beside the rifle.

"That's a good fella," the sheriff said. He turned to the other two men. "Don't be shy. Get them guns in the mud, and we'll go boil us a pot of coffee."

Inside the new Pullman car, the colonel paced like a caged bull, raving and cursing. He threw down his empty coffee cup and shouted, "Scotty! Scotty!"

When he got no reply, he shouted even louder, "Where the hell is my trail scout?"

"Colonel, sir," said Reese Donovan, who was standing beside the closed door, "Scotty

Dowell is still out there with Dr. Gray and the wagon."

"Damn it!" said the colonel. "My head feels like it's splitting!"

He caught himself, and for the benefit of anyone listening, he added, "But I'm feeling fine, though, all the same!" He eyed Donovan. "What were we saying?"

Donovan said, "We were talking about me taking a squad of good gunmen to find who's up there shooting our men, and kill him."

"Oh? And what else, Mr. Donovan?" the colonel asked haughtily.

"His head, sir?" Donovan said. "You told us to bring back his head or their heads, whichever the case may be, in a flour sack."

"Good, very good, Donovan!" the colonel said. "And remember." He raised a finger for emphasis. "You and your men ride unrelentingly!"

"Yes, Colonel," said Donovan. "We will, I assure you."

The colonel stepped in closer and said discreetly, "I don't suppose our good Dr. Gray left any medicinal supplies here for the rest of us? I have plenty of whiskey, but frankly, I could use something stronger."

"No, Colonel, he did not. But" — Donovan slipped a bottle of Blue River from under his long rain coat and held it out to Colonel Doss — "this is something I borrowed from a shipment of medical supplies he was expecting. I believe you'll find it does wonders for headaches as well as other pain and discomfort." He held the colonel's eyes with a knowing look.

"God bless our wonderful Dr. Gray," said Doss, taking the bottle and putting it out of sight in his coat pocket. "Now, get up on the hillside and kill whoever is doing the long shooting. Whoever it is, I want to see their head rolling across the loading platform."

He craned his head to look out the small window, his hand wrapped firmly around the bottle of Blue River in his coat pocket.

Chapter 23

On the pine- and juniper-filled hillside, a long way from the main street of New Water Stop One, Sven Handley sat under a sheltering large sheet of canvas Scotty Dowell had tied between three trees. The canvas tilted to one side enough to direct the flow of rain away from the front edge facing town. Just outside of the canvas shelter, Scotty Dowell had built a small fire, kindled from an emergency handful of dry leaves and pine needles he carried wrapped in wax paper deep down in his saddlebags.

Sven leaned against one of the trees, his big scoped rifle across his lap covered by a thin blanket. He watched the rail platform, the Pullman car and all things train station through a pair of binoculars he wore on a leather strap around his neck. Only now and then did he raise the rifle, scan from one end of town to the other, then set it back across his lap, wipe the lens and cover it.

Scotty bent down and stepped under the canvas out of the rain, holding out a wooden cup for Handley to drink.

"Here you go, Sven," Scotty said. "I always say, a man who can't live on elk needs to put these whole Rocky Mountains behind him." He grinned. "Watch it. It's hot!"

Handley took the hot broth and sipped it, leaving the small pieces of elk liver and heart at the bottom of the cup for now.

"Anything going on?" Scotty asked. "I don't hear any shooting."

"You will," said Handley. "They're reloading, getting ready for more." He relaxed, the warm cup resting on his leg.

"Are you feeling better some?" Scotty asked.

The evening before, the very thing Scotty had come along to guard against had happened. Sven Handley, weak, wounded, had fallen from his horse. He slid twenty feet down a slick, mushy path and would have gone over a cliff, had he not managed to hang on to a clump of wild grass until Scotty climbed down and saved him.

"I'm lots better. Thanks," Handley said.

He sipped and swallowed, set his cup down and raised his binoculars to his eyes.

"Okay, here we go," he said under his breath.

He watched a man in a long raincoat and bowler hat come out of the big shiny Pullman car. The man looked up toward the hillside, got in his saddle and rode slowly away, six waiting riders falling in behind him.

"Scotty, I think we've got company headed our way," Handley said.

Scotty squinted with his naked eyes to make out the toy-sized figures.

"Don't see the colonel. Do you?" he asked.

"No," said Handley. *But I'd like to.* "The colonel hasn't shown his face in quite a while," he observed.

He took off the binoculars and offered them to Scotty. "Want to take a look through these?"

"Naw, that's all right," Scotty said, watching the men ride down the trail. "If you say he's not there with them, there's no point in me looking."

Handley looked at Scotty for a moment. It was strange knowing that soon enough he would kill him. It was difficult knowing he would soon kill a man who had saved his life only the night before, but he called upon his darker side to dismiss the glimmer of goodness he'd seen and remember instead the man who had torturously beaten him, then buried him alive.

All of this, he reminded himself, on the orders of the demented fool down there in the shiny new Pullman car, Colonel Randolph Doss, security chief of Colorado Western Express Railroad.

"How long have you been the colonel's trail scout?" Handley asked.

"Since before the Civil War," Scotty replied. "Every decision he made was based on my personal assessment of the field and the battle ahead. I felt responsible for the colonel and every man under his command."

"You must be very proud," said Handley.

"Maybe sometimes," said Scotty, "but not always. We did things I knew would likely haunt me the rest of my life, and I was right. They have." He stood up and stepped close to the edge of the overhead canvas.

"Looks like this confounded rain's finally moving out," Scotty said. "Maybe this time it'll keep on moving." He paused for a moment, then asked, "Am I going to see another sunny day?"

"No," Handley said flatly.

Scotty sighed a deep breath.

"I knew you were him," he said quietly. "Are you going to ask me if I knew or not?"

"No," said Handley. "I thought about it. But I'd as soon never know."

"I understand," said Scotty. "I expect you ought just as well go ahead. I don't like to stand here wondering, waiting to —"

His words stopped as Handley's Colt roared out with one single shot.

Sven Handley limped slightly as he walked down the hillside to where Scotty Dowell had fallen. A string of dark blood slung wildly as Scotty rolled end over end. When he stopped, he sat slumped against a wet tree trunk, his head bowed on his chest.

Handley could see the .45-caliber bullet in the back of Scotty's head. *No need to check this one.* He flipped out his spent round and replaced it, spun the cylinder and slipped the Colt down into its holster. Knowing that the single gunshot would draw the riders in his direction like a pack of wolves, he hurried back to break down the campsite. He took down the canvas overhead and rolled it up. He put out the small fire, gathered the rest of the meager camp and tied it down atop Scotty's horse, making it his pack animal.

On his way down a hidden game path, he heard the colonel's riders coming up the hillside. When he knew they were getting very close, he swung wide and rode around, down toward the main trail. At the wider track of broken rock, down-washed and mud-covered gravel, he stopped and sat his horse silently.

At the distant sound of a mule braying, he backed his horse into wet trailside brush and waited until he saw Doc Gray and the medical supply wagon struggling up the muddy trail. The wagon mules, Elton and Champ, trudged forward, braying now and then in protest. On the driver's seat beside Doc sat Cal Lindsey, knocked out on laudanum, swaying with the slightest movement of the wagon. Farther up the hill in the direction of town, rifle fire, which had slowed almost to a stop earlier, now resumed as if in greater malice.

Fifteen feet in front of the wagon, Handley saw two of the colonel's riders, Ave Pettigo and Menard Baggs, scouting ahead, their clothes and horses streaked with mud.

Leading Scotty's horse beside him, Handley tapped the animal forward onto the trail at a walk. When he knew the two men could see him clearly, he turned his animals sideways to them and stopped.

"Hello the trail," he said, not too loud, but enough to be heard by the two scouts and the wagon driver.

"It's the quiet stranger," Pettigo muttered

to Baggs. To Handley he said, "Hello, traveler."

The two tapped their horses forward. From New Water Stop One, gunfire resounded.

"Sven Handley!" said Doc Gray. "Glad to see you and Scotty made it!"

"Just me, Doc," Handley said, stepping his and Scotty's horse closer to the wagon. "Somebody shot Scotty in the head. He's dead."

"Damn!" said Doc. "Who would shoot Scotty?"

"There're lots of the colonel's men riding around, flexing their gun hands," said Handley. "I wouldn't be surprised to hear one of them did it." He tugged the lead rope a little. "You can see I've got his horse. I didn't know where to take his body, so I left him right there. To tell the truth, I was a little concerned about being seen hauling him, the way all the rain has everybody acting."

"I don't blame you a bit," said Doc, his eyes a little watery and glazed.

Blue River? Yes, Handley thought.

There was no question Cal Lindsey, sitting limply and as pale as a corpse, was deeply under the laudanum's influence.

"Looks like the rain is out of here now,"

Doc said. "Let's hope so anyway."

Handley looked back along the trail, then at Doc Gray.

"Are you in trouble, Doc?" he said. "It looks like there's a couple of pirates following you."

"Pirates?" Doc chuffed, almost dreamily. He glanced back. "Aw, hell, they're not pirates. They're Comancheros. They came over with Baggs and Pettigo to deliver my Blue River. They found the three of us in a bad spot. They helped us get this rig up some slick hills back there."

"No offense to them, Doc," said Handley looking at the two men riding forward, "but they look like pirates."

"All right," said Doc Gray, "but there're seven more of them back there. All of them from their old stronghold in New Mexico."

Sven sat his horse, watching closely, ready for any trouble, but the two Comancheros didn't ride all the way up to the wagon; instead, they stopped fifty feet back and waited until Pettigo and Baggs rode back to them. After talking a few minutes, the two raised an openhanded adios to Doc Gray.

"Looks like they're headed home," Doc Gray said, returning their wave, then watching them fade into the wet brush and disappear.

"Must be they're wary of strangers," offered Handley.

Baggs and Pettigo returned to the wagon. "They seemed bent on getting out of here," said Doc Gray. "Was something wrong?"

Pettigo eyed Handley as he spoke.

"Danke, their leader, said he's seen the quiet stranger before. Said him and some of his men saw Sven climb up out of a grave, black vultures flittering around him like they were cousins from some otherworldly place!"

"What do you say to that, Sven?" Doc Gray asked with a curious look.

A tenseness set in. The three stared at Handley, who sat slumped and silent in his saddle.

Suddenly, Handley sprang upright and yelled, "Booo!" causing Baggs and Pettigo to jerk back in their saddles, almost causing their horses to spook and rear up beneath them. Doc Gray, also taken aback, caught himself quickly and laughed aloud.

"That ain't a damn bit funny!" Pettigo shouted angrily.

"Hell no, it's not!" said Baggs, his hand wrapping tight around the grip of his holstered Colt. "That's the kind of thing gets a man killed. We talked to those two! They were seriously upset!"

"All right," said Doc Gray, "everybody hold on to their water." He looked at Handley. "Black vultures flittering around you? You coming up out of a grave? Have you any idea what this is about?"

Handley saw the slightest shine of Blue River in Doc's eyes.

"I told you already what happened to me, Doc," said Handley. "I was caught off guard, waylaid, beaten, robbed, dragged and left for dead. I don't remember much else. Comancheros, maybe some of these who just left here, found me and kept me from dying."

"And that's all you remember?" said Doc.

"That's all," Handley replied. "Being dead and rising from the grave, I'm sure I'd remember all that." He looked at Pettigo. "I don't recall any vultures flittering, as you called it."

Pettigo's anger flared. "The hell's wrong with the word *flittering*?" he asked.

"Nothing at all," said Handley. "I'm just trying to recount the story. I don't remember any vultures. Not blaming you, but it sounds like some details have been stretched some."

He nodded in the direction the Comancheros had taken. "Are you saying I scared them off?"

"I don't know," Ave Pettigo said. "Why don't I go bring them back and you can ask them?"

"All right, I've had enough, Pettigo!" Doc said firmly." I remember when I met you, Sven. You couldn't talk. Your throat was sore and swollen from being choked."

"That's a fact," said Handley though he was lying.

His throat hadn't been sore from being choked; it had been from yelling so hard from the grave, hoping someone would hear him. But he'd stay with choking for now.

"If I could remember anything else at all, I'd tell you. I'm sorry to say, this is all I've got."

"And it'll do," Doc Gray put in.

He looked at Baggs and Pettigo in turn, holding their gaze until each of them nodded grudgingly.

"Ave?" Doc asked.

"Yeah, I'm good with it," he said, not even recalling now why the strange Comanchero story had upset him so bad. He tried forming a friendly smile. "Hell, these Comanchero traders have some big imaginations anyway."

"Good enough, then," said Doc Gray.

Rifle fire still resounded sporadically from

the direction of town.

"Stick with us, Sven. Nobody will give you any trouble. We'll keep going while this rain is stopped. I bet we've got a dozen wounded men waiting in line for us."

"Likely that ain't all we'll find waiting for us," said Ave Pettigo. He nudged his bootheels to his horse's wet sides.

They rode on.

Reese Donovan and his six riders had worked their way quietly up the soaked hillside. They'd shed their raincoats and tied them loose and unrolled across their saddle cantles now that the rain appeared to have stopped. At the three trees where Handley and Scotty Dowell had boiled coffee and heated elk broth over a small fire, Donovan signaled his men down from their saddles.

With one man leading their horses thirty feet away into a stand of juniper, the other five spread out around the campsite until one called quietly, "Uh-oh, there's a dead man over here, Mr. Donovan."

Reese Donovan and his men moved quickly and gathered around the body of Scotty Dowell slumped against a large pine tree.

"Poor ol' Scotty Dowell," said Reese Donovan. "This must've been the single gunshot we heard coming up the trail."

"The colonel's going to take this awfully hard," said one of the men. "Him and ol' Scotty rode many a hard frontier trail together."

"For a lot of years," said another.

"All right," said Reese Donovan, trying to remain coolheaded. This was his first time being in command of armed security men. "One of you go to the horses and bring back a spare raincoat. We'll wrap him and take him to the colonel."

A newer man named Darvin Settles hurried away to the horses. The others remained close together among the three trees.

A few minutes later, Donovan said, "Somebody go see what's taking Settles so long."

As a second man trotted away toward the horses, Donovan looked all around suspiciously and said, "Everybody spread out. We're standing too close —"

From behind a tree, a voice called out, "Everybody drop your guns! We've got you surrounded. We've got your horses and we've killed three of your men. You four are next if you don't do as you're told."

Four of them left! Reese Donovan glanced around wildly.

"Show yourselves, you cowards!" he

shouted at what looked like a vacant hillside.

But as he swung his Colt up from its holster, he heard gunfire from close up, all around him, in every direction, pounding him and his three remaining men lifelessly to the ground.

"Hold your fire, men. They're dead," the same voice called out.

Sonny Ryan stepped out into the open, his Colt smoking in his hand. He spun around when he heard wet brush rustle, and saw one of the men who'd gone for a raincoat stagger out, his bloody hands spread wide. The front of him drenched with blood from his cut throat, he staggered forward, his lips moving soundlessly.

To his left, a gunman stepped out of the brush holding his gun at arm's length, and fired a bullet though his head. The man fell limp. A fountain of blood rose high, then diminished. In seconds the thick blood shut down like a spigot turning off inside his head.

Chapter 24

Inside the small jail, the sheriff's three prisoners were housed in the cell on the left, two of them standing in the far corner, as far from the cell full of wet, muddy horses on the right as they could get. The third man sat on the hard, ragged bunk against the back wall, his hand wrapped around a tin cup of coffee. Because they had refused to tell Sheriff Boyd their names, the sheriff assigned them the first that came to his mind: Freeman, Arnold, and Big Boy.

"Sheriff," said one, "we don't like to complain about your jail, but these wet horses are stinking to high hell."

"Good thing you don't like to complain, Freeman," Boyd said. He sat at a window gunport with his double-barreled shotgun resting on his crossed knees.

"Why's that?" the man asked, one hand around the bars, his other holding his cup of coffee.

"Run your hand up and down the outside of those bars," said Max Boyd. "Then ask me what caused it."

With a smirk, the man ran his free hand up and down the bar. "It's rough as hell, Sheriff," he observed. "What caused it?"

"Those're buckshot scars, if you'll notice," the sheriff said, also sipping his hot coffee. "What caused it is I had a fella in there who, unlike yourself, did not mind harping and complaining. I threw a round of buckshot through the bars at him just to get him to shut the hell up."

The prisoners looked at one another and shut up instantly, having already decided that Sheriff Max Boyd was crazy. Boyd smiled subtly to himself. At the other battered desk, turned up on its end against the side door, Jackson Hoyt and Bailey McCool sat on wooden stools, cleaning their rifles.

On the floor, with saddles for pillows, lay the wounded Harvey Brewer and Poker Joe Elliot, both sleeping. Kid Santa Cruz and C.C. Ellis had been keeping a path clear between gunports in the window shutters and the middle of the thick front door.

Looking around the crowded jail, Kid Santa Cruz said to Ellis, "May-ma-maybe we should have gone on and taken the Pullman car like we started to?"

"No, Kid," said Ellis, "we had to turn back when the sheriff took on these prisoners. He had his hands full. He needed us — whether he knew it or not. Anyway, we've got a long shooter up in the hills taking our side. Now's the time to stick and see where it takes us. Don't you think so?"

The Kid nodded instead of trying to talk.

"We're good here, Kid," said Ellis. "When the time comes, we'll still take that train ride."

Somewhere along the front street, Deputies Wade Parnell and Robert Flitz were silently patrolling the town with shotguns.

They moved from one position to the next, every few minutes, staying out of sight, keeping watch on the roofline and either end of the street and always, of course, close watch on the big saloon tent, where the bartender occupied a low seat behind the long, thick bar. With a twelve-inch round mirror on the end of a stick, he managed to wait on customers and keep them coming and going. It hadn't rained now for a couple of hours and the town was drying, making a sucking sound like large insects breathing underground. The bartender kept a sawed-off shotgun on a shoulder strap. Near his left hand, under the bar top, lay a large ball-peen hammer. Beside it lay a pair of thick, studded knuckle-dusters.

Inside the new Pullman car at the rail platform, the colonel jumped to his feet at the sound of the wagon mules braying. "What the blazing hell?"

He looked out the small window, past his posted guards, and saw the mud-streaked faded green supply wagon swaying up the hill. On the driver's seat, Menard Baggs was struggling to keep Elton and Champ moving forward. On one side of the wagon rode Doc Gray, on Baggs's horse. On the other side rode Ave Pettigo and the man some of his security men referred to as the quiet stranger. Cal Lindsey lay facedown in the wagon, an arm hanging limply over the side.

Stepping out of the big Pullman car door onto the loading platform, Colonel Doss said to the guards, "Have a couple of these freight handlers drop the platform ramp. Help get that wagon up off the muddy trail!"

The colonel watched the burly freight handlers heave and shove the supply wagon up the loading ramp onto the platform.

Behind it Doc stepped down from the saddle and led Baggs's horse up the ramp, keeping it out of the sticking mud around the edge of the platform.

"Come inside, Dr. Gray, and give me a report," said the colonel. "We heard some hard shooting break out a while ago."

"We heard it too," said Doc, handing the horse's reins to one of the dockworkers as he followed Colonel Doss into the car. "It was higher up on the hillside."

"Thankfully it wasn't you or any of your men," said the colonel.

"Yes," Doc Gray said, "but I'm afraid I've got bad news for you anyway, Colonel."

Out front, the two door guards straightened and gripped their rifles smartly at the sound of the colonel cursing and shouting. Something made of glass crashed against the wall and shattered. After a moment they heard the colonel say in a calmer voice, "Oh, my, yes, Doctor! Thank heaven something has gone well this hellish day!"

The two guards gave each other a curious look, then snapped to a form of attention as the car door opened and Doc Gray stepped out.

"The colonel is resting, gentlemen," he said quietly to them both. "Please see to it he isn't disturbed for the next couple of hours?"

"Yes, Doctor, of course," said one of the guards. "Should I relay your instructions to Mr. Collins?"

He nodded toward Vincent Collins trudging along the street out front, leading his horse to the platform through the ankle-deep mud.

"No, I'll speak to him," said Doc.

He placed his battered bowler hat atop his head and walked out to meet Assistant Railroad Security Chief Vincent Collins as Collins led his reluctant horse up the loading ramp.

"The doctor looks like a man carrying a headful of bad news today," said one guard to the other.

"Yeah, well, at least it's stopped raining," the other said with a reserved smile. "Anyway, I hear he carries enough medication to soften every blow that life throws at him."

"Lucky him," said the other.

Across the street from the jail, his head half buried in the mud, Curly Burns's body stood upside down where he had fallen from the roofline hours earlier. A long tail of soiled white bandage hung loosely from his toeless foot and danced back and forth on a mild wind. For a while, he had struggled to free himself from the mud until Sheriff Max Boyd had mercifully, he thought, aimed a rifle out through the window gunport and put a bullet through Burns's heart.

"I should have done it sooner," the sheriff said, watching the hapless Burns slump a little, yet remain as upside down and mud stuck as before. "Had I killed him in the tent saloon instead of blowing his toes off, I would have saved him untold pain and bitter reflection."

"Not to mention the mud," Deputy Parnell said. He started to take his hat off, but caught himself and stopped.

Now the town was tense, yet, for the moment at least, restrained, and Deputy Parnell slipped back out and resumed patrolling. Poker Joe Elliot opened the front door a crack and looked out. He saw Doc Gray trudging toward the jail from the direction of the rail station. Doc had a white handkerchief tied around his bowler hat and wore his canvas medical bag over his shoulder.

Across the street two shovels stuck up from the mud beside Curly's body.

"Sheriff," said Poker Joe, "the doctor's coming."

Sheriff Boyd snapped out of a light doze and grabbed his rifle before grasping what Poker Joe had said.

He bent forward and looked out through the gunport. "Good, good. Get ready to let him in."

Then he noticed the two shovels and said, "The hell is this."

"Beats the hell out of me, Sheriff," said

Poker Joe. "Is it to mark his spot so a wagon won't run over him, you think?"

"Maybe," said the sheriff. He studied the two shovels through the gunport. "Whoever stuck the shovels there might have done so for show, then saddled up and cut out while nobody was watching."

"Oh . . . ," said Joe, who couldn't think of anything new to add to the speculation.

"I'm glad none of us is shooting right now," said the sheriff, "but don't let it deceive you. All the shooting we've heard in the distance is going to land on our heads before this is over."

Through the gunports, the sheriff and Poker Joe could see C.C. Ellis slip out of an alley and join Doc Gray. The sheriff glanced around as if to make sure Ellis wasn't still asleep on the floor where he had been. He shook his head. So did Poker Joe.

"I don't know how Ellis slips around the way he does," Boyd said. "He might be the devil."

"Watch your language, Sheriff," Poker Joe chuckled. "That's my jefe you're blaspheming."

"Let them in, Poker Joe," said Sheriff Boyd, "devil or not. We've got wounded here who need tending."

When Poker Joe swung the front door

open, Doc Gray stepped in quickly in spite of the white handkerchief around the band of his bowler. Nobody had authorized showing a white flag of truce. It had been his idea. *But if it saves lives, especially my own, so what?* he thought.

Behind Doc, Ellis stepped in, one hand on his Colt. Poker Joe started to close the door, but as if out of nowhere a big muddy boot came forward and held it open. Poker Joe looked into the half-hidden face of Sven Handley.

"Get on in here, quiet stranger," said Poker Joe, reopening the door. "I didn't see you coming out there!"

Sven Handley stepped inside quickly too, and Poker Joe closed the door behind him.

From his chair, Sheriff Boyd studied Handley's still healing, badly abused face.

"Gawd all mighty damn!" he said. "The more they come, the worse they look."

A soft rapping on the front door got Poker Joe's attention. Opening the door a crack, he recognized Cal Lindsey as one of Doc's helpers.

"Doc? I got to use the jakes," said Lindsey in a slurred voice.

"Doc, it's your man Lindsey," said Poker Joe. "Asked if he can use the jakes."

"It's around back," said Doc.

"Get out of the door before you get yourself shot," said Joe, and closed the front door in Lindsey's face.

Lindsey staggered away from the door and went around the side of the building.

In the falling afternoon shadows, Vincent Collins and six of his top employees met on horseback at the far end of town, out of sight of the Pullman car and the rail station.

"It's important for you to understand that I'm not doing this for any self-gain or promotion," Collins was saying. "I'm proposing we remove Randolph Doss from our operation here because if he's not stopped immediately, he will bring this railroad to its knees."

"Vincent, old friend," said one of the corporate board members, "I'm certain we all agree that the colonel," he said mockingly, "has to be stopped — stopped fast and strongly."

He pulled an empty laudanum bottle from his coat pocket and held it up. "If you look around, you'll see these little blue medicine bottles everywhere. The men call it Blue River, and while it is every bit as legal as alcohol, used together even in moderate amounts, it is proving to be a deadly combination."

A man cut in, saying, "When you say stop him fast and strongly, how fast do you mean?"

"Yes," asked another, "and how strongly are we talking about? Do you mean . . . ?"

The men fell silent.

"I can't say precisely how strongly this man needs to be stopped. I will say that our company will stand behind any and every step you take to keep our rail commerce going."

"How long will the company stand behind our efforts?" the same man asked. "Right up until they hang us?"

Dark laughter rippled among the mounted railroad men.

Collins gave a slight smile.

"That is correct," he said. "And I'll go so far as to say, I will be there, my hat under my arm, on the day they hang you."

When the laughter fell away, Collins said, "All right, then, we won't go into details this evening. Suffice it to say that tomorrow I will handle whatever we need to do the way I did with the informants we found in our ranks."

The men gave what amounted to a quiet cheer in agreement.

"Yeah!" one said. "That's the kind of fast

and strong we all like!"

Laughter rippled again, then settled.

Another voice said, "Say, did they ever find out any more about what became of Preston Horn's son-in-law?"

"No," Vincent Collins said flatly, dismissing the matter out of hand. "Now, if we are all in agreement, as I feel certain we are, I plan on seeing to it that both our management problem and our outlaw problem will be dealt with tomorrow morning."

It seemed unusual, Ellis thought, when along around dark, the railroad security men allowed a couple of women from the tent saloon to bring two wicker baskets filled with food for the now fourteen people inside the small jail building.

Two men who had accompanied the women from the saloon carried in two large buckets of fresh water from the town well for the horses occupying one cell. Lindsey, who had become clearheaded enough to muck the horses' cell, wandered out and brought a fresh bale of hay from the town livery.

Ellis watched everything happening but trusted none of it. True, the railroad had no charges to bring against him and his men, neither did the Gadsen Mine. Yet knowing the railroad, he felt there was something slippery afoot.

"I don't trust them either," said the sheriff, seeing the way Ellis kept an eye on everything. "They're busy working something to their advantage. Soon as they do, they'll fly into what I call a railroad rage." He smiled. "There's a trick up every sleeve. I felt better when they were trying to kill us. Now that they're feeding us dinner and watering our horses, I expect them to do just about anything —"

"C.C. Ellis," said one of the prisoners, "there's a fella outside here wants to talk to you." He motioned at the barred cell window.

"Yeah? Who is it?" Ellis said just for the hell of it.

The prisoner stepped up on the bunk, then turned and said, "Says his name is Willie Town. Another fella says he's Juan Sanchez."

Ellis, Jackson, Poker Joe and Bailey all traded glances. Ellis stood up. Sheriff Boyd handed him the cell key.

Inside the cell Ellis stepped up on the bunk and looked into the two outlaws' faces through the bars.

"Howdy, Willie," he said to Town, "and, Juan, it's good to see ya. I figured you for dead by now."

"No, I am healing good," said Juan. "I am riding with Sonny."

"How is Sonny?" Ellis asked.

"Ask me yourself," said Sonny Ryan. He eased his horse up close to the back wall. "I'll put it this way," he said. "I'm not in jail." He laughed to himself, glancing around the cell through the window. "What'd they get you for?" he asked.

"Nothing, Sonny," said C.C. Ellis. "I'm not under arrest for anything. Look." He held his Colt up. "See?"

"Yeah, I see," Sonny said. "I've always thought arming prisoners was a good idea."

"Fact is, the new sheriff's in here too, Sonny. A few of us rode in to help him. Railroad security men have been trying to run him over."

Sheriff Boyd looked around from his chair and touched his hat brim toward the window.

"Evening, Sheriff," Sonny said.

"The railroad gunmen are getting out of hand," the sheriff replied. "It's a long story. Anyway, here we are, railroad gunmen all around us. Hell, they're everywhere. But we've held them off well enough so far."

"I know," said Sonny. "News travels. I've kept up on things. We heard some of them got ambushed up in the hills today." He gave Ellis a look, letting him know he and his men were the ones who had done it. "Are you about ready to put this place behind you?"

"Yes, if I have to," said Ellis with fake regret, "whether the sheriff and his men go with us or not. But I know it's going to be slick and muddy traveling for the next few days. Hard getaway riding. So I've been biding our time."

"Do you want to stay a little longer?" Sonny asked. "You and your sheriff friend can play checkers."

"It sounds tempting," said Ellis, "but no, we're taking the train down to some flatlands. If we go by horse, we'll be sliding and fighting all the way down."

"Train, huh?" said Sonny. "Do you know how to operate an engine?"

"No," said Ellis, "but I reckon I can figure it out. Speed up on the flatlands, slow down on the curves."

"Sounds right to me," Sonny said. "Did Jackson Hoyt teach you that?"

"We talked some," said Ellis. "I promise you, if it gets us out of here, I will run that machine."

"So much for operating the big engine. What about your horses?" Sonny asked.

"It's a big Pullman car," said Ellis. "We can get them in it. How many men are riding with you?"

Sonny shrugged. "A dozen more or less. Soon as word got around, they started coming out of everywhere, wanting to lend a hand."

"A gun hand, I hope," said Ellis.

"Sure. What other kind?" Sonny smiled.

"All right, then," Ellis said, "first thing in the morning?"

"Yep, first thing in the morning," said Sonny. "I might even have a man who can operate a rail engine for us."

In an abandoned tack shed behind the livery barn, the Lorys had covered the single window with dark canvas to keep any lantern light from seeping out into the night. Adam and Peyton knocked quietly three times on the door and waited until Billy and Brady, and cousin Jason Smith, trimmed the lantern wick down dark and raised their cocked pistols. The three crept close enough to look through a crack and see the other two brothers in the pale moonlight.

"It's them," Jason whispered. He lifted the latch and opened the door to let the them in.

Billy turned the lantern back up, creating

a circle of soft light.

Adam, the eldest of the Lory brothers, let out a breath and said, "I knew if we sat back and watched and waited we'd catch these jakes up to something."

Stalling, prolonging the suspense, he raised his Colt, checked it, and slipped it back down in his holster.

"Well . . . ?" prodded Brady.

"Mr. C.C. Ellis, the chief long rider himself, had a visitor while I watched from behind a tree." He grinned proudly and waited.

"Lord, man!" said Brady. "Are we going to have to wait and read about it in the newspaper? Tell us, gawddamn it!"

"All right!" Adam collected himself and spoke a little faster. "Sonny Ryan and some riders came visiting at the back window. I heard enough to know they're making a break come morning!"

The three looked at him.

"Making a break?" said Brady. "Hell, they ain't locked up! They ain't under arrest! They're carrying guns just like we are! For all we know, they could all be church deacons!"

"But remember, Colonel Doss does have a bounty on their heads," said Adam. "Forget the rest of it. They are in jail. Sonny and a bunch of his riders are here to get them out before the railroad security men drag them out and rip them apart like wild dogs!"

"Bull!" said Brady. "From what I've seen, these railroad security men are scared half to death of them. The long riders just about have them outnumbered by now. And the telegraph lines are down, so they can't wire out for any more help!"

"What are you saying, Brady?" said Adam. "You want to forget killing them and ride away? Leave that private bounty money behind?"

Brady thought about it.

"No, damn it!" he said. "The colonel wants them dead, not dead or alive. And I hate leaving that kind of money laying on the table."

"So do I," said Adam. He looked from face to face in the circling glow of light. "So everybody wake up with a boiling mad-on in the morning. We're gonna kill the hell out of these sumbitches."

Chapter 25

Moments before dawn, Jackson Hoyt and Bailey McCool lay sleeping on a pallet made up of blankets and empty flour sacks. With old saddles for pillows, their entire makeshift bed leaned partly against the desk that had once again been upturned against the side door just in case. The roofline across the street had been quiet throughout the night. The rain was gone. Any men still up behind the clapboard facade were keeping down out of sight. The window gunport shutters had been latched in place. The shutters in the cells were back in place and latched. At the left front window, Poker Joe Elliot stood watch, his side wound healing, feeling better. Before he'd started standing watch, he'd straightened a blanket and spread it over Jax and Bailey, who slept with arms and legs entwined, naked as newborns.

The body of Curly Burns had been raised from the sucking mud and moved somewhere out of sight. One shovel was gone; the other remained stuck in the street. Burns's only boot lay on its side, its worn sole crusted heavily with drying mud.

"Poker Joe," Sheriff Boyd said in a low voice, "here, take this coffee."

"Obliged," said Joe, accepting the steaming coffee mug. He set it on the windowsill just before it grew too hot to hold.

"I make it hot and strong!" the sheriff said with a little chuckle. "Hot as a dancer's drawers and strong enough to bend a branding iron."

"I'll attest to the hot part," said Poker Joe. "I'll let you know on the branding iron."

He'd noted earlier that the door to the cell with the three would-be gunmen in it stood half open. The men slept in heaps, two on the floor, one on the wall bunk.

"Do you lose many prisoners like that?" Joe asked, jutting his chin at the open door.

The sheriff chuffed. "Not as many as you might think," he said. "Lots of times a man sees an open door to freedom, he right away thinks it's a trick — you know, an ambush where somebody shoots him in the back before he can get out the door. Years ago it was a town sheriff's way of keeping the budget trimmed. It ain't so much the case anymore," he sighed.

"I expect you've seen it all, Sheriff," Joe said, putting the disturbing jailbreak-ambush story out of his mind. It still felt funny being in a jail fully armed, able to walk out the door anytime he damn well pleased.

"Yep," said Max Boyd, "I expect I have just about seen it all at one time or another. Some of it good, some of it bad. Some of it just downright strange."

"Strange, huh?" said Joe.

"Yep," the sheriff said. "Strange as socks on a rooster."

"That is strange," said Joe, trying to picture it.

He sipped the boiled coffee, which was still too scalding to be touched by a living man's tongue. "Whew! Are you and your deputies leaving with us, Sheriff?" he asked, feeling his mouth wilting as he spoke.

"If it was only me, I'd stay," Boyd said. "I'm seventy-four years old. At my age life has a way of winding down quicker than a cheap pocket watch. But with Parnell and Flitz to think of, I'd better get us all down the trail until everything simmers down here for a while."

"That sounds like a wise thing to do, Sheriff."

At the rear window, someone made a

sound like a cat begging for milk. Joe walked into the cell and over to the edge of the bunk.

"Scoot over!" he said, nudging the sleeping prisoner with the toe of his boot. The man barely moved an inch. "Damn it!"

Stepping up on the bunk, Joe looked out the window at Willie Town sitting atop his horse against the outside of the wall, a coil of rope and a long chain draped over his shoulder.

"I'm fixin' to pluck out this whole window, Joe," Willie whispered. "Tell your pal there to get out of the way. If this rope happened to break, it'll snap his head clean off!"

"Let her snap, Willie," said Joe. "He ain't my pal, and I can't get the sumbitch to move."

"Let me help you, Poker Joe," Sven Handley said under his breath.

Stepping inside the cell, he straightened the sleeping man, took both his feet and dragged him straight off the bunk. The man's head smacked hard on the stone floor.

The man came awake with a start. As his eyes fluttered open, he looked up at Handley's grim, misshapen face and stifled a gasp.

"Hope I didn't hurt you," Handley said.

"No, no! Please! Not at all," the would-be

gunman said, scooting farther and farther away from Sven Handley, who was trying to offer him assistance getting up. "I'm good here! Real good," the man said shakily, a hand going to the back of his head. "Just fine! Thanks! Thank you!"

There was a hard vibrating snap, and Handley looked at the window to see that its thick frame of bars was gone. A few scraps of mortar and cement lay on the bunk below it.

"That wasn't too loud at all," Poker Joe said.

"All right, let's get going," said Ellis, levering a fresh round into the chamber of the rifle he'd finished loading. "Open the other cell door. Let these horses out. Everybody else go out through the cell window."

Behind the jail, Sonny Ryan and his men were still mounted, but when the occupants of the jail started climbing out the cell window, they jumped down from their horses and slapped them on their rumps, sending them running in every direction. Across the street the few railroad men still left on the roofline opened fire, then stopped in confusion when they saw the horses were riderless. The long riders could be glimpsed only as they crossed the alleys on their way toward the rail station.

In the street, riflemen in bowler hats stepped out of alleyways and set up a heavy line of fire, despite the outlaws' horses running wild all around them. Other horses had been riled up to follow them, some of them pulling their reins free.

Ellis was running hard at the head of the gang, Sonny right beside him, firing as they ran.

"The train engine is running!" Sonny shouted. "My man is there waiting and ready. When we make it there, we're as good as gold!"

Assistant Security Chief Vincent Collins and his select group of men sat mounted, ready to charge C.C. Ellis and his long riders. But just as they roared out of the alley onto the muddy street, the double-wide gates of a crowded cattle corral flew open and four hundred head of wild longhorn Texas brush cattle spilled out wide-eyed and bawling as some of Sonny's men fired rifles in the air above their heads.

Firing at Collins and his riders on the other side of the stampeding cattle, and the riflemen who had come down from the roofline to charge at them from behind, Ellis and his gang fought their way onto the rail platform. Ellis, Jackson Hoyt and Sonny

Ryan took up a firing position behind a stack of thick wooden crates, which provided good cover for the others who came running and firing up onto the platform, toward the big idling engine and the open door of the Pullman car.

"Let's do some traveling!" shouted Bailey McCool.

Amidst the heads of cattle, the galloping horses and the running gunmen, Ellis saw Colonel Doss stumbling up the outside stairs to the second story of the New Water Stop One Hotel, firing his Colt wildly down into the throng of bowler hats below. Return fire came up from the crowd and thumped against the clapboard building.

Poker Joe Elliot and Sheriff Max Boyd tumbled in beside Ellis behind the stack of crates. Three guns fired at them. Poker Joe covered the sheriff, but Max Boyd was having none of it. He shoved Joe away and shot one of the attackers in the forehead. Boyd laughed as the man's bowler spun in the air on a spray of blood. Ellis and Sonny Ryan fired and shot the other two men.

Seeing a lot of blood on Boyd's chest, Ellis shouted, "Take the sheriff to the Pullman car! Doc is on his way there!"

Joe tried to take the sheriff's arm, but the sheriff pushed him away.

"Get away from me!" he said. "Dying here beats the hell out of a rocking chair!"

"All right, go see Doc yourself, Joe!" said Ellis, alarmed by the amount of dark blood on Poker Joe's chest, his neck, his shoulder.

"I'm done for, jefe!" said Joe. "I'm fighting right here till my string runs out!"

Cal Lindsey wandered up out of the crowd and plopped down on a crate, dangling a long Smith & Wesson pistol from his hand.

"Anybody seen Doc Gray?" he asked, unfazed when a shot from the crowd hit the frame of the crate he was sitting on.

"He's on his way to the Pullman car," said Ellis.

"From where?" Lindsey asked in his laudanum stupor.

"I don't know!" said Ellis. "Out there somewhere?"

Another bullet hit the crate Lindsey was sitting on.

"If you're going to sit there, Cal," said Ellis, "you might want to do some shooting back."

"Damn!" said Jackson Hoyt, looking Cal Lindsey up and down. "Do I act like that when I'm drinking Blue River?"

"No, Jax, you act even stupider," said Ellis.

Cal Lindsey stood up, wobbled, then fell

just as Doc Gray came running up onto the platform and jumped behind the cover of the large shipping crates.

"Here, Cal, let me help you up." Gray pulled Lindsey behind a crate offering a little better cover. Looking down at Sheriff Max Boyd, Doc saw all the blood and asked, "Are you hit bad, Sheriff?"

"Kind of, maybe," said the sheriff, "but I ain't leaving here, so forget that." He tried to shove Doc away from him. "I'm a citizen of this nation. I've got the right to die wheresoever I dang well please!"

"We're going back there to the Pullman car, Sheriff Boyd," Ellis said sharply. "You're going with us. Poker Joe won't go unless you go. So if you don't go, it's not just your life at stake. It's Joe's."

"Come on, Sheriff," said Sonny Ryan, picking the sheriff up in his arms like he was a small child. "We can fight from back there same as we can from here."

"Now you're talking my language, young man," said the sheriff.

"Poker Joe," Ellis asked, "can you walk?"

"I can if you and Jax help me along," said Poker Joe.

"All right." Ellis and Hoyt took Joe under his arms. "It's time we move this party indoors."

■ ■ ■ ■

In the lobby of the New Water Stop One Hotel, Vincent Collins sat leaning on his side on a short sofa. The room was empty, the lamplight dim. Outside, the morning sun warmed the blue sky. Although the crowd had become smaller, the muddy streets were still filled with men on horseback. Even though he was alone, Collins spoke as if addressing his railroad security employees.

"Gentlemen, I have been shot. I fear I may be dying." With tears in his eyes, he sighed and continued. "Shot by a woman no less. As loath as I am to admit it, these so-called long riders have outthought and outfought us. I say us although these are my men, and I alone must accept responsibility for this extraordinary defeat."

He touched a tear as it broke free and ran down the length of his cheek. His voice began to fail him. Still, he continued. "I only wish I had had the forethought to write all of this down. Now it is far too late."

He stretched out on the small sofa and died there, warm blood pooling against his wounded side.

Chapter 26

C.C. Ellis, Jackson Hoyt and Sonny Ryan stood three abreast on the big rail platform, looking along the main street of New Water Stop One. An hour earlier, a telegram from the railroad home office had shown up urging everyone involved to pull back and wait awhile until all the fighting had subsided and the town combatants had drifted away, some to their homes, even more to the tent saloon. Dead men and dead horses and even the body of one aged foxhound had been moved out of sight.

A wheelbarrow load of unclaimed firearms and bowler hats had been gathered and would be held at the barbershop to be sorted out and claimed by their owners. A large bass drum of a kind worn against a musician's chest and used in parades lay broken in the mud. Beside it lay a twisted and broken trombone, a bottle of cheap rye stuck into its brassy throat. On a few wagons that had risked the mud, bodies lay stacked two deep covered with canvas tarpaulins belonging to the railroad.

The three — Ellis, Jackson and Sonny — each held a rifle loosely in their hand, the smell of burned gunpowder wafting strong around them.

"What about Harvey Brewer?" Sonny asked quietly.

"Alive," said Jax, "just a little shot up."

"Kid Santa Cruz?" Sonny asked.

"Alive," said C.C. Ellis.

"And he's talking as straight as the next man," Jax threw in. "That's how it goes sometimes with stuttering."

"I've heard that," said Sonny. "What about Poker Joe Elliot?"

"He's good," said Jax. "Patched up like a preacher's fiddle. But good." He looked at Sonny. "Are you going to ask me about every-damn-body?"

"You mean like Doc Gray, Sheriff Boyd, his deputies, Cal Lindley, the quiet stranger?"

"Everybody's alive! We're all alive if you call this living," said Jax.

"What about —"

"Forget it, Sonny," said Jax. "I'm going to the saloon tent and get some beers to drink on our way down the hills."

"Watch for railroad men," Ellis said, joking.

"Ha!" said Jax. "They burn flowers and herbs and hope to never meet me."

"That's what I heard," said Sonny. "Don't forget some beer for Bailey."

"I won't," said Jax. "She knows I've got her covered."

Ellis and Sonny looked all around, amazed, seeing how quickly the town had come back from what anybody had to admit had been a hell of a gun battle.

Sonny chuckled and said, "Can you believe that we managed to beat the living hell out of a railroad security force?"

"First time for everything," Ellis said.

As they talked, they watched the five Lorys walk toward them along the platform, spread out, their dusters pulled back behind their holstered Colts.

"Hey! C.C. Ellis. Sonny Ryan! You long rider cowards think we forgot about you?"

"It slipped my mind, Adam," said Ellis. "It is Adam, right?" he asked Sonny.

"Beats me," said Sonny. "Sounds familiar, though."

"You damn well know we've got a reckoning coming. The colonel has private bounty on all of you. Today, we're cashing you in!"

From the engine, one of the riders called

out, "All aboard. Hey over there. All aboard. Are you taking this gawddamn train or not?"

"We're coming," shouted Ellis, knowing the train wasn't leaving without Sonny and the rest of them on board.

"Well, Adam, that's for us. You hear them. We've got to go," said Ellis.

"Like hell!" Adam Lory shouted. "We're taking you in dead on a board or a head in a flour sack! We're through talking. Now you either —"

Ellis's shot nailed him high in the chest. Sonny Ryan drew at the same time and shot Brady through his head. Without stopping for a second, Ellis shot Peyton Lory and saw him drop on the spot, his right hand flying open to drop his big Colt. Brother Billy and cousin Jason turned and ran. When they tried shoving their way through some dockworkers who were nailing a large shipping crate shut, the workers fell upon them with hammers and pry bars and beat them down onto the hard planks.

"C'mon, Ellis," said Sonny. "So you know, we're stopping near the Stoy Meachum place and taking some of them stray horses off your and Rena's hands." He pointed at a livestock car that had been coupled to the engine and firebox. "We've even got a livestock car if we need it. It'll keep the horses off the furniture."

"Okay, just a minute, Sonny," Ellis said.

He looked back in the direction of the New Water Stop One Hotel, where a moment ago, he had seen Sven Handley slipping up the stairs, the same stairs the colonel had climbed earlier. Handley held his gun down at his side and disappeared into the second floor.

Jax came back from the tent saloon with his arms full of large bottles of beer.

"You're a good man, Jax!" said Ellis, taking one of the beers and opening it.

But before he could drink, a shot resounded from the second floor of the hotel. As he watched Sven Handley appear back on the stairs and start down, Ellis raised the bottle to him, not too high, but just high enough for Handley to see. Sven raised his gun to the same height and tipped it in return.

Jackson Hoyt was struggling to hold on to the beers against his chest.

"Hey! Are we taking the train or what?"

"Yes, we are taking the train!" Ellis said. He took a large swig of cool, foamy beer, let out a hiss and said, "Ready when you are!"

ABOUT THE AUTHOR

Ralph Cotton has been an ironworker, a second mate on a commercial barge, a teamster, a horse trainer, and a lay minister with the Lutheran Church. He's now a bestselling author who's written more than 70 western novels, including the Pulitzer Prize nominated *While Angels Dance*. He lives in Corydon, Illinois.

The employees of Thorndike Press hope you have enjoyed this Large Print book. All our Thorndike, Wheeler, and Kennebec Large Print titles are designed for easy reading, and all our books are made to last. Other Thorndike Press Large Print books are available at your library, through selected bookstores, or directly from us.

For information about titles, please call:
(800) 223-1244

or visit our website at:
gale.com/thorndike

To share your comments, please write:
Publisher
Thorndike Press
10 Water St., Suite 310
Waterville, ME 04901